Secrets in the Shadows

TOR PARANORMAL ROMANCE BOOKS
BY JENNA BLACK

Watchers in the Night
Secrets in the Shadows
Shadows on the Soul
Hungers of the Heart

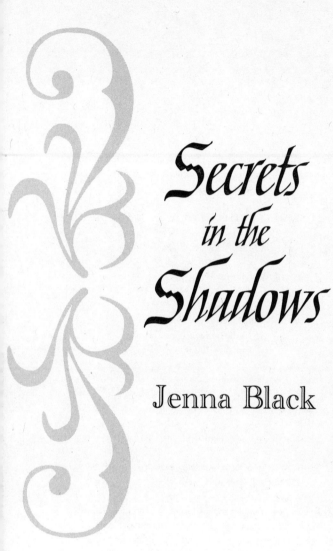

Secrets
in the
Shadows

Jenna Black

TOR®

A TOM DOHERTY ASSOCIATES BOOK
NEW YORK

SECRETS IN THE SHADOWS

Copyright © 2007 by Jenna Black

A Tor Book
Published by Tom Doherty Associates, LLC
175 Fifth Avenue
New York, NY 10010

www.tor-forge.com

Tor® is a registered trademark of Tom Doherty Associates, LLC.

The Library of Congress Cataloging-in-Publication Data is available upon request.

ISBN 978-0-7653-3801-3 (trade paperback)
ISBN 978-1-4668-1049-5 (e-book)

Tor books may be purchased for educational, business, or promotional use.
For information on bulk purchases, please contact Macmillan Corporate
and Premium Sales Department at 1-800-221-7945, extension 5442,
or write specialmarkets@macmillan.com.

First Trade Paperback Edition: April 2014

Printed in the United States of America

0 9 8 7 6 5 4 3 2 1

In loving memory of my father, Alvin O. Bellak.

I wish you could be here
to see the dream you helped foster come true.

Acknowledgments

I'd like to thank Gayle Glass and Kelly Gay, who served as my first readers on this book. Your insights helped keep me on target as I battled the demons of self-doubt. Thanks also to my agent, Miriam Kriss, who nursed me through several bouts of Neurotic Writer Syndrome. And a special thanks to my editor, Anna Genoese. Your incisive comments and suggestions helped make this a much better book.

Secrets in the Shadows

1

JULES WASN'T THE NERVOUS type. In fact, he prided himself on his façade of calm confidence—what most people considered arrogance. But tonight his nerves were making a rare and unwelcome appearance. When he arrived at the gate of Eli's mansion on the Delaware River and checked his watch, he saw that he was actually *early* for the weekly meeting. He was usually the last to arrive. He couldn't remember the last time he'd been early.

Eli buzzed him in, and Jules made his way down the moonlit path through the gardens that surrounded the house. Lights blazed from the windows of the ballroom that Eli had converted into a meeting hall when he'd founded the Guardians of the Night, before Jules was born. Through those windows, he could see that although he was early, he was far from the first to arrive. It looked like more than half the Guardians were already here. Patting his coat pocket to reassure himself he'd brought the papers, he went inside.

Heads turned when he stepped into the meeting hall. Eli,

sitting in his customary chair by the fireplace, raised his eyebrows in inquiry, but Jules pretended not to notice.

"Is the city burning down?" Gray James, Jules's least-favorite Guardian, asked in mock horror. "A nuclear threat? Terrorists? *Something* must be horribly wrong if you're here on time."

A couple of the other Guardians snickered.

"*Trou d'cul,*" Jules said, though by now everyone in the room knew that meant "asshole," so some of the fun had faded from cursing Gray in Québécois.

Gray opened his mouth to say something else, but Carolyn, his mortal fiancée, elbowed him in the ribs and he shut up. Just as well. Jules would have loved an excuse to pummel the bastard, but Eli would never have allowed it. He took a seat as far across the room from Gray as possible and folded his arms across his chest. He felt Eli's eyes on him, but he refused to meet the Founder's gaze.

Tonight was going to be a mess, and Jules wished it were over already.

The last to arrive was Drake, the only one in their midst who'd succumbed to the blood addiction. While the Guardians fed on lamb blood mixed with milk, Drake fed on and killed mortals. Only those he considered the scum of the earth, but Jules had never been able to gracefully accept alliance with a Killer. Before last year's reign of terror, Eli had invited Drake to meetings only when his services as a true vampire—with greater physical and psychic strength fueled by the kill—were desperately needed. Now, he showed up every week.

"You have something on your mind," Eli said, and Jules

could no longer avoid his eyes. "Let's have it out in the open now."

Jules squirmed, his carefully rehearsed speech forgotten.

"What's the matter Jules?" Gray James taunted from across the room. "Cat got your tongue?"

Jules bared his teeth at the asshole, even as Carolyn gave him another elbow to the ribs. In the months that had passed since Jules had suspected Gray of being a serial killer, they'd reached something approximating a truce. That didn't mean they had to like each other.

He didn't dignify Gray's taunt with an answer, instead turning his attention to Eli. "I've found evidence of another Killer," he announced, pulling the handful of neatly folded printouts from his breast pocket. He held the papers up, but didn't unfold them. "I've found about a dozen newspaper articles online that document murders that look suspiciously like vampire kills."

"The hell you have!" Michael Freeman said. "I've been on paper patrol duty for the last six months. If there were a dozen suspicious murders, I'd have noticed it." He glared at Jules, as if Jules had directly questioned his competence. But Michael's youthful appearance did not lend itself to intimidation.

Jules made a calming gesture with his hand. "If they'd happened in Philadelphia, I'm sure you would have noticed." Once more, he turned his attention to Eli. "The murders occurred in and around Baltimore."

A few of the Guardians started murmuring softly to one another. If a Killer dared set foot in the Philadelphia area, the Guardians would destroy him or her as soon as they could. But they'd always been at heart a local organization, and they'd never gone as far afield as Baltimore.

Eli narrowed his eyes and peered at Jules with his too-knowing stare. "And why have you been scouring the Baltimore papers, Jules? I don't remember assigning you the task."

Jules wanted to look away, but Eli wouldn't let him. Damn the old man and his glamour! Eli's eyes narrowed even more at whatever he read in Jules's gaze.

"It wouldn't have anything to do with the fact that Ian Squires lives in Baltimore, would it?"

Eli finally let him go, and Jules dropped his gaze to his feet. He was as transparent as plastic wrap! But where Ian was concerned, he found himself incapable of keeping his emotions under control.

Shaking his head, Jules looked up. "You saw the article in the *Inquirer.*"

"Of course."

"Excuse me," Carolyn interrupted. "For those of us who are new to the Guardian world—who is Ian Squires?"

Jules hoped Eli would answer the question, but he remained annoyingly silent, and all attention was focused on Jules. Memories battered at the barriers in his mind, but he kept them at bay. "He's the vampire who made me." His voice came out flat, though no doubt his eyes glowed with the hatred he'd harbored all these long years. "When the Guardians rescued me, Ian got away. I'd hoped he was dead. But he isn't."

"There was an article in the *Inquirer* last week," Eli said. "It had a picture of a 'philanthropist' who made a generous donation to the University of Pennsylvania."

Jules snorted. "If Ian is a philanthropist, then I'm the Easter Bunny. The article said Ian lived in Baltimore, so I started scanning the Baltimore papers. Like I said, I've already found a dozen suspicious murders. And if Ian has been living there for almost eighty years . . ." How many people had died at Ian's hands? And how badly had his victims suffered before the sadistic bastard killed them? At least half the kills Jules had uncovered involved rape and torture—Ian's specialties.

"So you would like me to send some Guardians down to Baltimore to hunt down Ian Squires and kill him," Eli said.

"In a word, yes." He tensed and held his breath, preparing himself as best he could for Eli's inevitable decision. Eli would send his Guardians to Baltimore, but he'd order Jules to stay here. He'd never put anyone on the task force who had a personal agenda. But Jules was damned if he was staying in Philadelphia while others got the pleasure of killing Ian. And he was prepared to face Eli's considerable wrath when he insisted on going.

"I hate to break this to you, Jules, but there are vampires in every major city in every country in the world. They're naturally drawn to the big cities, where their kills can go unnoticed. There aren't enough of us to police the whole world, or even the whole country."

Jules blinked. "Excuse me? I've just brought you concrete evidence that a Killer has been murdering people for eighty years, and you're telling me we're *not* going to go after him?" He tried to keep the outrage out of his voice, though he doubted he succeeded. Surely he must be hearing Eli wrong.

"If he were to come anywhere near Philadelphia, we would hunt him down and destroy him. But no, I'm not sending anyone to Baltimore after him." Eli held up his hand to forestall the protest Jules was about to make. "In case you haven't noticed, we're a little short on manpower right now."

"Oh for Christ's sake, Eli!" Jules shot out of his chair, unable to keep still. He'd thought he'd been prepared for the worst, but never in his wildest dreams had he supposed Eli would hear this evidence and do *nothing*. "It's not like we've got a daily influx of Killers we've got to deal with. We can spare a few Guardians for the hunt."

Eli's expression hardened, but he didn't otherwise react to Jules's outburst. "I also must say I find it terribly suspicious that Squires would suddenly make a large donation to the university. Vampires are hardly known for their philanthropy."

The other Guardians chuckled, but Jules didn't find it funny. "What's your point?"

"My point is it smells like a trap of some kind. Either Squires is hoping to lure you to Baltimore, or he's trying to lure some Guardians away from Philadelphia. I don't like either possibility."

"I can't believe what I'm hearing. You'll just allow him to keep killing, and killing, and—"

"We have to choose our battles carefully, for solid, logical reasons. *Not* merely based on emotions."

From deep in his belly, Jules felt the rage bubbling and boiling. He wanted Ian dead. For a moment, he'd allowed himself to think he might get his wish, might get to kill the son of a bitch who'd fucked with his mind so badly that eighty years wasn't enough to mend the damage. And now, Eli had snatched that hope away with hardly a care.

The beast stirred within him, a primal force that didn't give a shit about logic. His throat tightened, his breath came quick and short as he battled for calm. His focus narrowed until all the Guardians save Eli faded from his vision.

"Control yourself, Jules," Eli said, his voice somewhere between a warning and a threat.

Last year, when Jules had been convinced Gray James was the Broad Street Banger, he'd found himself battling his temper on an almost daily basis. He'd thought he'd learned to control it, but now it felt almost like a separate being. One that longed to split his skin and burst out into the light.

"Eli, please," he croaked. God, how he hated to beg! Especially in front of all his fellow Guardians. "You don't know how much this means to me."

"Yes, I do." He'd dropped his voice to a soothing croon. "You've been carrying this hatred for a very long time. And you're feeling particularly volatile since—"

"Don't say it!" The words came out a snarl, and he was shaking with the effort of fighting his temper. He *had* to control himself. Eli could squash him like a bug. *Would* squash him, if he thought Jules would go rogue on him.

"—since the death of your son," Eli finished insistently.

Jules clenched both his fists as Eli's words sent a stabbing pain through his chest. It had been two months since Luc died, and Jules hated that the thought could wound him so. Luc had been only two when Jules was forced to abandon him and his mother because he'd been transformed. He'd never really known his son, though he hadn't been able to resist keeping an eye on him from afar. How could the death of a man he barely knew hurt so much? Especially when Luc had suffered from Alzheimer's for years, his death a foregone conclusion.

But Eli had repeatedly warned him the end would hurt, and as usual, he'd been right.

"That has nothing to do with this," Jules insisted. He'd dreamed of revenge against Ian since the day Ian had bitten him.

"I think it does. I think it makes you vulnerable to your emotions. It's your emotions that tell you we should march on Baltimore, when your rational mind has to know—"

"Bullshit!" Jules paced the room in great, angry strides, so furious he wanted to hit something. In some pocket of his mind, he was aware he and Eli weren't alone, but all his attention was focused on the Founder. He caught a glimpse of movement out of the corner of his eye, someone approaching him. Drake.

Jules turned toward the Killer. The rational part of his mind expected Eli to intervene any moment, but that didn't stop him from taking up a defensive position. Drake held his hands up in a placating gesture, but he'd lowered his fangs.

"Sit down, Jules," Drake said.

Adrenaline pumped through Jules's system, and he pulled his lips away from his fangs. "Make me."

Drake rolled his eyes. "You're being juvenile. But if you'd like me to make you sit down, I'd be happy to oblige."

Jules launched himself at the Killer, glad to have an outlet for his rage even while he expected Eli to stop him. But instead of meeting his charge, Drake side-stepped.

Jules hurtled into the cluster of Guardians behind Drake. Hands grabbed hold of him, either hoping to restrain him or to keep them all from falling in a heap. He jerked away from the clutching hands, and his elbow smacked into someone behind him.

Then suddenly his feet weren't on the floor anymore. He flew through the air until he smashed into a wall. His back hit first, then his head. Pain exploded in his skull and his breath whooshed out of him. He slid limply down the wall, just barely conscious, fighting to suck air into his lungs.

Eli hadn't even gotten out of his chair, though all the other Guardians were on their feet. Gray James was snarling at him, fangs bared, but it seemed he was either in better control of his temper than Jules, or Eli was holding him back with glamour.

Jules winced when he saw Carolyn, tucked under Gray's arm, hand clapped to the side of her face.

Was that who he'd hit with his elbow? He shuddered, and the rage drained out of him as quickly as it had come.

Once more, he was lifted into the air by unseen hands. Another shudder rippled through him. How the hell was Eli doing this to him? Glamour gave a vampire the ability to manipulate the minds of mortals—and less powerful vampires. But not the power to lift a man off his feet without touching him! He braced himself, thinking Eli was going to smash him into the wall again. But Eli seemed to see that reason had returned. He released Jules from his glamour—or whatever it was—while Jules was still two or three feet in the air.

Jules tumbled to the floor once more. He refused to meet anyone's eyes. He couldn't have screwed this up any worse if he'd tried.

"Meeting adjourned," Eli said. "For everyone but Jules. We'll reschedule for tomorrow."

No one said a word as the Guardians filed out of the room. Jules kept his eyes fixed on the fleur-de-lis pattern of the rug, not wanting to see the various pitying or maliciously smug expressions he assumed were being tossed his way. He recognized Gray's ratty sneakers coming his way, and he recognized Carolyn's sensible pumps as she headed him off. He was going to have to apologize to her, though how he'd manage it with Gray around was anyone's guess.

But he was getting ahead of himself. First, he had to survive this little tête-à-tête with Eli.

The door to the meeting hall closed with a solid thunk, and Jules forced his gaze up. The look on Eli's face was not promising.

The Founder's physical age appeared to be around sixty. Of only medium height and a little on the thin side, he cultivated a harmless-old-man look. But no one could look at those deep, stormy eyes of his and think he was harmless. Jules shivered. The room always seemed to grow cold when Eli was angry, and he was mad as hell at the moment.

"We've discussed your temper before, Jules," he said, his voice deceptively mild while his eyes blazed and the temperature continued to drop.

Jules had always thought the chill that accompanied Eli's anger was a trick of the mind—until he saw his frosty breath in the air. *Marde!* Just how angry *was* the Founder, anyway? Jules swallowed hard, his heart pounding. He wasn't entirely sure he wasn't about to die, though probably if Eli were going to kill him he'd have done it already.

Well, if he was about to face his death, he wouldn't do it on his knees. Jules forced himself to his feet, his back still aching from the impact with the wall. "I'm sorry, Eli." He almost snorted at his own pathetic words.

"If I'd known you were going to make such an ass of yourself, I would have called you in here last week the moment I saw that article in the paper. Foolish optimist that I am, I thought you'd gained a measure of maturity."

Eli's criticism stung. But worse was knowing he deserved it. He was almost a hundred and ten years old—you'd think he'd have learned more self-control by now. But seeing Ian's face in the paper—so soon after he'd lost Luc—had dug up issues he couldn't seem to rebury.

"I have no maturity where Ian is concerned," he admitted. "You don't know what he did to me."

"Yes, I do."

Jules shook his head, but didn't bother to argue. Yes, he'd told Eli some of the story, told him how Ian had once been his closest friend and then betrayed and bitten him. But he hadn't come close to telling it all.

"Come sit down," Eli said.

Jules noticed with relief that the room was warming again. He took a seat on the sofa nearest Eli's chair and waited for the lecture. But Eli just stared at him with those knowing, piercing eyes of his until Jules squirmed.

"You're at a very dangerous time of your life, my friend," Eli said with surprising gentleness. "Many vampires have . . . strong reactions when the last of the people they knew as mortals die. It can cause something of a vampire mid-life crisis, as it were."

Jules couldn't help a little bark of laughter. "Should I go out and buy a red sports car?"

The corners of Eli's eyes crinkled slightly. "The red might clash with your hair. I'd advise black."

This time the laugh came more naturally. That Eli would

tease him about his vanity relieved him to no end. Yes, he'd fucked up tonight. But Eli could forgive him for it.

"Mortals in mid-life crisis can do stupid things," Eli continued, "like destroying their marriages by looking for something better. Something that doesn't exist."

"And what kind of stupid things do vampires do?"

"Indulge in pointless revenge quests. Alienate the only friends they have by behaving like assholes. The worst of them can go rogue and start killing, but I know you wouldn't do that."

Jules winced, remembering how mindless he'd been in his rage. He'd hit Carolyn, for Christ's sake. He couldn't stand Gray, but he *liked* Carolyn. Not that he'd done it on purpose, but if he'd been in his right mind it never would have happened. He glanced at Eli.

"Why didn't you stop me when I went after Drake?" Keeping the Guardians from fighting with each other was usually part of Eli's job description. Vampires tended to grate on each other's nerves on some primal level, which made cooperation something of a challenge. If it weren't for Eli, the Guardians would have gone their separate ways—or killed each other— long ago.

"I wanted to see if you would stop yourself. You can't *always* rely on me to control your temper for you."

Jules forced a deep breath. He couldn't deny that Eli had a point. "I still don't understand why you won't send a task force to Baltimore. I understand why you won't send *me*, but—"

"Why Baltimore?"

Jules blinked in confusion. "Uh, because Ian is there, killing people, and we're supposedly dedicated to stopping people like him."

Eli shrugged. "Why not New York, then? I guarantee you there are Killers in New York. It's far too good a hiding place for Killers not to take advantage of it. I'm sure there's a bigger population there than in Baltimore. Or what about D.C.? Boston?" He shook his head. "There are too few of us. If we start taking on the world, we'll be destroyed."

"I'm not asking you to take on the world! Just Baltimore."

"Just so you can personally get your revenge. It's not a good enough reason, *especially* when the circumstances are so suspicious. It's not impossible for other vampires to band together against us, especially if they institute a divide-and-conquer strategy." He shook his head once more. "No, Jules. I can't risk it. I'm sorry."

Jules felt his temper rising again and ruthlessly tamped it back down. This was obviously an argument he couldn't win.

He didn't know how he was going to swallow the bitter pill of Ian alive and well and killing in Baltimore. But somehow he was going to have to. Because only the worst kind of idiot would defy Eli's direct orders and single-handedly take on a mature Killer on his home turf.

2

At three o'clock in the morning, Jules decided it was pointless to lie to himself any longer. Whatever had awakened inside him when he'd first seen Ian's picture in the paper was not about to go back to sleep. No matter what Eli ordered.

He sighed heavily as he folded a cashmere sweater into his suitcase. Eli did not tolerate rebellion. At the turn of the last century, he'd let a Guardian leave the organization. A century of living outside Eli's calming influence had turned Archer Montgomery, a former Guardian, into the Broad Street Banger. Eli wouldn't chance something like that happening again. If Jules made it out of Philly alive, he knew he could never come back.

The thought of never coming back made Jules's throat ache, and he cursed Ian for the millionth time for so thoroughly destroying his life. He was giving up everything that made his immortal life feel worthwhile by defying Eli's orders. And yet, he had enough self-awareness to realize he had no choice. Tonight's explosion of temper wasn't his first, and it wouldn't be his last, as long as Ian lived. He'd rather damn himself in his quest for vengeance than risk killing one of his fellow Guardians in a fit of rage. Only Eli and Drake were powerful enough to subdue him if his control lapsed again, and he couldn't count on them being there next time it did.

Jules closed his bulging suitcase and yanked the zipper, practically pulling it off in his agitation. He got down on his hands and knees and pulled another suitcase out from under his bed. If he was never coming back, he might as well take as much luggage as he could carry.

The doorbell rang just as he stood up with the second suitcase in hand. He started. Had Eli guessed his intentions and sent a party of Guardians to stop him—which would likely mean a death sentence?

No, he thought as he slowly descended the narrow staircase to the first floor of his house. Eli was capable of ruthlessness when necessary, but it was a subtle ruthlessness. For instance, everyone knew Eli had killed Tim Carter, a Guardian who'd rebelled against him during the Banger case last year. But Eli had never said a word about it to anyone. It was as if Carter had never existed. Jules had nerved himself up to ask Eli about it once, but the Founder's only answer had been a long, silent stare.

Jules reached out with his senses as he approached the door and discovered that, as he'd expected, there was no party of vampires on his doorstep. All he sensed was a single mortal presence. His brows drew together as he leaned toward the peephole. What mortal would be coming to his house at three in the morning?

"Come on, Jules, open up already. It's cold out here."

Standing on his doorstep was the *last* person he'd expect to see at a time like this. He threw the door open and stood aside to let Carolyn come in out of the cold. A brief psychic survey reassured him that Gray wasn't lurking nearby.

"Brr," Carolyn said, tucking her hands under her arms and hunching in on herself. She wore a warm-looking—if not particularly flattering—puffy coat, but no hat and no scarf and no gloves. No wonder she was cold.

She turned to face him in his foyer. The cold had reddened her cheeks and chapped her lips, but what caught his eye and made guilt kick him in the gut was the bruise darkening on her chin.

He forced himself to meet her eyes. "I'm very sorry about what happened," he said, wincing involuntarily as he remembered the feel of his elbow making contact. "I—"

She held up both hands. "Don't worry about it. It was an accident." She flashed him a rueful smile. "I was a cop for eight years. This is hardly the first bruise I've gotten in the line of duty."

He grimaced and gestured her into the living room, wishing he could offer her something to drink to ward off the chill. But the only thing he had in the house was milk and blood, and he felt quite certain she wouldn't want any of that.

Carolyn opened her coat, but didn't take it off. Then she sat on his butter-yellow leather sofa and looked up at him inquiringly. He was too edgy to want to sit, but he could hardly stand here looming over her, so he lowered himself onto an arm chair

"So, what brings you to this part of town?" he asked.

She shrugged. "Just coming to see if you were all right."

"Me?" He wondered if there were anything she could have said that would have taken him aback more. "You're the one with the battle scars."

Her smile was warm and sweet. "I think yours are internal and harder to treat." The smile faded and she leaned forward, peering at his face intently. "How's your back?"

He stretched tentatively, but felt no twinge of lingering pain. Luckily for him, Eli hadn't hit him hard enough to break anything, and bruises healed in a manner of minutes. "It's fine."

Her forehead furrowed. "What happened in there exactly?"

He wished he knew. "Eli's one scary dude. Even *I* didn't know he could do that."

"Makes you wonder what else he can do that we don't know about."

"I suggest you don't think about it. That's what I've decided to do."

She smiled faintly. "So, you're all right?"

"I'm fine. Really. Thanks for caring enough to check on me. You're a really nice person." A lump formed in his throat. He had to shut up immediately, before he said something else that sounded suspiciously like a goodbye.

"You're not going to do anything stupid, are you Jules?"

He hoped he managed to keep his expression bland and unconcerned. "You mean like take off for Baltimore?" He grinned at her, trying for his usual easy sarcasm, not at all sure he was pulling it off. "Only an idiot would do something like that."

She pushed a lock of blonde hair out of her face. He could hear the crackle of static as she did, and when she took her hand away, several stray strands floated with their electrical charge. Amazing how she still managed to look so pretty with her cold-reddened skin, a bruise on her chin, and her hair standing on end. She was *way* too good for the likes of Gray James.

"So the question becomes, are you an idiot?"

Once again he forced himself to make eye contact. Her detective instincts would go on high alert if he didn't. "No, I'm not an idiot," he said, looking her straight in the eye and trying to sound a hundred percent certain. If Carolyn caught wind of his plan, she'd very likely rat him out before he could get out of town. She'd think it was for his own good, but she'd be wrong.

He couldn't tell from the look on her face whether she believed him or not, but she seemed willing to let the subject drop. "I'm glad to hear that," she said, rising to her feet and zipping her coat once more.

"I still don't quite get why you're here," he said as he walked her to the door.

"I just wanted to let you know there were no hard feelings."

"You *should* have hard feelings. I should never have let my temper get the better of me like that."

She patted his shoulder. "If it makes you feel any better," she said with a wry grin, "Gray has enough hard feelings for both of us."

"I'll bet. Does he know you're here?"

She laughed and opened the door, stepping out into the cold. "If you tell him, I'll deny it to my dying day." She reached out a hand. "Now let's shake on the no-hard-feelings thing."

Her contagious good humor momentarily lightened his

heart. Instead of shaking her hand as she'd intended, he raised it to his lips and with exaggerated ceremony planted a courtly kiss on her knuckles. She rolled her eyes, extricating her hand from his.

"You're a *hopeless* charmer, Jules," she teased

He put his hand over his heart and bowed his head. "Thank you. And if you ever get tired of Gray . . ."

She smacked his shoulder with the back of her hand, but he thought she was secretly a little pleased with his flirting. Or maybe, he thought as he watched her walk away, she was just relieved because the flirting was more "normal" behavior for him.

Knowing his performance for Carolyn wasn't exactly Oscar material, Jules decided he'd better leave town as soon as possible. Too bad he'd never bothered learning to drive, but it hadn't seemed worth the trouble. It's not like he ever *went* anywhere. Now he was stuck taking the train, which wasn't running at three in the morning. But as soon as the sun set tomorrow night, he'd be on the first train out of there.

Wishing he had a little more time to plan his strategy, he hurried back to his bedroom to continue packing.

తు

Hannah Moore's office always seemed huge and empty, now that she was going it on her own. She'd donated Carolyn's desk to charity so she wouldn't have to be reminded daily that her former business partner had moved on to a bizarre new career as a vampire hunter. Hannah wondered if she ought to go looking for another partner, but she wasn't sure she could stand working with anyone other than Carolyn. She chuckled to herself as she unlocked the door and flipped the light on.

Okay, so maybe it was more of a problem that no one else could stand working with *her*.

Her first task of the morning—as always—was to start a big pot of coffee, of which she would drink way too many cups before the morning was even halfway past. She inhaled the rich, heady scent of the freshly ground coffee as she scooped it into the basket. Then she pushed the brew button and waited impatiently for the carafe to fill.

"Extra strength, as usual?" a voice asked from behind her.

A little shriek of surprise escaped her as she whirled around to see Carolyn standing in the doorway. Hannah put a hand to her heart and glared at her best friend.

"Geez, Carolyn! You've been hanging around with Dracula too long. Don't you know better than to sneak up on someone?" Hannah hated just about everything about vampires, but that quiet, sneaky way they moved was at the top of the list.

"I thought we had an agreement that you weren't going to call Gray Dracula anymore. Or Vlad."

Hannah sniffed and pushed her new glasses—damn, she hated those things!—back up her nose. "I forgot. So sue me." There was a mug's worth of coffee in the bottom of the carafe, so she stuck her mug in the stream and poured, sticking the carafe back on the warmer with only a few drops spilled. "Want a cup?"

"No thanks," Carolyn said, holding up her hand. "It's too close to bedtime."

"Ah, so this is still yesterday for you." Doing daytime investigation work for the Guardians while spending quality time with Gray at night, Carolyn had adopted a bizarre sleep schedule that Hannah still hadn't quite figured out.

"Something like that," her friend laughed, taking a seat on the couch that served as a waiting room.

Cupping her hands around her coffee mug, Hannah joined her. And that was when she got a good look at the side of her face. Hannah thunked her mug down on the coffee table, heedless of the coffee that spilled over the edge and dampened the *Sports Illustrated* beneath it.

"If Gray did that to you, there's nowhere on this earth he can run that I won't find him." She hadn't liked Gray when he was mortal—in her opinion, he'd been way too much of a stick-in-the-mud for Carolyn—and she didn't like him any better as a vampire. He wasn't a stick-in-the-mud anymore, but he'd morphed into a testosterone-laden alpha male. The kind of guy who was guaranteed to rub Hannah the wrong way.

Carolyn waved off her concern. "Don't worry, it wasn't Gray."

"Then who was it?"

"Don't worry about it, Hannah. That's not what I'm here to talk about."

Hannah bit her tongue. She'd always felt this overwhelming urge to protect her friend, but she was trying to learn to back off. There was something about Carolyn's petiteness, her fragile, china-doll looks that made Hannah want to mother her. Only Carolyn didn't *need* mothering. Despite her delicate looks, she was perfectly capable of taking care of herself. And now that Gray was back in her life, filling the great emotional void he'd left when he'd jilted her . . . Hannah had to admit she kind of missed being needed.

She picked up her coffee cup, ignoring the drips that ran

down its side, and took a gratifying sip. From the seriousness of Carolyn's expression, she guessed she'd need the caffeine. "So, what's going on? Another vamp invasion?" Usually, Hannah resisted asking about Carolyn's vampire-hunting job. When at all possible, she'd rather pretend that vampires were just a myth. Hey, what she didn't know wouldn't hurt her, right?

"No, nothing like that." Carolyn rubbed her hands together in a gesture that looked suspiciously nervous.

Uh-oh. This didn't look good at all. "Come on, honey. Out with it." She couldn't help harboring a secret hope that Carolyn had decided to dump Gray. And all the rest of the Guardians, for that matter. Yes, Gray undeniably made her happy, and Hannah was correspondingly happy for her. But unlike Carolyn, who was living very much in the now, Hannah couldn't help peeking into the future.

What would happen when Carolyn aged, and Gray didn't? Gray had broken her heart once—would he do it again?

"Okay," Carolyn said. "This is going to sound kind of weird."

Hannah groaned. "Man, if *you* think it's weird, I'm in big trouble!"

Her friend grinned at that. "You've got a point there. But seriously. It's about Jules."

Definitely *not* something Hannah'd been expecting. "Jules? You mean Mr. I'm-prettier-than-you-are?"

Carolyn stifled a laugh. "You know anyone else named Jules? Yes, him."

Hannah hadn't set eyes on any vamp but Gray since last

year's excitement. And that was just the way she wanted things. Actually, if she could have skipped Gray, too, life would have been just about perfect. "So, what about him? Did he break a nail?"

"Hannah," Carolyn said reproachfully.

"Hey, I can't help it. First impressions die hard." And Jules made quite a first impression. His wardrobe must cost more than the gross national product of several small countries. And he probably spent hours in front of a mirror to get his hair just so—the casually wind-blown look that he no doubt thought was sexy.

Okay, so maybe it *was* kinda sexy, but his obvious pride in his appearance ruined the effect.

"Okay, go on. What about Jules?"

Carolyn bit her lip. "I think he's in trouble."

Frowning, Hannah listened as Carolyn told her about the outburst at Eli's. She had to admit, she kind of agreed with Jules. There was something downright *wrong* about letting this Squires guy just keep killing people with impunity. Still, it wasn't like there was anything anyone could do about it if the Great and Powerful Oz put his foot down.

"Okay, so Jules is going off the deep end. So what?"

"So I think he's going to run off to Baltimore after this guy without Eli's permission."

"I repeat, so what?"

Carolyn wouldn't meet her eyes. Yet another bad sign. "So you can imagine what kind of trouble a vampire could get himself into in a strange city. He won't have a house to spend the day in, and hotels are dangerous places."

"Let me get this straight—the guy's going down to Balti-more to try to kill a vampire who's stronger than he is, and you're worried about him staying in a hotel?"

Carolyn's lips twitched into a smile that swiftly faded. "I think he's going to get himself killed. Eli thinks it's some kind of trap and I tend to agree." She met Hannah's gaze. "We can't afford to lose him, Hannah. Next to Eli, he's the oldest, most powerful Guardian."

"Except for that Drake guy, right? The serial Killer with a heart of gold?"

Carolyn acknowledged that with a slight nod. "Drake's great, but . . ." She shrugged. "The Guardians work with him because Eli says they have to. They'll never fully accept him. We need Jules."

Hannah narrowed her eyes at her friend. "Okay. Let's say you're right. Why are you telling me?" But she already had a damn good idea, and Carolyn's sheepish grin confirmed it. "So, you'd like me to dump all the cases I'm working on right now and follow Jules to Baltimore. And do what, exactly?"

"Keep him safe during the day when he's completely help-less. And if you could talk sense into him, that would be great." Carolyn grinned. "Though somehow, I don't think that's hap-pening.

"I'll pay your retainer, of course. I'd go myself, but I don't think Gray would quite understand. And I think Eli might understand even less."

Hannah had never met the founder of the Guardians, and she profoundly hoped to keep it that way. He sounded like a real weirdo. The guy was some kind of über-vamp, but he refused to leave his house even when people were getting killed right and left and he might have been able to stop it. She was less than impressed with him, no matter how much Carolyn and Gray seemed to revere him.

"He's not the kind of guy I want to piss off," Carolyn concluded. "No other Guardian would dare go with Jules now, but going down there alone is incredibly foolish."

"So why don't you just tell Yoda what you think is up? He can lock Jules in his room or something."

But Carolyn shook her head, not even cracking a smile at the Yoda reference. "I'd feel like the worst kind of tattletale doing that."

"And telling me doesn't count as tattling."

"Right. It's up to you, Hannah. I know you don't want anything to do with the Guardians, and I know you didn't like Jules much. I won't hold it against you if you don't want to do this." Her features turned stern. "And I *will* hold it against you if you decide to go down there and give Jules more than just a little daytime logistical support."

With a sigh, Hannah leaned back into the cushions of the couch, sipping at her coffee. Why should she stick her neck out for Jules? She barely knew the guy, and like Carolyn said, she wasn't exactly fond of him. She had a full case load at the moment, though admittedly nothing that couldn't wait.

It was Carolyn who got her jollies fighting the good fight, making the world safe for truth, justice, and the American way, or whatever. Hannah was happy in her own little corner of the world, hunting down deadbeat dads and photographing cheating husbands.

"I'll think about it," she said.

Carolyn smiled at her. "That's all I could ask for."

But Hannah had a pretty good idea Carolyn was hoping for more. Worse, she had a pretty good idea she was going to get it.

3

Drake wasn't surprised when Eli asked him to stay after the meeting adjourned. When Jules had failed to put in an appearance, he'd known there would be trouble. Eli had waited until all reasonable hope that Jules would show up was gone, then started the meeting without comment. No doubt everyone in the room had reached the same conclusion—the damn fool was on his way to Baltimore to get himself killed.

When the last of the Guardians left the room, Drake sat on the couch facing Eli, waiting for the Founder to speak. But Eli just looked at him, an assessing gaze that made Drake want to crawl under the sofa and hide. He fought his instinctive reaction and scowled.

"Stop looking at me like that!" he said.

Eli blinked, and the penetrating stare turned into a slight smile. "Like what?"

Like you're trying to peel the flesh away and get a peek at my soul, he thought, but refrained from saying. "You know damn well what I mean. If you want to know something, just come straight out and ask me." Unlike the true Guardians, Drake refused to let Eli intimidate him. He'd known Eli too long, and understood him far better than anyone else. Not that that was saying much.

"I need you to go to Baltimore," Eli said.

Drake nodded. "Yeah, I kind of figured that's what you had in mind."

"You have to bring Jules back."

Drake met the Founder's steady gaze. "Why?"

"He has no idea what he's walking into."

It was Drake's turn for the long, hard stare, but Eli seemed disinclined to volunteer any more information. "And you do?"

Eli's chin tilted down in the slightest of nods. "The task he's set himself is beyond him."

Drake mulled that over. When he wanted to, Eli could wipe even the faintest trace of emotion—or humanity—from his expression. He was doing it now, his eyes strangely blank, all the muscles of his face immobilized. Even Drake found that look unnerving, and despite his assertion that he wasn't intimidated by Eli, it was hard to push words out of his throat. He forced himself to speak anyway.

"What's going on, Eli? You have to give me a little more to go on."

"It's very simple. I want you to bring Jules back. As soon as possible."

Eli made a habit of being close-mouthed, but this was an extreme even for him. "So it's okay for *me* to have no idea what I'm walking into, but it's not okay for Jules? Is that what you're telling me?"

Eli visibly debated with himself before speaking again. "My

intention—and my hope—is that you bring him back before any trouble starts."

In other words, Eli wasn't going to give Drake even a hint of what was happening in Baltimore and why he was so eager to save Jules from his own idiocy. "Not enough info, Eli." Drake was in a unique position amongst the Guardians in that they needed him more than he needed them. Considerably more. Which gave him a strong enough bargaining position to say no when he wanted to.

The temperature in the room dropped, and Eli's face no longer wore that disturbingly impassive expression. "Once upon a time, people respected me enough to take things on faith."

It was true that before last year's troubles, the Guardians—and even Drake himself—had followed Eli's orders with barely a question. But things had changed. Eli no longer seemed in-fallible, and that necessarily weakened his authority.

Drake chose his words carefully. "I respect you a great deal, or I wouldn't be here. I know you have secrets." He allowed himself a faint smile. "I might even know what some of them are, and I'm not about to share them with anyone. But you're asking me to do something that my every instinct tells me is dangerous, and I'm sorry, Eli, but I'm not walking blindly into it."

With an irritable grunt, Eli rose from his chair and turned to face the fire. For long minutes, he stood silently watching the flames while Drake waited for him to speak. No doubt the Founder was trying to decide how much to tell. Drake wished Eli would trust him enough to tell him the whole truth, rather than calculating what was the least amount of information he could reveal while still getting his way.

Finally, Eli turned to face him once more, shaking his head. "I can't afford to have Jules kill Ian Squires." He returned to his seat, his expression grim. "He's more likely to get himself killed than actually succeed in his quest, but I can't take any chances."

Drake cocked his head. "And why, pray tell, do you feel a need to protect Squires?"

"I'm not protecting him, *per se*." He heaved a heavy sigh. "You know more about vampire societies outside Philadelphia than any of the Guardians. You know how . . . territorial . . . master vampires can be."

It was true that before he'd encountered Eli, Drake had had dealings with the outside world that the Guardians knew nothing about. In every major city he knew, there were one or more vampire "families"—a master vampire and his or her fledglings. In some cities, these families acted remarkably like street gangs, claiming territory and fighting amongst themselves to expand their boundaries. It went without saying that Jules, as a foreign vampire, would not be welcomed with open arms in the city of Baltimore.

"Yes, I know," Drake agreed, his mind still trying to puzzle out what Eli was getting at. "Jules will step on toes the moment he sets foot in Baltimore. What of it? And why does it matter if he kills Squires?"

Eli squirmed and looked remarkably uncomfortable. "I have an agreement with the Master of Baltimore," he admitted. "A non-interference agreement. If Jules kills one of her fledglings, that will most definitely break our agreement."

Drake sagged in his chair, more shocked by Eli's confession than he'd like to admit. He'd always thought he himself was the only Killer Eli would tolerate, and that he was tolerated because of his strong moral code. But a master vampire wouldn't have the same kind of scruples. He'd thought Eli's commitment to destroying Killers was unshakable. Of course, Eli had refrained from killing Drake, so that should have been his first clue that the Founder was more flexible than one might originally have thought.

"I've disillusioned you," Eli said, with a sad little smile. "For that I'm deeply sorry."

Drake waved the apology off. "No need. I understand that the world isn't painted in black and white."

"I've had to make certain concessions to ensure the survival of the Guardians. I don't *like* it, but there you have it."

"So you have agreements with other masters as well. That's why you never send the Guardians out of the area."

But to Drake's surprise, Eli shook his head. "I don't send them out of the area because they're not strong enough to overcome a master with a gang of fledglings. My only special agreement is with the Master of Baltimore, with whom I was . . . acquainted long ago."

Drake's curiosity was most definitely piqued, but Eli continued before Drake could ask any questions.

"Camille could destroy the Guardians if she wanted too. She's quite old, and quite powerful, and she knows—" Eli cut himself off with a frown. "She knows how to exploit our vulnerabilities."

But that hadn't been what he'd originally meant to say. A suspicion crept into Drake's mind and took root. All the years he'd known Eli, Drake had managed to keep his suspicions to himself. No doubt he should do the same now, but his tongue seemed to have a different idea.

"She knows you're a Killer," he said, and saw Eli tense.

Personally, Drake was amazed the thought never seemed to occur to the rest of the Guardians. How could someone who didn't feed on the kill possibly have the kind of massive power that Eli had more than once demonstrated? But the Guardians didn't *want* to know the truth about their Founder, and so they allowed themselves to believe he was some kind of mysterious anomaly, an immensely powerful Guardian who'd never killed a mortal soul.

Now that he'd opened his mouth, Drake figured he might as well keep talking, despite the noticeable chill in the air. "I would guess that you're old enough to venture out and about in broad daylight, so you can kill when your Guardians don't know about it. And you've built this fable that you never leave the grounds of your house to provide yourself a ready alibi.

"I'm not one to throw stones, Eli. I'm certainly not going to tell anyone, if that's why you're glaring at me like that."

A long, tense silence followed. The air had grown positively arctic, and Drake wondered if he'd overstepped his bounds. Perhaps now that Eli realized the extent of Drake's knowledge, he'd decide Drake had to go. But even in the face of Eli's anger, Drake didn't quite feel afraid of him. Wary, yes, but not afraid.

With another heavy sigh, Eli swallowed the bitter pill. "My authority has been weakened enough already. If the Guardians were to suspect me of any hypocrisy . . ."

Drake knew exactly where Eli was coming from. In the outside world, master vampires held their "families" together via the bond between master and fledgling. Eli had no such bond with his Guardians. As he'd said in the past, he led only as long as the Guardians let him lead. If the Guardians were to learn the distasteful truth, he might not be able to hold them together anymore.

Eli was right. Jules couldn't be allowed to kill Squires, not when the Master of Baltimore held such a terrible threat over Eli's head. The Guardians' mission was too important, and they'd never survive without Eli.

"I'll go to Baltimore," Drake said, "and I'll do my best to bring Jules back."

"And if you can't persuade him to come back?" Eli's face had gone impassive again, his thoughts and emotions shuttered tightly.

"I won't kill him, Eli. I have to draw the line somewhere." Jules was an arrogant, annoying prick, but at heart he was relatively decent. *Not* someone Drake's conscience could handle killing.

Eli nodded. "All right, then. You'd better be at your most persuasive. And keep in mind what's at stake."

Drake knew Eli hoped that if push came to shove, Drake would make the "right" decision and kill Jules if he refused to abandon his vendetta. But that just wasn't going to happen. He'd find some way to get Jules out of Baltimore, even if he had to tie him up and stash him in the trunk of a car to drag him back to Eli. It would be up to Eli to decide what to do with him then.

అం

IT HAD BEEN ONE hell of a hectic day. After contacting all her clients to let them know she'd been called out of town for an emergency, Hannah'd gotten right to work figuring out where Jules was staying in Baltimore. A surprisingly easy task, actually. He wasn't making any particular attempt to be sneaky. She'd guessed—correctly—that someone as fastidious as he would stay at a high-class hotel.

She'd called two hotels and asked to be connected to Jules Gerard with no success. Then she'd called the Harbor Court hotel. After the operator's "one moment, I'll connect you," Hannah had hastily hung up.

As she packed her bags, she thought long and hard about whether to take her gun with her. After the Banger incident, when her lucky shot with Carolyn's borrowed gun had saved the day, she'd reluctantly decided it was time to get a gun of her own and learn to shoot it. But she hated the damn thing. When she was ten, she'd gotten hold of her father's gun and almost shot her brother's foot off while playing with it to prove she wasn't a sissy. She still occasionally had nightmares, hearing her brother scream, seeing the blood oozing from the wound. He bore the scar to this day, but now the damn fool thought it was a funny story. Ever since that day, she'd decided guns and her were a bad combination. But now that she knew about vampires, she found she felt safer armed and dangerous.

Of course, she had no permit to carry a concealed weapon in Baltimore. She could get into deep shit if she was caught with it. But how could she possibly go down there with no weapon?

Crossing her fingers, she tossed the gun and a box of bullets into her suitcase.

Her lemon of a car was in the shop for the umpteenth

time, so she decided to rent a nice, shiny Taurus for the trip. She loaded up with maps at the rental place, but she was a tad . . . directionally challenged. Three hours and too many wrong turns to count later, she gratefully pulled up to the front doors of the hotel. The gratefulness turned to unease when she got a good look at the place. She'd known from her research that it was a nice hotel, but she hadn't realized *how* nice. She made a good living, but this place was definitely *not* in her price range. She almost lost her lunch when she found out parking would cost her twenty-one dollars a day. Maybe she should have taken the train after all.

Her discomfort rose another notch when she stepped into the lobby. "Holy shit," she muttered under her breath. The place was a freakin' *palace.* Her shoes made soft clinking noises as she crossed the floor of creamy ivory tile. The gorgeous flower arrangement that dominated the room was bigger than she was, and overflowed with sunflowers and lilies and exotic greens. A graceful curving staircase, complete with red-patterned carpet, gave the lobby a *Gone with the Wind* feel. And there was a crystal chandelier. In the *lobby.* Motel 6 this was not. Why couldn't Jules have been a cheapskate?

Trying not to look awed at her surroundings, she made her way to the reception desk. She could just use a house phone and ask to be connected to Jules's room, but thinking about what this trip was going to cost her made her grumpy enough to want to give him a hard time. So instead of calling his room, she went to the front desk and asked them to leave a message, saying only that an "old friend" would meet him in the bar. No doubt Jules would think the message was from Squires.

As she should have expected, the bar was as classy as the rest of the hotel. It was called the Explorer's Lounge, and was decorated in an elegant safari motif, with murals on the walls and antiques everywhere. She felt like some kind of barbarian ordering a beer—this was more of a cognac kind of joint. But a Corona was about as high falutin' a drink as she could handle, so she ordered one and tried to look inconspicuous as she waited for Jules to make an appearance.

Minutes ticked slowly by as she nursed her beer. She smiled faintly to herself, trying to imagine what kind of face Jules was going to make when he saw her. And how grateful he was going to be to have her help. Not!

Some of her self-assurance fled when she glanced at her watch and noticed it was six-thirty already. She'd thought for sure he'd be down by now. Certainly he was awake. Maybe he hadn't noticed the message light on his phone? She debated calling, but decided against it, at least for now. She ordered another beer and settled in to wait some more.

She'd just decided she'd have to call after all when Jules finally made his appearance. No attempt at stealth—he was striding toward the bar with calculated purpose, his face set in a deep scowl that would be unbecoming on anyone else. Damn, she'd forgotten what eye-candy he was. He didn't see Hannah at first, so she took a moment to ogle before the games began.

It was no wonder it had taken him so long to come down— he'd obviously spent a good deal of time in front of the mirror. His dress was casual—for Jules, at least—but screamed of money and good taste. Hannah imagined each item had a designer label on it, but not being a connoisseur of men's fashion, she couldn't have said which ones. His long-sleeved forest-green shirt had the sheen of fine silk. The color was a perfect complement to his artfully tousled auburn hair. She couldn't help wondering how much mousse it had taken to get those fine locks into such perfect disarray. Charcoal gray trousers hugged his hips, and she knew if he turned around the rear view would be spectacular.

His features and his clothes should have given him a pretty-boy look, and yet Hannah would never dream of describing him that way. Maybe it was just his expression, his sensuous lips pressed into a thin line of anger, his expressive eyes narrowed as he scanned the small crowd at the bar. Or maybe it was just that she knew he was a vampire, and therefore supremely dangerous.

When Jules finally caught sight of her, Hannah smiled brightly and waved. His expression darkened even more, and something inside Hannah quailed. Instinct told her to run like hell as he stalked toward her table, his anger a palpable force. But from long experience, she'd learned to hide her vulnerabilities well, so instead of cowering, she raised her beer bottle in a mock toast.

He came to a stop directly in front of her, glowering down at her ferociously.

"Yeah, glad to see you too," she said. "Have a seat—I'm getting neck strain looking up at you like this."

One corner of his lips lifted in something like a snarl. He jerked a chair out from under the table and sat. "What do you think you're doing?" He leaned forward to crowd her space, and his voice was a low growl he expected to intimidate her.

She sniffed the air and grinned at him. "You know, you'd

be much scarier if you skipped the mousse and perfume." She sniffed again, catching the warm, spicy scent of him. "Not that I'm complaining." Whatever he was wearing smelled damn good.

A muscle ticked in his jaw. "It's aftershave, not perfume." He sounded like he was one step shy of strangling her.

She shrugged. "Whatever. It smells nice, anyway. But it really detracts from your terror-factor."

"All right, how about this?" He pulled his lips away from his teeth, giving her a glimpse of the long, sharp fangs he'd lowered.

She shuddered deep inside. She'd seen vampire fangs before, of course, but that didn't make the sight of them any easier to swallow. "Ooh, I'm scared," she mocked, though she wasn't sure she was entirely convincing. "You planning to use those on me?" An image came to her mind—her neck stretched out and vulnerable while Jules lowered his head to her throat. The image was strangely, unnervingly erotic.

He leaned back in his chair, shaking his head at her. "I'd forgotten what a pain in the ass you were. What do you want?"

"I'm on assignment in Baltimore and thought I'd look you up."

"*Hostie d'idiot,*" he growled.

Jules got a great kick out of insulting people in French, or Quebecian, or whatever it was he spoke. Hannah figured he did it because he always got such a reaction from people—there was something creepy about being insulted but not knowing what exactly the insult was. Well, she wasn't about to give him the pleasure of reacting!

"I'm here as your guardian angel." She giggled. "*Guardian* angel. Gee, I made a joke and didn't know it."

"Your clever wit astounds me." A cocktail waitress made her way to their table and asked Jules if he wanted anything to drink. He waved her off. "Ah, for the days when I could drown my sorrows in alcohol!" he said when she'd wandered away.

Hannah furrowed her brow at him. "What sorrows would those be? Me? Or the ones that brought you to Baltimore in the first place?"

Not surprisingly, he didn't answer. "I know Eli wouldn't have sent you after me, so I must presume Carolyn's the culprit."

"Yeah. She's got this funny thing where she feels grateful to you for saving her and Gray's lives. And she seems to think you'll have a tough time all alone in a strange city."

For the first time, he smiled, an expression that softened his face and took the glint of anger out of his eyes. "She's a remarkable woman."

He sounded so wistful, Hannah's suspicions were aroused. "You don't have a thing for her, do you?"

She'd expected a quick denial, so when his expression turned pensive she was surprised. "If she were to climb into my bed, I wouldn't kick her out," he said finally. "But I wouldn't say I have a *thing* for her."

Hannah was surprised at the zing of jealousy that admission caused. Stupid! Carolyn was so damn sweet and pretty Hannah doubted there was a straight male on the planet who would kick her out of bed. Besides, it wasn't as if Hannah had any interest in Jules. The guy was good-looking, but that was about all he had going for him.

"So Carolyn sent you here to look after me while I hunt my maker, is that the gist of things?"

"In a nutshell."

"Of course you realize I don't need your help."

"Of course," she said and almost laughed at how concerned he looked by her easy agreement. She let her words hang for a moment just to savor his discomfiture. "You're a lone Guardian in an unfamiliar city, hunting a Killer who's way more powerful than you and who may be trying to set a trap for you. How could you possibly need any help?" She swigged the last of her beer, and sighed in contentment. One thing she had to admit—it was fun to yank Jules's chain. And easy, too.

The dark, brooding look was back on his face. "I'll find a way to get to him. And the last thing I need is a helpless mortal tagging along, getting in the way and distracting me."

"Yeah, that's what you said last year, too. Remember? When you went running off to take on the Banger and commanded me to stay in the hotel?"

He'd bullied and badgered her until she'd agreed to stay behind, but of course she'd been lying through her teeth. If she hadn't arrived at the scene when she did, very likely there wouldn't be a single Guardian left alive today.

"You said yourself it was a lucky shot."

"Yeah, well, you make your own luck." But she knew Jules would remain stuck on his 'helpless mortal' idea, so she decided to try another tack. "So tell me, do you know where Squires lives?"

She could see at once that she'd hit a nerve. His face was too expressive to hide his chagrin. "Not at the moment, but I'll find him."

"How?"

Jules squirmed and didn't answer.

Hannah pounded her point home. "I already checked to see if he was listed in the phone book and came up with a big fat nothing. So tell me, Sherlock, what's your first step going to be?"

He heaved an exasperated sigh and ran a hand through his hair, ruining its orderly disarray. "Okay, you're right, I don't know. I didn't have much time for planning before I had to get out of town quick. But I'll figure something out."

"Hmm. Too bad you don't have a professional private investigator around to help you out."

"I'll hire one!"

"What? Hire a helpless mortal? One who doesn't even know what he's up against? Jules, that seems a bit shitty even for you."

He looked like he wanted to shake her. "How did Carolyn put up with you for so long? I swear, if you'd been *my* business partner, I'd have killed you before the first month was up."

"Yeah, I'm sure Carolyn felt that temptation off and on. But I was kinda handy to have around, so she let me live."

In truth, Carolyn was one of the few female friends Hannah'd had since her college days. Her family was a bastion of testosterone, her father a firefighter and her three brothers all policemen. Sometimes she thought testosterone was a communicable disease and she'd caught it. She couldn't quite get into all the girly stuff other women were into. Shopping was a painful chore that needed to be done, not an enjoyable social engagement. Cooking was best done by microwave with as little effort as possible. She'd rather watch *Die Hard* than *Sleepless in Seattle,* and she was a regular at Eagles and Phillies games. And that wasn't even mentioning her smart mouth, which had on occasion lost her friends of both sexes.

"What would be *your* next step if you were on this case?" Jules asked, every word dragged from his mouth with obvious reluctance.

She shrugged. "I'd start by calling the *Inquirer.* If they did an article on Squires, they may well have his contact information."

"Surely it won't be that easy."

"Probably not. Still, it's worth a try. You never know."

"Fine. I'll call them tonight."

"No you won't." She chuckled at the way Jules bristled. "First off, the likelihood that you'd be able to get in touch with anyone who knows anything at this hour is next to nil. Secondly, if you just ask them straight out for his address or phone number, no one will give you diddly."

His eyes narrowed. "I presume you have a counter-suggestion?"

"You betcha. We wait until tomorrow. In the morning, while you're getting your beauty sleep, I'll call the paper and charm them into giving me the info."

"You? *Charm* them? Are you mad?" Amusement soothed away the angry line between his brows. His eyes were such a beautiful warm shade of brown when they weren't narrowed in anger.

"I can be charming when I want to be," Hannah said, smiling despite herself. She had to admit, she kind of enjoyed sparring with Jules. When she stuck her verbal pins in Gray, he'd just get curt and irritable, but Jules actually fought back.

"I'd have to see it to believe it."

"Too bad you'll be fast asleep at the time."

He sobered quickly, giving her a penetrating look. "This is very dangerous, Hannah. If Ian really has lured me down here, then if you start poking around you'll probably set off some kind of alarm. Believe me, you don't want to find yourself face-to-face with this son of a bitch."

It chilled Hannah more than she liked to admit that she saw what looked like a flicker of fear in his eyes. Jules wasn't the kind of guy to reveal his vulnerabilities. Hannah knew all about hiding beneath a façade of confidence, could recognize the symptoms when she saw it in others. For that façade to slip for even a moment was not a good sign at all.

For half a minute, she refrained from poking into the crack in the façade, but she'd never been one to let tact get in the way of what she wanted. "So, this guy Ian. He's the one who made you a vampire, right?"

Jules stiffened. "That's right."

"May I ask what happened?"

"No, you may not."

"Why?"

His fierce glare was back again, in full force. "Don't press me on this," he said, leaning forward. This time, she really *did* feel intimidated by his anger. His eyes seemed almost to glow with it, and the air fairly shimmered around him. "If I have to use glamour to make you shut up, I will. And I can guarantee you won't like the results."

No light-hearted quip would come to her, and she hated that she probably looked as shaken as she felt. She'd felt the effects of glamour before, and she most definitely didn't want to feel them again. There wasn't much in the world creepier than having someone turn you into a temporary vegetable. And from what she'd gathered, vamps could even make you *do* things under the influence of their glamour. She doubted Jules would actually hurt her, but she could imagine him doing any number of things she'd really, really rather avoid. Like getting her to strip naked in a public place—this hotel lobby, for instance.

"I believe we have an understanding," Jules said, leaning back in his chair, his expression still closed and chilly.

"Yeah, I guess we do," Hannah answered, keeping her voice low so it wouldn't shake. She flagged the waitress down and ordered a third Corona. Probably not the smartest thing to do on an empty stomach, but she needed the alcohol after that little conversation.

What had Ian Squires done to Jules to inspire that kind of hatred and fear? That it was more than just the natural hatred many unwilling vampires felt for the ones who made them was obvious. *Something* more had happened between them to make Jules take the stupid risks he was taking right now.

And though for the moment Hannah had to cede the field, she was far from finished trying to pry Jules's secrets loose.

Maybe she was glad she'd come on this trip after all. She had to admit, it was more interesting and exciting than tracking down cheating husbands. Unfortunately, it didn't pay too well and it was also far more likely to get her killed. . . .

4

Ian paused on the doorstep, reminding himself that Camille's reign was soon to end. He could stand to kiss her ass for just a little longer. Hating the dread that churned in his stomach, he rang the doorbell. Whatever the bitch wanted from him tonight, he was sure not to like it.

Her mortal butler answered the door, dressed in somber black livery and looking down his nose at Ian. What a *servant* had to feel superior about was anyone's guess. Ian ground his teeth and promised himself that when he took over Baltimore, Jeeves—he'd never bothered to learn the guy's real name— would die a slow and painful death. The prospect made Ian's gums tingle. But Camille would permit no hostility toward her mortal pets, and years of brutal punishment had taught him to keep his fangs sheathed no matter how strong the urge to lower them.

"Please do come in, Mr. Squires," Jeeves said. How he managed to imbue those words with such condescension Ian couldn't imagine.

Ian stepped over the threshold and had to fight another wave of resentment. Once, this had been *his* house. He'd designed the stately gray marble foyer, with its sunburst of warmer orange marble at its center. He'd hired the carpenter who'd carved each mahogany baluster by hand. He'd supervised the painting of the walls, and selected each piece of furniture with meticulous care. But when three months ago Camille had suddenly taken a fancy to the place, he'd had no choice but to let her move in, evicting him. Now he was a guest in his own goddamn home!

"This way, sir," the butler said, leading Ian toward the living room as though Ian hadn't lived in this house for more than half a century himself.

He braced himself for the assault on his senses that was Camille's redecoration of his home. Even so, he winced when he caught sight of his former living room. Camille was unfamiliar with the term "simple elegance." Or "tasteful." But he supposed her taste for the garish was a blessing in disguise—he'd gotten to keep most of his furniture when she'd taken over the house.

His distaste for this summons increased exponentially when he saw that Camille was not alone. It took all of his considerable willpower not to groan when he saw Gabriel, her son and right-hand man, lounging in the one item of his furniture she'd kept—his favorite Stickley chair.

Gabriel's permanent sulk became a smile when he caught sight of Ian. Not a good sign at all.

For the most part, Gabriel looked surprisingly harmless. His young physical age was part of it—he looked like he was barely in his twenties—and the sulk wasn't particularly conducive to menace. He dressed like a tough guy in silver-studded black leather jacket and boots, and he wore his short blond hair in messy spikes, but none of that was what made him look like the badass he was.

Maybe it was his eyes. Those light gray-green eyes of his could chill a brave man to the marrow. Or maybe it was the long white scar marring his pretty cheek that inspired fear despite his otherwise less-than-frightening features.

Whatever it was about him that gave him his aura, it was hard for Ian to hold his ground when the son of a bitch unfolded from his chair and approached at a predatory stalk. The gray-green eyes pierced him, causing a nearly physical pain in Ian's head.

Gabriel came to a stop well inside the boundaries of Ian's personal space. Ian hated that he had to look up to meet his adversary's gaze, but he wasn't about to back down from a challenge, even when Gabriel bared his fangs.

"What are you up to, you little shit?" Gabriel growled, leaning even farther into Ian's space.

Sweat broke out on Ian's brow and he cursed his body's too-human responses. Gabriel's nostrils flared, scenting fear in the air. How much did he know?

"I don't know what you're talking about," Ian said, his voice sounding scared even to his own ears.

"Wrong answer." Gabriel grabbed a double handful of Ian's shirt. Ian made a fruitless effort to pry his fingers loose, but soon found himself slammed against a wall, his feet dangling, Gabriel's nose a fraction of an inch from his.

"May I hurt him, Mother? He's been a naughty boy."

"A wrist-slap only, for now," Camille said.

Ian swallowed hard, trying to control his dread as Gabriel's cruel smile widened. He lost all sense of fear when Gabriel's knee connected brutally with his groin. There was no room for fear then, only pain. Pain that left him retching helplessly, gasping for breath, his vision swimming with stars.

When he regained his senses, Ian found himself in a heap on the floor, his body curled into itself in an effort to protect his most vulnerable parts. If he'd been mortal, that knee would have made a eunuch of him.

As he was still trying to recover his breath, he saw Gabriel's studded motorcycle boots approaching. He almost begged for mercy, but Camille and son would enjoy that too much.

Instead of kicking him as Ian had expected, Gabriel dropped a newspaper in front of his nose. Ian groaned when he saw his own picture staring back at him. His calculated risk had come back to bite him in the ass.

"Explain, please," Camille said, her voice silky-soft, but deadly just the same.

Ian tried to push himself to his feet, but Gabriel wouldn't let him rise.

"You can stay on your knees," Gabriel said. "It's where you belong."

Ian shuddered even as his hate boiled higher. Neither Camille nor her son had ever forgiven Ian for fleeing to Philadelphia almost a century ago. But he'd never intended to stay in Baltimore after she'd transformed him. He'd played the good little toady for the two years she'd made him wait for the gift of her bite. He'd seen what a tyrant she was, gleefully grinding her fledglings under her heel. And they worshipped her for it, kissed her ass and begged for more. But not Ian. He planned to let her transform him, and then get the hell away from her and her pervert of a son.

He'd thought to start his own "family" in Philadelphia, starting with golden boy Jules Gerard, his one-time "best friend." The man who always seemed to have it all when Ian had shit. Two years of kowtowing and groveling had seemed a small price to pay for the power she would give him. He'd imagined himself as the king of Philadelphia, with Jules as his whipping boy and a harem of tempting young morsels bound to him by the blood tie between master and fledgling.

But Ian had been woefully ignorant about vampire society at the time, and he'd barely escaped Philadelphia with his life. Realizing he'd never survive as a lone fledgling in a world crawling with stronger vampires, he'd been forced to slink back to Baltimore. And Camille.

She and Gabriel had been making him pay for his desertion ever since. He'd endured every torment they'd thrown his way, paying for his life with his last scrap of dignity. But Ian was not an idiot. He was now the oldest of Camille's fledglings. And he wasn't that old, not for a vampire. No, Camille would never allow her fledglings to get old enough to challenge her power. And no one but Ian seemed to be disturbed by the fact that although she made a new fledgling every few years, she never seemed to have more than eight to ten of them serving her at any one time.

Some of them were killed for misbehaving. But what about the rest, the ones who just . . . disappeared? If pressed, she'd hint that she'd sent her oldest fledglings out into the world to start their own "families." But that was pure bullshit.

How long did he have before she decided to kill him?

It could be a matter of minutes, depending on how well he explained away his recent activities.

Staying obediently on his knees, Ian fixed his eyes on Camille's exquisite Jimmy Choo shoes. *Only the best for the Master of Baltimore,* he thought with distaste. He hated even more that he could actually recognize them as Jimmy Choos; he frequently served as a bearer on her shopping trips, and he could name the label on just about every item of clothing she owned.

"I have some unfinished business with my fledgling," he said, his heart fluttering in his chest. Would she believe him? Would she think him bold enough to try to depose her? Surely not! He was a beaten cur—she couldn't possibly expect him to bite back. "It's been festering for nearly eight decades. I thought it was time to end it. I knew you wouldn't let me go to him, so I arranged to appear in the paper and hoped he'd come to me." He raised his head and met Camille's cool stare.

Camille regarded him with glacier-blue eyes. "You mean to tell me it never occurred to you that you should ask permission before bringing your fledgling into my city?" Camille would tolerate no fledglings but her own in Baltimore—a fact she'd pounded into her fledglings' sensibilities with no attempt at subtlety. Create an unauthorized fledgling and die. It was as simple as that. The only reason she'd let Ian live was that he hadn't made his fledgling in Baltimore.

"It occurred to me," Ian admitted boldly. "I knew you wouldn't allow it. I'd hoped he'd be dead before you knew he'd come."

Camille leaned forward in her chair, her lovely face marred by fury. "You mean to tell me you have willfully defied me?"

Better to admit to this than to admit the full truth. He *might* live through whatever punishment she meted out for his defiance.

"I gave him the greatest gift a mortal man can receive, and in return he tried to get me killed. I can't bear the thought that he still lives," he said, bowing his head once more. "I've managed to swallow that reality for a long, long time, and I just couldn't do it anymore. All I can do now is throw myself on your mercy."

As if Camille had ever shown a hint of mercy in her life.

He waited an interminable amount of time while Camille pondered her judgment. Beside him, Gabriel cracked his knuckles loudly. A sense of calm settled over Ian, a brief reprieve from the terror. It was out of his hands now. He would either live or die at Camille's whim. There were times when he thought death might be the lesser of the two evils, if living meant remaining under Camille and Gabriel's heels. But then he reminded himself what he had to live for—the day when they died and Baltimore became his.

"What do you think, my son?" she asked. "Shall I spare his miserable life?"

"I must say, I would miss his special . . . talents were he to die."

Again, a shudder rippled through Ian's whole body. If he lived through this, and if he took the city, he swore he would cut Gabriel's dick off before he killed him.

Camille feigned a wistful sigh. "As would I." Mother and son shared a malicious chuckle at Ian's expense.

Camille rose and drifted toward the door leading out of the living room. She preferred not to watch Gabriel at work, though she had no qualms about giving the orders. "Beat him until he sees the error of his ways," she commanded from the doorway. "Bring him to me when he's thoroughly chastened. You can have him back when I'm finished with him."

Out of the corner of his eye, Ian saw Gabriel put his hand to his heart and bow from the waist. "As you command, so shall it be."

Then Camille was gone, and Ian's private hell began.

๛

HANNAH YAWNED AS SHE sat on the bed cradling her third cup of coffee. As Carolyn had once warned her, hanging out with a vampire was tough on the sleep schedule.

After Hannah had browbeaten Jules into letting her help, she'd invited herself to stay in Jules's hotel room. He'd made the expected protests, but she'd gone into persuasion overdrive because she flat out couldn't afford this hotel. Technically, she could charge Carolyn for her expenses, but this felt more like a favor than a job. Besides, if they shared a room, Hannah could look out for Jules during the day, make sure he didn't get deep fried by a stray ray of sunshine.

As she'd expected, she'd worn him down—eventually it became more of a pain to argue with her than to just give in to the inevitable. Besides, there were two beds, so she wouldn't cramp his style too badly. Then Jules had had to ruin her little glow of satisfaction by heading out for the night. Just to explore, he'd said, but she thought exploring might be a bad idea. She didn't much understand how it worked, but she knew vampires had some way of "sensing" each other. Some kind of psychic shit that she only sometimes allowed herself to believe in. Vamp-dar, she decided to call it.

Jules had won that little argument by playing dirty. A touch of glamour had left her gazing at her navel until he'd gotten far enough away that she couldn't follow him. She'd stayed up half the night waiting for him, wondering if that weird feeling in her stomach was actually worry. She didn't like to think so, but she supposed it was understandable. Certainly she'd feel like an incompetent if the guy managed to get himself killed on the first night of her watch.

She'd fallen asleep in her clothes, then awakened just before dawn when Jules returned to the room. Through slitted eyes, she'd noticed that the man slept in black silk pajamas, and it was all she could do not to start laughing.

Not until he'd buried himself under the covers and hadn't moved for about fifteen minutes did she get up.

The first priority was coffee, and though she was usually a coffee snob, this morning she settled for the crap they served in the room. Then her baser instincts got the better of her, and she started snooping. She wasn't exactly doing it behind Jules's back. Not technically, when he was in the room.

Her first objective was his shaving kit. She whistled in amazement when she opened it. The guy actually shaved with a straight razor! Of course, she supposed if he cut himself shaving, it would heal before it had a chance to bleed much.

There were three kinds of aftershave stowed in that little kit. Hannah sniffed all three and had to applaud his taste. Each spicy scent was supremely masculine—despite her teasing about his "perfume" last night. Another toiletries kit contained a tube of hair gel and a can of men's aerosol hair spray. She figured with hair as long and fine-textured as his the gel was a must, but she confiscated his hair spray. He'd look even sexier if his hair moved a little in the breeze, and she planned to teach him the error of his ways.

She raised her eyebrows when she discovered a handful of condoms in the bottom of the kit.

Why the hell did a vampire need condoms? She had it on good authority that they couldn't father children. Surely they weren't vulnerable to STDs. Then she noticed the expiration date on them was nine months past. Did this mean Jules hadn't been getting any lately?

Hannah met her own eyes in the mirror. "His sex life is none of your business, young lady," she said, shaking her finger at her reflection. But since Hannah hadn't gotten laid since the Pleistocene era, she supposed she had a bad case of sex-on-the-brain. And the fact that Jules was sex on two legs didn't help.

Annoyed with herself, she quit her snooping and got down to work. She called the *Inquirer* and got transferred around until she reached a harried-sounding cub reporter. She told the reporter that she was trying to get in touch with Ian Squires because there'd been a death in his family and asked if there was any contact information on record. The reporter was terribly sympathetic, and while she didn't have an address for him, she was able to find a phone number from when he'd done a telephone interview. Hannah took down the number, smirking at Jules's unconscious form. Thought she was helpless and useless, did he?

Next, she called the number. She figured her chances of success were minimal—it wasn't like vamps were up and about at this hour—but nothing ventured nothing gained, right?

She nearly dropped the phone when someone actually

picked up, but she recovered her cool quickly. "Hi, this is Sheila from UPS. I have a damaged package for a Mr. Ian Squires, and I have this as a contact number."

There was a long pause on the other end of the line. "Really?"

It was a man's voice, with a slight trace of a British accent. Could this be Squires himself? She glanced at the bedside clock. Not at nine in the morning it couldn't be.

"Yes, sir," she said, sounding chipper. "There's been some water damage, and the address is pretty much unreadable."

"Who is it from?"

This was the fun part. Hannah cleared her throat and mumbled a bit, sounding embarrassed. "Um, it appears to be from a company called Sextasy." On the assumption that she wasn't speaking to Squires himself, she figured that would be enough to quell whatever curiosity the gentleman on the phone might have. "I can return it to the sender, if you'd rather. But I don't think the water soaked through the box, so the contents are probably all right."

After a brief hesitation, the guy gave her an address, which she looked up online. The address was in the ritzy Federal Hill neighborhood, near the Inner Harbor. And, coincidentally, relatively near the hotel. She wasn't entirely sure whether that was a good thing or a bad thing. How strong was the vamp-dar anyway? She knew the Killers had better range than the Guardians. So did Ian already know Jules was in town and where he was staying? She sure hoped not.

Common sense told her she should take a nap, seeing as she was going to be on a nocturnal schedule for the foreseeable future. However, caffeine and nerves had other ideas, so she gave up trying to sleep after only half an hour.

It was going to be a long day as she hung around here waiting for Jules to wake up. But tonight might turn out to be very interesting indeed. She just hoped it wasn't *too* interesting.

Just to have something to do, she opened up the closet and looked over Jules's luggage. And discovered he'd packed enough clothes for an army. Just how long a field trip was he planning, anyway? Apparently, things were already more interesting than she'd realized.

๛

JULES SLIPPED OUT OF bed at five-fifteen. Hannah lay across the other double bed, fully clothed and fast asleep. Her riot of curly black hair had come loose from the barrette she'd used to control it. Her glasses had slipped down to the tip of her nose. If she turned over, she'd either knock them off or break them.

Smiling with what he might have termed affection if she weren't such a pain in the ass, he reached out and gently plucked the glasses off, folding them onto the night stand. She hadn't worn glasses last year, when he'd first met her. Was her eyesight worsening, or had she worn contacts before? He was old enough to remember a time when women who wore glasses—spectacles, as they were more commonly known then—were automatically considered homely. He rather liked them on Hannah, though. They added a hint of vulnerability to her tough-as-nails exterior.

He was still smiling—the hell with the mess he was making of his life—when he stepped into the bathroom. The smile disappeared immediately.

[67]

His shaving kit was open, as was his toiletries bag. He knew he'd closed them after using them last night. He made no bones about being scrupulously tidy. His temper stirring, he left the bathroom and opened the closet. Sure enough, his suitcases both lay on their sides. When he popped one open, he discovered his neatly folded wardrobe had most definitely been disturbed.

"*Marde*," he grumbled, his hands clenching into fists. He'd meant to unpack immediately when he'd arrived, but when he realized practically everything would need ironing, he'd changed his mind and only unpacked the bare necessities. When Hannah had shown up last night, he'd been glad he hadn't unpacked—if she saw how much he'd brought with him, no doubt she'd start asking questions he didn't want to answer. He should have known she was the snooping kind.

Behind him, Hannah yawned. Trying to control yet another burst of temper, he turned slowly, gritting his teeth.

She was sitting up now, running a hand through her messy curls as if that would tame them. He started toward her, and she picked up her glasses and put them on.

Smothering another yawn, she looked up at him with a tentative grin. "You wouldn't hit a girl with glasses, would you?"

He let out an exasperated hiss. "No, but I might strangle her. What gave you the idea it was okay to rummage through my things?"

"I'm a PI, Jules. And I was a reporter before that. I'm congenitally nosy. So tell me, do you change clothes every hour, or are you planning to be here a while?"

"Keep your nose out of my business!" he snapped. He should have held his ground last night and made her get her own room, but he'd fallen victim to his own uncertainty. The bedroom in his house had such heavy curtains there was no risk of daylight seeping into the room, but the curtains here weren't so heavy. He'd had visions of tossing in his sleep, dislodging the covers and letting the sunlight sear him.

Hannah had to crane her neck to look at him as he towered over her. Not surprisingly, she wasn't cowed by his temper. "You've really got to work on your technique. See, if you want to be all manly and intimidating, you'd be much more effective in something other than silk jammies." She leaned back on her hands, grinning up at him. "Not that you don't look good in them, but they're kind of prissy."

He actually flinched at the description. "*Prissy?*" he asked with a curl of his lip. He wanted to tear the damn pajamas from his body right that moment, more stung than he'd like to admit. He'd thought of them as elegant and sophisticated. Certainly not *prissy*!

Hannah frowned and cocked her head at him. "Relax, Jules. You look like I just told you you have terminal cancer."

He tried to school his features, regain his usual nonchalance. "I'm very particular about my wardrobe, and—"

"No shit?" she said with a laugh. "I've never known a straight man who dresses near as well as you."

So much for nonchalance. He actually *felt* the blood draining from his face, and he took a step back from her.

Her eyes widened. "What? What did I say?"

He wanted to conjure a glib answer, but his heart was

pounding and his throat was tight and he couldn't force a word out.

Hannah stood up, her head tilted to the side once more. "I didn't say I thought you weren't straight," she said carefully, watching his face with intense concentration.

He swallowed hard. "No, of course not."

Her lips tilted up in a half-smile, but her eyes still shone with curiosity. And perhaps a hint of worry. "Homophobic a bit?"

Calm was returning slowly, and he was able to answer in a more normal tone of voice. "Not at all. But I might need to re-evaluate my wardrobe if it gives women the impression I'm gay."

Hannah's half-smile turned into a full grin. "I don't think there's much danger of that, Jules babe. You pretty much ooze testosterone."

He sniffed. "Nonetheless, I'm going to have to burn these pajamas."

"Just the top."

"Huh?"

"Burn the top, keep the bottoms. There's nothing sexier than a hot guy in black silk pajama bottoms."

To his surprise, she actually blushed, which fully restored his good humor. "Oh really?" He began unbuttoning the top. "Let's test that theory, shall we?"

She held up both hands and averted her eyes. "I thought you were a gentleman! And gentlemen don't undress in front of women they hardly know."

But even with her eyes averted, he could see the color in her cheeks. No, she didn't object to seeing him without his shirt. The idea set off a corresponding stir in his groin. He had to get out of the room before he made a too-visible statement of his sexual preferences.

"I'm going to take a shower," he said, heading toward the bathroom once more. "When I get out, you and I are going to have a talk about respecting each other's boundaries."

"I can hardly wait!" Hannah called after him.

5

Jules stayed in the shower longer than usual, hoping the steam would clear his mind. Fat chance.

What a fool he'd made of himself. He'd thought he was well beyond the point in his life where mere words could hurt him. But the thought that the way he dressed might make people think he was gay . . . okay, so maybe he was a little homophobic. What did it say about him that the idea of being mistaken for a gay man could stir such a sense of horror in his gut?

He snorted. He couldn't even count the number of girlfriends he'd had in his life, and not one of them had seemed to question his virility. And it wasn't like he got a hard-on when he looked at other men. But the poison Ian had poured into his veins long ago never seemed to disappear from his system.

Maybe when Ian died at his hands he could finally put the past behind him and go on with his life. After all, if he actually survived this little field trip he had quite a lot of life left to live.

He was disturbed enough by his memories that he actually nicked his cheek when shaving, something he almost never did. Though the nick healed immediately, he decided to leave a goatee-shaped area of fuzz around his mouth. He leaned forward and peered at his reflection in the mirror. The auburn fuzz gave him a scruffy look that made his fingers itch for the razor, but he resisted the urge.

Ignoring Hannah's crack about his "perfume," he splashed some aftershave on his cheeks, then dried his hair. Gel gave the fine strands some body, but he couldn't find his hair spray. What had Hannah done with it? He leaned his fists on the counter and fumed at the thought of her pawing through his things. But he wasn't about to make a fuss about the missing hair spray—he could only imagine what she'd have to say about *that*.

The flyaway hair went with the scruffy semi-beard, so he supposed he didn't look too bad in an unkempt, blue-collar sort of way. Of course, the tailored wool trousers and Armani jacket he'd chosen didn't go with the look. Daring Hannah to tease him, he boldly strode into the room and dug through his suitcase until he found his lone pair of jeans, then retreated to the bathroom once more before she had a chance to comment.

When he emerged again, he stood still while she gave him a visual inspection from head to toe. Color warmed her cheeks again, and she touched her tongue to her upper lip in what he felt sure was an unconscious gesture.

"Not bad," she said, the hoarseness in her voice giving evidence of her true opinion.

He couldn't help smiling. It had been too long since he'd had a woman. But Courtney's death last year had hit him hard, and his conscience hadn't let him bring a woman to his bed since. He refused to let another mortal woman come to harm because of her association with him. True, he hadn't loved Courtney, but there'd been an emotional connection between them. When they'd made love, it was more than just sex. It was hard to settle for less now. Which meant he'd been celibate for a frighteningly long time.

Which, in turn, meant that Hannah's obvious attraction to him held a great deal more appeal than it should.

"I'm glad you approve," he said dryly, breaking the awkward moment.

"Yeah, well, you've got quite a wardrobe to choose from in there." She jerked her finger toward the closet. "What's the deal? Oh, and by the way, I snooped in your cooler too."

He'd left the cooler—loaded with bottles of blood—on the floor of the closet under a huge bath towel he'd brought from home. He'd have put the blood in the mini-fridge, but he'd been afraid a maid might ignore the do-not-disturb sign on the door and try to restock the bar. Probably paranoia, and eventually he'd have to risk it. There was only so long he could keep the blood fresh in the cooler.

"For future reference," Hannah said, "when a neat-freak leaves a towel lying around in a heap, it makes us nosy types really, really suspicious."

He sighed. "Leave it alone, Hannah."

"Gray only feeds twice a week, and you're a lot older than he is, so I'm guessing you don't have to feed as often. There's a hell of a lot of blood in that cooler."

What was the point of fighting it? Hannah was going to chew his ears off until he told her what she wanted to know. Besides, she'd no doubt already reached the logical conclusion.

"I'm not going back to Philadelphia," he said.

"Ever?"

His throat tightened. "Ever." But of course, she'd want an explanation, so he couldn't just leave it at that. "I've disobeyed a direct order from Eli. There's a good chance that if I go back to Philly, he'll kill me."

Hannah gasped. "No way!" She looked horrified. "You're not serious, are you?"

He nodded tightly.

"Geez, I knew the guy was a weirdo, but I thought he was a weirdo with a heart of gold."

His hackles rose to hear the Founder so insulted, but he answered mildly enough. "Eli *does* have a heart of gold. But he's learned his lesson after what happened with the Banger. It's damn hard for a Guardian to stay on the straight and narrow on his own. I'll do it, of course. I'd stake myself out in the sunlight before I'd let myself go rogue. But I can't blame Eli for distrusting my motives after the way I've acted lately."

"Well, *I* have no trouble blaming him! And I don't want Carolyn or even Gray having anything to do with the sicko."

She was grabbing for the phone as she spoke, outrage pouring from her in waves. Jules crossed the distance between them and wrested the phone from her hand.

"Settle down," he said, hanging up the phone. "Carolyn and Gray know perfectly well what Eli's like. Believe me, if you'd ever met him, you'd know in a heartbeat he isn't someone you want to fuck with."

Hannah sat heavily on the edge of the bed, crossing her

arms over her chest. "Well, I just lost the last hint of respect I ever had for the guy. Which wasn't much in the first place."

How could he expect her to understand Eli? Hell, he couldn't really claim to understand the man himself. What he *did* understand was that Eli was a good man who considered his cause more important than any individual. Everyone was expendable. And that was as it should be.

"Let's agree to disagree on this, okay? We have more important things to talk about right now. Did you learn anything today?"

Hannah's fierce glower turned into a smug smile. "Only Ian Squires's address and phone number. Will that do?" She held up a little pad of paper with the hotel's logo on it, under which she had written the address and phone number in surprisingly tidy script.

His mouth dropped open. Though he probably should have known better, he hadn't truly expected her to have much luck. How had she gotten the newspaper to give out Ian's unlisted number? He closed his mouth with an audible click. "All right. I'm impressed," he admitted grudgingly.

"I'll try not to gloat. But one weird thing—when I called the house at nine this morning, someone actually answered the phone."

He'd thought he was getting used to being shocked by Hannah, but obviously he'd been dead wrong. "You called the house? Are you insane? No, wait." He held up both hands. "That goes without saying."

"So is this Squires guy old enough to be up and about at nine in the morning?"

Jules shook his head. "He's only been vampire a few years longer than me. He must have a mortal working for him." No surprise there—Ian had been an aspiring snob when Jules had known him. He probably had a houseful of servants by now, just because he could. Did this mortal have any idea what he was working for? Jules knew from long experience that it was relatively easy to pull the wool over most mortals' eyes, as long as they weren't too terribly smart. Courtney had been his girlfriend for six months and had never guessed there was anything unusual about him.

"So, what's our next step, Professor Van Helsing?"

"*My* next step is to check out that house and confirm there's a vampire living there."

"Isn't that kind of a stupid way of going about it? I mean, isn't his vamp-dar stronger than yours?"

"Vamp-dar?" Being with Hannah could make his head ache.

"Yeah, you know—the way you guys can sense each other. Kind of like gay-dar." Hannah paused, "Vampire radar," she said slowly. "Get it?"

Yes, his head was definitely starting to pound. "It takes a conscious effort for us to sense each other. Unless he's sitting in his house concentrating on surveillance, he won't know I'm there."

"Uh-huh. And if you were him, what would you be doing if you'd set up a trap for a fellow vampire?"

She had a point, but it didn't much matter. "I don't have a lot of options. My first step has to be to locate him. I'll worry about what to do when I find him later."

"Or what to do when he finds you," Hannah retorted. She popped up from her seat on the bed and crossed the room to flip open her suitcase.

When she pulled out a gun and a box of bullets, he realized she meant to come along on his hunt. That led to two more realizations—one, that he couldn't allow it. And two, there was nothing he could say to persuade her to stay put.

She turned to him. "You'll be happy to know I actually know how to use this now, so—"

Her words trailed off when she met his eyes and he trapped her with his glamour.

∾

DRAKE HAD DONE A great many distasteful things in his life, but going to visit with the Master of Baltimore ranked pretty high on the list. Eli had told him almost nothing about her, except that she was very powerful and territorial. Eli'd also said she would honor their agreement and not kill Drake for having the audacity to trespass in her territory, but he found himself less than thrilled by the prospect of facing her.

He'd arrived in Baltimore just before dawn, and had immediately called Camille to announce his presence, as Eli had instructed. It had been too close to sunup for them to meet, but she'd asked him to call on her at his earliest convenience. His earliest convenience, of course, was the moment the sun set.

Leaving his rental car parked at the hotel, he made his way around the tourist-packed Inner Harbor toward Federal Hill, the wealthy historic neighborhood where Camille lived. He'd barely set foot out of Philadelphia in the last century. On any other occasion, he would have enjoyed the new and different surroundings.

A wide pedestrian walkway allowed him to take the scenic route along the water, but though he tried to drink in the atmosphere, he failed miserably. There was just no getting around the fact that he didn't want to be here.

Past the bustling, highly commercialized harbor lay Federal Hill, where restored historic houses abounded, homes that spoke of old money and power. Drake paused to reach out with his senses, wondering how many of these elegant homes were vampire lairs. He immediately sensed a pair of vampires not very far away. At a guess, he'd say he was sensing Camille and some unknown other, for her house was less than three blocks from here in the correct direction. Other than that, the area was vampire-free. He supposed that was a good thing. The only thing worse than meeting with Camille would be meeting with Camille and her cadre of fledgling Killers.

Drake walked the last three blocks quickly, ready to face whatever was to come because he was tired of thinking about it.

Even if he hadn't known the address, and even if he hadn't sensed the presence of vampires, he would have known which house belonged to the Master of Baltimore. Surrounded by the ubiquitous brick row houses, this house was about three times the size of any around it. The arched entryway was actually flanked with granite columns. The place gave the impression of a palace—exactly the kind of home a master vampire would choose for herself to showcase her importance.

He paused again on the doorstep, checking to see if any more vampires had made an appearance, but there were still only two in the house, along with a single mortal. Unfortunately, he now sensed another vampire about a block from here. Could that be Jules?

Drake took a step away from the door, meaning to check out the vampire at his back, but the door suddenly opened. A mortal stood in the doorway, looking Drake up and down.

"Good evening," the mortal—a butler, apparently—said. "You are expected."

So much for checking out the stray. Obviously, Camille was quite anxious to see him. "So I gathered." He stepped over the threshold as though he called on master vampires on a regular basis.

"I'll take your coat, sir," the butler said.

"That's all right. I'll keep it." Although he was no possible threat to Camille, he had no idea who the second vampire was, and he didn't want to give up any possible intimidation factor. His black leather jacket, matched with his black leather pants, lent him a menacing aura that often made others uncomfortable.

The butler made a disapproving face, then led Drake down a carpeted hallway to a huge living room that looked like something out of Versailles. It even had a gilt ceiling.

Ostentation was obviously Camille's middle name.

An intricate—or busy, depending on your tastes—Persian rug draped the dark hardwood floor, and the room was furnished in genuine Louis XV antiques, with the exception of a single chair that looked more like an early-twentieth-century piece. Dark, brooding oil paintings in ornate gold frames lined the walls, and a crystal chandelier that no doubt had originally held candles lit the room.

At one end of the room, Camille sat in a high-backed chair, her legs crossed at the knees as she regarded him with undisguised curiosity.

She was a handsome woman, if not exactly pretty. It looked like she'd been in her mid-thirties when she'd been bitten. Despite flawless makeup, there were tiny crows feet at the corners of her eyes. Her hair was long and platinum blonde, and she wore it loose about her shoulders—beautiful, really, though Drake thought the color chemically altered. Her eyebrows were a distinctly darker shade of blonde, almost brown. An expensive-looking dress of midnight-blue silk clung to her alluring curves, displaying an enticing expanse of décolletage while the hemline stopped a couple inches above her knees. Drake resisted the urge to stare at her legs.

The other vampire was in many ways Camille's exact opposite. Where she sat tall and straight in her chair, he slouched and draped one leg over his chair's arm. Where her hair was classic and tidy, his was short and spiky, with the spikes sticking every which way. An ugly scar marred what would otherwise have been a handsome face. To Drake's chagrin, the other vampire also wore a black leather jacket. So much for intimidation.

"So," Camille said, her voice silky and just a tad sly. "You're Eli's exception to the rule."

He wondered how much Eli had told her about him. Apparently, more than he'd told Drake about her.

"Please do come in," she said, beckoning with her hand.

He obeyed the summons and gave her a respectful bow. No doubt she was old enough to appreciate the gesture that had once been the only acceptable way for a gentleman to greet a lady.

"Yes, I work with Eli," he said, acknowledging only part of her greeting.

She smiled at him then gestured toward the sullen-looking young vampire who slouched in the incongruous twentieth-century chair. "This is my son, Gabriel."

Drake did his best to hide his surprise and revulsion. The woman had made her own *son* into a vampire? And a Killer, at that. "Pleased to meet you," he said, and hoped he sounded more pleased than he was.

Gabriel grunted but didn't bother to make a more formal greeting. He didn't even move his leg off the arm of his chair.

Currents of power rippled the air as mother and son regarded him with very different expressions—hers of curiosity, his of unbridled resentment. Drake decided he'd had enough posturing for now, so he took a seat without waiting to be invited. Gabriel's expression darkened even more, but Camille merely arched a brow and let it go.

"So," she said, "you are here to retrieve Eli's prodigal son."

For whatever reason, Gabriel's lip twitched in a snarl. Drake caught the lightning-quick repressive glance Camille shot Gabriel's way. It seemed clear Camille and her son were not in agreement on how to handle the trespassers.

"That's right," Drake answered. "I'll remove him from your territory as soon as inhumanly possible."

The corners of her mouth curled upward at his joke. "Have you located him yet?"

Drake shook his head. "Not yet. As you know, I've only just arrived. But I know the kind of hotel that would appeal to him, so I doubt it will take me more than a night or two to find him."

"If he succeeds in killing my fledgling before you find him, then you are *not* to remove him from Baltimore. While there are times that Ian tries my patience, if anyone's going to kill him, it will be me."

"Or me," Gabriel put in with another snarl.

Apparently, the pup didn't like anyone. Which was probably just as well, because it was hard to imagine anyone liking *him*.

Camille ignored his interruption. "Are we clear on that?"

"We're clear." Drake wasn't sure how he'd live with himself if he abandoned Jules to this unpleasant duo once he'd taken on the task of saving him, but he wasn't going to put the entire society of Guardians at risk to protect him.

"I'm glad to hear it. Now, it's best you start your search as soon as possible, so I won't keep you. Gabriel will see you to the door."

Oh, shit, Drake thought as Gabriel's eyes lit with pleasure at the prospect. It seemed he was about to be given a small demonstration of what might happen to him if he didn't toe the line. If Gabriel was Camille's son, then he must be old indeed, despite his baby face, which meant Drake would be no match for him. But there was nothing for it, so Drake shrugged slightly and took his leave, following Gabriel out of the room.

Not surprisingly, Gabriel came to a stop shortly after they'd left the room, in a narrow, unfurnished hallway. No breakables. He turned to Drake, those pouty lips stretched into a cruel smile.

"Am I allowed to fight back, or am I just supposed to take it?" Drake asked. He managed to sound completely unruffled. He wasn't looking forward to whatever was to come, but he'd never seen much use in complaining about things he couldn't control.

To his surprise, Gabriel laughed. The laughter washed every trace of cruelty from his face like a magical transformation. For just a moment, he was another person entirely, a handsome young man with a glint of good humor in his eyes. It faded quickly.

"I'm so used to dealing with idiots and ass-kissers," he said, a hint of laughter still in his voice. "What a refreshing change." The humor faded. "You can try to fight back if you want. I won't hold it against you. How old are you? A hundred? Maybe a little more?"

How could he tell? It was impossible to guess a vampire's age—or power—by his psychic footprint. Then again, maybe Eli had told Camille his age.

"About that," Drake admitted. Instinct urged him to make a preemptive strike, but he wasn't sure of the house rules. If he struck first, would Camille take that as an inappropriately hostile act and make good on her threats to reveal Eli's secret?

Gabriel shook his head. "Then I wouldn't bother fighting back if I were you. It'll be over quicker if you just hold still." Something ugly and eager gleamed in his eyes.

Drake might not be able to take the older vampire, but he'd be damned if he'd just "hold still." Pride demanded he land a punch or two for the asshole to remember him by.

Gabriel flashed him a goading grin, then motioned for him to take a swing. At this point, he was happy to oblige.

What happened next was disorienting even for Drake, who'd battled his fair share of older, stronger vampires in Eli's service. One moment, his fist was heading straight toward Gabriel's jaw. The next, his fist was flying through empty air and a brutal jab connected with his kidney from behind.

He went down—as much from the force of his own swing as the blow he'd taken. Gabriel laughed again, but this was a cold, nasty laughter.

"I warned you to hold still. You won't lay a finger on me, kid."

That someone who looked to be little more than a teenager would call Drake "kid" was nearly unbearable. Never mind that Gabriel was probably at least twice his age.

Unfortunately, once Gabriel connected with that first blow, Drake was never able to recover. The older vampire moved so fast it was almost impossible to see him, and it *was* impossible to make contact. That didn't stop Drake from trying, though he knew he was probably making things worse for himself.

Eventually, Gabriel's surgical strikes sapped too much of Drake's breath and strength, and he had no choice but to take whatever was dished out. Protecting his head as best he could, he gritted his teeth and rode it out until Gabriel finished making his point.

After the blows stopped coming, Drake took a minute to regain his breath before he sat up tentatively. Considering how long and hard Gabriel had beaten him, he was amazed that nothing seemed to be broken.

Gabriel offered him a hand up, and Drake reluctantly accepted. Gabriel hauled him to his feet, then kept hold of his hand, squeezing just short of hard enough to break bones.

"Just so we're clear," he said, "I pulled my punches tonight. If you fuck with me, if you fuck with my mother, or if your little friend does anything that pisses me off, I'll show you what I'm really capable of. Got it?"

Drake nodded but didn't trust himself to speak. He might say something he'd regret.

Gabriel smiled and turned his bone-crushing grip into a handshake. "It's been a pleasure meeting you."

Drake had to call on every ounce of his self-discipline not to take a futile, ill-advised swing at the condescending ass.

6

Hannah cursed Jules at the top of her lungs, making a big show of struggling against the bonds. He'd used a couple of his fancy designer ties to bind her hands behind her back and tie her ankles together. When he used another to gag her, she tried to bite him, but he just grinned at her.

"It's for your own good, Hannah," he said, really proud of himself. "You're right, I'm no match for Ian if he takes me unawares, but you're even less so. I'm more than a hundred years old. If he kills me, I'll still have lived more than my fair share of years." His Gallic shrug suggested he could care less if he died. The expression in his eyes suggested he cared more than he wanted to admit.

He smoothed away a lock of hair that had gotten stuck in her mouth and was held in place by the gag. It was a surprisingly tender gesture.

"I'll take the do-not-disturb sign off when I leave. If something happens to me, a maid will be by in the morning to untie you."

She tried to force the words "fuck you" through the gag, but all that came out was a vague grunting noise. She was sure he caught the sentiment, however. He didn't seem annoyed by it, or even amused. Instead, there was a hint of sadness on his face, and for just a moment, her heart ached for him. What kind of pain was eating away at his insides to make him throw his life away to try to get revenge?

Then she decided she couldn't afford sympathy at the moment. She made a snarling noise and struggled against the bonds again, letting him see that she couldn't possibly get her hands free when he'd tied them so thoroughly.

"*Reste tranquille,*" he said in a voice barely louder than a whisper. For once, she suspected his French was neither a curse nor an insult. Then he bent and pressed his lips to her forehead.

The touch of his lips stilled her struggles immediately. It was only the briefest of kisses, planted on a part of her body she didn't consider an erogenous zone, but it electrified her all the same. Her skin tingled with it and her heart accelerated and she inhaled deeply the aftershave-and-man scent of him.

Then, with another sad little smile, he was gone, the door thunking closed behind him with what was meant to be finality.

Hannah shook off her moment of girlishness. There was no time to lose. Trying to relax all her muscles while hurrying wasn't the easiest thing in the world, but she was determined. She'd studied martial arts since she was a little girl—a very useful pastime for a girl with three older brothers—and while she was kind of a jack of all trades, master of none, she *was* naturally limber. Besides, she might not have survived

childhood with the Three Musketeers if she hadn't learned to
be an escape artist.

Rolling her shoulders to loosen them as much as possible,
she slowly and painfully worked her bound hands downward.
Once she got them down below her butt, she tucked her body
in on itself, making the smallest possible bundle, until she could
stick her feet through the circle of her arms.

Adrenaline surged, but getting her hands in front of her
was only half the battle. Raising her hands to her mouth, she
cursed Jules again for the damn gag, which made it hard for
her teeth to get a hold. Then she cursed herself for flailing
about so much and tightening the knots. Every minute she was
delayed was another minute Jules had on her. Thank goodness
she knew where he was going, or she'd never have any hope of
catching up with him.

Desperation lent her speed, and Jules had been too nice to
tie her very tightly anyway, so after what felt like forever and a
day, she was finally able to pry the tie off her wrists. After that,
it took mere seconds to strip away the gag and the tie at her ankles. Hoping like hell she wasn't too late, she grabbed her gun
and stuck it in the inner pocket of her coat. Then she bolted out
the door and made for the parking deck at warp speed.

JULES STOPPED FREQUENTLY ON his walk to reach out with his
senses, but his vamp-dar, as Hannah called it, wasn't all that
strong. He could be surrounded and not even know it, as long
as the enemy kept more than a block away. But he'd known
going into this that it was a long shot, and he was prepared to
face the consequences if things went badly.

There was no reason to expect things to go badly tonight, though. This was merely a reconnaissance mission, not an attack. And though Ian might well be expecting him, Jules couldn't believe his maker had nothing better to do than to sit in his house concentrating on sensing other vampires.

He'd asked the concierge at the hotel for a map of downtown, but of course the map was more concerned with tourist attractions than with places trespassing vampires could hide, so it hadn't done him much good. As he approached the block where Ian's house stood, though, he kept his eye out for unobtrusive hiding places and was gratified to see that like most cities, Baltimore had its share of dark, secluded alleys.

As he neared the house, he paused again, closing his eyes to block out all other senses as he reached out in search of vampires.

His eyes popped open as his pulse accelerated. He'd been looking for Ian, expecting to sense *one* vampire. Instead, his senses told him there were *three* vampires up ahead. What the hell was he walking into? He let out a stream of expletives in Québécois, his body trembling in fury. Taking on *one* Killer on his own had been a fool's errand. Taking on three was just plain suicide. Eli was right—he was in over his head. He cursed some more, but it didn't relieve his sense of impotent fury. He'd thrown everything that was good in his life away so he could have his revenge, and, damn it, he would have satisfaction!

But not tonight. No, tonight it was time for the strategic retreat. He'd accomplished what he'd come for, confirmed that vampires lived here. Now, it was wisest to make himself scarce before one of those three vampires sensed him. He took a couple of reluctant steps backward.

He was about to turn and make his escape when a pair of hands clamped down on the tops of his shoulders, fingers digging in deep. He wanted to whirl around and face whoever was behind him, but his limbs wouldn't obey him. He couldn't even turn his head.

Sweat beaded his brow despite the chilly winter air. It had to be glamour that held him motionless, and yet his senses insisted there was no vampire behind him.

A warm, moist puff of air tickled the side of his neck, and Jules felt the warmth of a body standing way too close for comfort.

"I've learned a few things since last we met, Jules," a voice whispered practically in his ear.

His stomach clenched tight, his heart pounded, and for a moment Jules thought he was actually in danger of passing out, for he recognized that voice.

"You see," Ian continued, his lips so close to Jules's ear that he could almost feel them moving against his skin, "a master vampire can learn to mask his psychic footprint from his fledglings. I'll bet you didn't know that, did you, old friend?"

Blood pounded in his temples, but though he wanted to utter some kind of nonchalant reply, his tongue seemed glued to the roof of his mouth. Worst of all, that *wasn't* a result of the glamour. Ian's presence sapped every ounce of his strength and courage and he trembled deep inside. He loathed the sound of his maker's voice, loathed the touch of his hands, loathed the invasion of his personal space.

"Let's have a chat, shall we?" Ian said, his hands sliding away. Unfortunately, he then threw an arm around Jules's shoulders, and there was nothing Jules could do to shrug it off or twist away.

Ian steered them toward one of the dark alleys Jules had spotted, his glamour forcing Jules to move with him. Why oh why hadn't he listened to Eli? He'd *known* what a fool he was being, and he'd come anyway. Walked right into Ian's goddamn trap.

With a monumental effort of will, Jules forced words from his throat. "How could you possibly find me so quickly?" He really hadn't believed Ian would be so single-mindedly seeking him out, even though this *was* a trap.

"Like I said, I've learned some things in the last eight decades." They'd reached the mouth of the alley now, and Ian continued on into the darkness, drawing Jules with him. "It's amazing how much power a master has over his fledgling. As I've learned the hard way, many times." The bitterness in his voice was almost comical to Jules's ears. After what Ian had done to him, he deserved the worst that could happen. He hoped Ian's maker tormented him daily.

"I can feel your presence without even trying. Hell, I pretty much *own* you. I would have come for you last night, but I was . . . detained." Did Jules imagine it, or did Ian just shudder?

Ian finally removed his arm from around Jules's shoulders, then gave him a hard shove so that his back was up against the brick wall of the alley. Ian's glamour still held him immobilized, and he quailed inside. The sensation of helplessness nearly unmanned him, and he felt a sudden stirring of remorse for the times he'd used his own glamour to overcome and taunt Gray James. But then, it was no doubt his history with Ian that made the glamour such a violation.

"So," Ian said, crossing his arms over his chest, "are you really alone? Tell me even *you* aren't that stupid."

Jules supposed he should tell Ian there was a troop of Guardians on their way to him as they spoke, but there didn't seem to be much point in lying. Ian could obviously tell he was alone, seeing as the only other vampires in the vicinity were in Ian's house. He decided to say nothing at all.

"Imbecile!" Ian said. He struck Jules across the face with the back of his hand, but the blow was an ineffectual one, barely hard enough to hurt. Ian never had been much good with his fists. When they'd been friends in college, Jules had more than once had to extract him from fights he couldn't win. Fights Ian had started because he knew Jules would play the role of big brother and rescue him. Now, Jules wished he could go back in time and help Ian's opponents beat the shit out of him.

"I'd hoped you'd give me at least a *little* challenge," Ian complained. "Eighty years of waiting, and all the fun will be over in one short night."

That Ian would want revenge on *him* had never occurred to Jules. Ian had already glutted himself on revenge for what he perceived as Jules's sins—being stronger, being richer, being *liked*.

"I'm very sorry to disappoint you," Jules said, mustering his sarcasm. "It just breaks my heart."

Ian smiled and clucked his tongue. "Oh, you're not sorry now, I know. But I'm going to make you sorry. Very, *very* sorry."

So, his would not be a quick death. Jules was hardly surprised. As a vampire, Ian had shrugged off the constraints of polite society. His transformation had unleashed his sadism, a revolting appetite that Jules had been too naive to notice lurking below Ian's formerly urbane manner.

Ian crowded into Jules's space, putting his face within inches of Jules's nose. His breath reeked of blood from a recent kill. "Say you're sorry, my friend. Say it like you mean it and perhaps I'll have a change of heart and kill you quickly."

Jules couldn't help the shiver of fear and revulsion that tore through his body as he read the intent in his maker's eyes. The false apology would buy him nothing but humiliation. Better to suffer in silence.

For the first time ever, Jules cursed his immortality, which would allow Ian to commit terrible atrocities without killing him. But he should have known just what kind of atrocity Ian had in mind.

"I think I'm going to have a little fun with you before I start hurting you," Ian said, his eyes glowing with decidedly unwholesome pleasure. "What do you think, old friend? Once more, for old time's sake."

The blood drained from Jules's face as his heart clenched painfully in his chest. Sweat bathed his body and he fought futilely against Ian's control. He was about to relive the nightmare he'd been fleeing for eighty years. Ian smiled in sadistic pleasure, savoring the fear and revulsion Jules couldn't hide.

With dread pooling in his gut, Jules felt his maker's glamour take a more intimate control of his body. He swallowed hard on a dry throat, fighting with all the will he could summon. But Ian's glamour was far too strong, and there was no resisting it. Ian's lips twisted into a cruel smile as Jules's cock began to rise no matter how hard he fought.

He closed his eyes, his mind yammering at him. *It's just glamour.* he reminded himself, fighting the panic. Even if he really did have a thing for men, he certainly wouldn't be aroused by *Ian.* His conscious mind knew this—though when Ian had first done this to him, Jules had been mortal, and didn't even know what glamour was. He'd found himself doing things with Ian he'd never imagined doing with a man, and Ian's glamour had made it seem like it was all Jules's idea. No amount of logic could overcome the memory of how his body had betrayed him under Ian's influence.

"My maker and her goddamn son have taught me a thing or two about degradation and humiliation in the years I've had to live under her thumb," Ian said, planting a hand in the center of Jules's chest. "I'm going to teach every one of them to you before you die."

"I don't think so."

Jules's eyes popped open and Ian gasped in surprise. Jules had to blink a time or two to clear his vision, assure himself that his eyes weren't lying to him. But no, that really was Hannah, standing there in the alley right behind Ian, her gun less than an inch from the back of his head.

"You move, I shoot," she said. "And I know it'll take a second or two at least for your glamour to get to me without eye contact. I feel any hint you're trying it, and I'll shoot."

Hannah now had Ian's full concentration, allowing Jules to move his limbs. And, thank God, he instantly lost the erection Ian had forced on him.

"Shoot him, Hannah," he said. "He's at least as evil as the Banger, maybe even worse."

He glanced over Ian's shoulder at Hannah's face and saw how pale her cheeks were. She'd shot the Banger in the heat of battle. Did she really have what it took to shoot a man in the back of his head in cold blood? Jules fervently hoped so.

"I'm sure we can reach some sort of agreement," Ian said, holding his hands up in a gesture of surrender.

"If you let him go, we'll lose our one and only edge," Jules urged. "He'll kill us both." A quick mental survey of the area showed him the alarming fact that another vampire was fast approaching. "Hurry, Hannah, someone else is coming."

Hannah licked her lips, her eyes wide and terrified. Her hands shook with her conflict and Jules willed her to shoot before it was too late.

Then it *was* too late, for the other vampire had rounded the corner and was sprinting down the alley toward them.

❧

HANNAH HATED HER OWN squeamishness. She stood in that alley holding the gun to a Killer's head and couldn't make herself pull the damn trigger. He was a murderer many times over, and he'd just threatened to torture Jules. She *had* to shoot him. Her finger twitched on the trigger and yet still she didn't fire. Buffy, she was not.

"Damn it, Hannah!" Jules shouted, "shoot him *now*!"

"No!" another voice yelled, this one from behind her. "Don't shoot."

The voice was vaguely familiar, but Hannah didn't dare turn to see who it was. She couldn't afford to be distracted, or Squires would turn the tables on her.

"Drake?" Jules said, sounding confused. "What are you doing here?"

"Saving you from yourself."

Yes, Hannah recognized the voice of the Killer who worked with the Guardians. The guy creeped her out big time, but she tentatively numbered him among the good guys.

"Please don't shoot him, Hannah," Drake said. It sounded like he was about five feet behind her now.

She blinked away a bead of sweat that trickled down her forehead. And she kept her gun right where it was.

Jules snarled at Drake. "Keep out of this! Hannah, shoot. Now!"

"Don't shoot," Drake countered.

Jules drew breath to bark another command, but Hannah cut him off. "Okay, guys, you can stop now. I'm not doing anything just because one of you says so. I know why Jules wants me to shoot. Why don't you want me to, Drake?"

"If you shoot him, we're all dead. He's far from the only vampire in Baltimore, and they'll avenge him if you kill him."

Jules let loose a stream of French. She didn't understand a word, but she sure as hell got the gist of it. "Shut up, Jules. Let him finish. So, what's to stop him from killing us if I don't have my gun to his head?"

"Me, for one," Drake said. Jules started up again and Drake raised his voice to be heard over the cursing. "But I'll try for something more concrete. Hold tight for a minute."

She heard little beeping noises she recognized as cell phone buttons being pressed. She let out a slow breath to calm the pounding of her heart, wishing she could spare a hand to wipe the sweat from her brow. Drake's presence calmed some of the anxiety, but she wasn't what you would call at ease. Her fingers started to cramp from holding the gun so tightly, and she forced herself to loosen her grip.

"I need to speak to Camille," Drake said into his phone. "It's an emergency." There was a brief pause, then Drake made an irritated-sounding grunt. "Put your mother on, Gabriel." Another pause. "Oh, all right. Tell her that if she wants Ian alive, she'd better call him off right this moment. My friend has a gun to his head and every reason to fear for her safety if she lowers it. Eventually she's going to get tired of waiting and shoot."

Another beep from the phone as Drake hung it up. Seconds later, Squires made a choking sound, and despite Hannah's order for him not to move, he staggered sideways toward the mouth of the alley. She kept her gun trained on him, but he barely seemed aware of her. He'd put both hands to his throat, and his eyes bulged. Hannah shivered as she realized he was choking himself. What the hell was going on?

Drake's hand landed on her arm. "Put the gun down and let's get out of here."

Jules stepped away from the wall, eyes glowing with purpose as he strode toward Ian.

"Stop it, Jules!" Drake barked. "If you want to risk your own life, fine, but Hannah will pay the price with you if you kill him now."

Jules turned back toward them, his lips stretched away from his teeth to display the fangs, a feral, frantic look on his face. For the first time ever, Hannah actually felt afraid of him. Her hand flexed on the gun and she wondered if she'd end up having to use it on Jules.

She'd forgotten that as a Killer, Drake was much stronger than Jules. She could see the moment Drake's glamour hit— Jules's face suddenly went slack and his eyes glazed. Behind them, Ian was struggling to move down the alley, still clutching his throat.

"Let's go," Drake said softly, tugging on Hannah's arm.

Shaking with nerves, she lowered the gun and allowed him to lead her to the other end of the alley, Jules following behind with a dazed look on his face.

When they reached the main street, Hannah cut a look at Drake from under her lashes. What she saw caused her steps to falter, and he turned fully toward her.

"Geez!" she said. "What happened to you?" Both his eyes were blackened, and another large bruise spread over his jaw. She didn't even know vampires could *get* bruises.

He shook his head. "We've stepped into the middle of some kind of mess here. I'm not sure I understand the details. Come on, let's keep moving, shall we?"

"My car's that way," she said, pointing. She'd thought driving would get her to the scene faster, which had turned out to be a miscalculation since she'd had to find a place to park.

Drake nodded and gestured for her to lead the way. Jules was still following like a zombie. She supposed she should be trying to get Drake to let up on the glamour, but after the madness she'd seen in Jules's eyes in the alley, she wasn't sure what he'd do.

"Are you all right?" she asked Drake, more disturbed than she liked to admit to see a vampire of his power with black eyes.

"I'll be fine. The bruises will heal in a few minutes."

"Oh, crap," Hannah said.

"What?"

She heaved a sigh. "You see that policeman over there? The one writing out a ticket? Well, that's my car." With the clock ticking, she'd finally decided an illegal parking spot would have to do, and she'd parked smack dab in front of a fire hydrant.

Drake actually smiled at that. "I'd change his mind for you, but I'd have to let go of Jules and I don't think that's a good idea right now."

She glanced at Jules and his slack jaw and shivered. "You going to keep him like that indefinitely?"

"Tempting," he muttered under his breath. "No," he said aloud. "Just till we get back to the hotel. Let's skip the car. We don't want to be talking to cops right now."

With the highly illegal concealed weapon on her person, and a PI license that would be revoked in a heartbeat if she was caught with it, Hannah had to agree, so the three of them strolled right on past her car. It wasn't that far to the hotel anyway.

"So," Drake said, "I was expecting to find Jules alone. What are you doing here?"

"Carolyn was afraid Jules was going to do something stupid like this, so she sent me to look after him. You know, make sure he didn't accidentally fry in his hotel room, stuff like that. What's your story?"

"Eli sent me to haul Jules back to Philly."

Hannah bit her lip, remembering Jules's assertion that Eli

would kill him if he ever went back to Philadelphia. Was he right? Or had that just been a bad case of paranoia?

They walked in silence the rest of the way to the hotel. By the time they stepped into the elevator, she noticed Drake's bruises were completely gone.

7

Pᴇᴏᴘʟᴇ ʟᴏᴏᴋᴇᴅ ᴀᴛ Iᴀɴ strangely as he staggered and stumbled down the street toward the house, his hands, under Camille's command, cutting off most of his air. Gabriel met him halfway, grabbing his upper arm in a brutally hard grip and dragging him along.

Ian cursed his moron of a fledgling, and he cursed the interfering mortal who'd stopped him from getting his satisfaction. Despite the distraction of Camille's forceful summons, he'd taken a long, hard look at the woman. He would recognize her if he saw her again, and he would make her suffer for what she'd done.

And Jules! Who'd ever guess the bastard was stupid enough to have come down here alone? No, he was *supposed* to bring a nice, big squad of Guardians with him, and they were *supposed* to find the house that, on paper, Ian still owned. And they were *supposed* to kill the bitch who lived there! Leave it to Jules to fuck everything up so thoroughly.

Gabriel ushered him into the living room, then gave him a

shove that left him lying face down at Camille's feet. At least she finally let up on making him choke himself. He lay still, sucking in air, grateful to be alive, and not sure how long that would last, seething with fury that his plan had failed.

"I thought you were supposed to be hunting me up a juicy morsel for dinner," Camille said. "Yes, I specifically remember asking you to do that for me. And yet, it seems that you had other priorities."

The bitch was too lazy to do her own hunting half the time. And, unlike Ian, she was picky. Male or female, her meals had to be pretty or she'd throw a fit.

Camille hadn't given him permission to get up, so Ian remained prostrate at her feet. "I was hunting for you," he lied. "I'd found one I thought you would like and was bringing her back when Jules found me."

"*Jules* found *you?*" she said, her voice dripping with incredulity. "Sit up so I can see your eyes."

He sat up and obediently met her eyes. She thought her ability to read his eyes was infallible, but she was wrong. Years of trial and error had taught him how to mask his thoughts with reasonable success. He did his best now to project sincerity even as he frantically planned his next steps. He might convince her for the time being, but that was unlikely to last.

Camille sat back, looking disappointed that she had read no lie in his eyes. He almost allowed himself a breath of relief, but she spoke before he did.

"Would your little fledgling tell the same story if I questioned him?"

Oh, no. She *couldn't* be allowed to speak to Jules. She was, unfortunately, anything but stupid. If she talked to Jules, she'd figure out what Ian was up to eventually.

He hoped his fear didn't show in his eyes. "Probably not," he said, "if he sensed saying otherwise would get me in trouble."

"Hmm," she said with a little pout reminiscent of Gabriel's. "I suppose I'll have to make the interview subtle enough that he won't know which answer would precipitate your death, won't I?"

If she talked to Jules, he was dead. Simple as that.

"I was looking forward to a nice, quiet evening. Now you've gone and spoiled it for me." She fixed Ian with her coldest stare. "I'm tired of looking at you. And I'm hungry. If you don't bring me dinner soon, I'll be *most* displeased with you."

He swallowed hard. "I'll take care of it," he promised. *Go get your own dinner, you fucking bitch,* he thought. If she wanted to talk to Jules tonight, then it would happen. Which meant Ian had to get the hell out of Dodge.

He felt a moment of profound relief that he hadn't pinned all his hopes on Jules. He'd been thinking about and planning his coup for years now, and the notice in the paper about the death of Jules's son had seemed like it might be a godsend, making his job exponentially easier. But he had a plan B, one Camille hadn't even begun to guess at.

His other fledglings were younger than he would have liked, but it seemed he had no choice but to step up the time line. If he lost a few fledglings in the process, well, they could be replaced once the city was his.

When next he saw Camille and Gabriel, he would *not* be helpless.

JULES CAME BACK TO himself with a start and a gasp. The last thing he remembered was standing in that alley in the middle of a mess of a standoff. He shook his head to clear the cobwebs and realized he was sitting on the edge of a bed. With his hands tied behind his back and his legs tied at the ankles. Hannah sat Indian-style on the other bed, and Drake hovered in the entryway.

Familiar rage boiled in Jules's gut, moments away from eruption. He tugged at his bonds. It would take a great burst of strength, but he thought he could break them.

"Drake wanted me to leave the room," Hannah said. "He said you're going to have a temper tantrum and get in a fight with him and I might get caught in the middle and get hurt. I told him you were more mature than that. Which one of us do you want to prove right?"

That checked his temper in a hurry. In the entryway, Drake laughed, covering his eyes and shaking his head. Jules made a growling sound deep in his throat, but Drake was too amused to care. And Hannah was grinning from ear to ear, proud of herself for knowing how to defuse him. Jules ground his teeth and shut up before he said something he'd regret.

Drake seemed to be convinced Jules wasn't going to do anything monumentally stupid and came fully into the room, pulling the chair out from under the writing desk and sitting down. The Killer folded his arms across his chest and rocked back in his chair.

"You can untie me now," Jules said, looking at Hannah. She hesitated only a moment before hopping onto the bed behind him and loosening his bonds. The brush of her fingers over his wrists made his skin tingle pleasantly.

"What are you doing here?" Jules asked Drake as Hannah worked the knot loose.

"Eli sent me."

To do what? Jules wondered. Hannah finished untying his hands and laid his crumpled Yves St. Laurent tie on the comforter. He quickly freed his feet from another of his silk ties, then stared hard at Drake, trying to guess his intent. Drake's face gave away nothing. Neither spoke, and the stare turned into a silent challenge.

"Ooh," Hannah said. "I can just *feel* the testosterone in the air. It's so fun to watch a couple of alpha males doing the macho stare-down thing. Sexy as hell. If you want, I'll go find a ruler—you can whip 'em out and I'll let you know which one is bigger."

Jules and Drake broke off the stare at the same moment, both sets of eyes turning to Hannah who was looking disgustingly perky. Jules glared at her, but Drake laughed again.

"A ruler might do for Jules, but you'll need a yardstick for me."

Hannah laughed right along with the asshole, and Jules squirmed, strangely jealous of what seemed like a sudden, easy camaraderie between the two. He'd never known Drake to have much of a sense of humor; as for Hannah, it was either laugh with her or kill her, and right now, the latter held a certain appeal.

"Okay, comedy hour is over," Jules said. "You've got some major explaining to do, Drake." He remembered the distinctly disturbing sight of Ian's hands squeezing his own throat. Obviously he'd been under the influence of some kind of glamour, but Jules had never heard of a vampire who could use glamour without even being in sight of his victim.

Drake raised a single dark brow. "I don't see why I'd have to explain anything to you. You're the one who—"

"Who the hell did you call?"

Drake's expression was one of long-suffering patience. "Ian's maker, of course."

"And what exactly happened after that?" Hannah asked before Jules could.

"Camille—that would be Ian's maker—called him off."

Hannah looked down her nose at him. "By making him choke himself. Or was that some kind of optical illusion?"

"No, that seems to be what happened." He turned to Jules. "Your maker has a lot more power over you than anyone else. Camille couldn't have managed a glamour like that against anyone but her fledgling. Do I have to spell it out to you that Ian has similar powers over you? Not as strong as Camille's, for sure. But you're in way over your head."

"How do you know all this?" Jules demanded.

"I had a life before I joined the Guardians."

Jules had always disliked Drake on principle, hating that the man killed without apparent remorse. The dislike had overshadowed any curiosity he might have felt, and he couldn't remember having a single conversation with him that wasn't directly related to a case. Why had it never crossed his mind that he knew *nothing* about Drake?

"Are you going to elaborate?" he asked, already knowing from the closed expression on Drake's face that he wasn't.

"I prefer to keep the past in the past whenever possible.

But I do understand things about how vampires outside of Philadelphia function. The ones we get are the lone wolves. They come from the country or the suburbs or cities too small to sustain a significant vampire presence. But you won't find lone vampires in cities the size of Baltimore.

"Places like this, you find master vampires with varying numbers of fledglings serving them. Camille is the Master of Baltimore, and Ian is far from her only fledgling. I don't know how many she has, but I have encountered one of them and he overpowered me with frightening ease."

"So that's where you got the shiners?" Hannah asked.

Jules frowned. He'd never gotten a good look at Drake back in that alley. Despite his dislike for the Killer, there was something distinctly unnerving about knowing there was a vampire in the city strong enough to beat him in a fight.

"Yes," Drake answered. "He was making a point about who was in charge here and what would happen if I stepped out of line."

"Hold on," Jules said. "Back up a minute. There's still a lot you haven't told us. How come you knew this Camille person? And how come you just happened to be there to stop me from killing Ian?"

Drake snorted. "You mean stop him from killing you, don't you? Like I said, I had a life before I joined the Guardians. I knew about Camille, and I knew only a vampire with a death wish would set foot in the city without checking in with her. I'd just gotten her permission to stay in the city until I found you and dragged you home when I sensed a couple of vampires nearby. I thought it wise to check it out, so I did."

The coincidences seemed too numerous for Jules. "So you

just happened to know who the Master of Baltimore was and where to find her? And you just happened to know you were supposed to check in with her, and you just happened to be checking in with her when Ian found me? Is that what you're telling me."

"Something like that."

Jules fully intended to pry more information out of Drake, but Hannah interrupted.

"Never mind all that. Let's get back to the important stuff. Like what happens now?"

Not a topic Jules was anxious to discuss. He wasn't ready to face the shambles he'd made of his life. He'd burned his bridges with Eli, and now he'd learned that his quest for revenge had been doomed from the beginning. He'd always known it was a longshot, but he'd never allowed himself to believe it was *impossible*.

"We get the hell out of Baltimore as soon as possible," Drake said.

"And go where?" Jules asked.

Drake frowned at him. "Back to Philadelphia, of course. Where else?"

Jules shook his head. "I can't go back."

"Of course you can, you ass."

Jules raised his chin. "I disobeyed his direct orders. And he was already angry at me for not controlling my temper better."

Drake shrugged. "So?"

"Don't play stupid! If I go back to Philly, he'll kill me."

Drake snorted. "God, what a moron you are. How have you managed to live this long?"

Usually, Jules's temper would have made an appearance just now, but he was too drained to rise to the challenge. Regret weighed his shoulders down, and his chest ached with something that just might have been despair. "We all know he's not the kind of man you want to cross, and I've crossed him. Big time."

"Jules, he's not going to kill you."

"Why shouldn't he? He set a precedent with Tim Carter, didn't he?"

Drake was silent for a long moment, staring at him with a strange expression on his face. Then he sighed and looked like he was bracing himself for something. "No, he didn't. *I* killed Tim Carter."

Surprise sucked the air from Jules's lungs. He might have thought Drake was lying, either to shield the Founder or to persuade Jules it was safe to go back, but there was a haunted look in Drake's eyes that said it was the truth.

Jules should have felt at least a little outrage over the murder of his fellow Guardian. Instead, he just felt confused. And curious.

"Why?"

Drake stared at his fingernails with great concentration. "He showed his true colors when he refused to obey Eli."

"Drake, *I* just refused to obey Eli. Are you going to kill me too?"

"Carter was different. He turned on us. And he incited others to join him."

"But you didn't kill the others." The small cadre who had deserted along with Carter had all come back to the Guardians. There was a lingering taint of desertion that clung to them, but for the most part they'd been accepted back with open arms.

"They were just confused, and following someone who could be very persuasive. But Carter was never coming back. And he'd shown how much hate was inside him. It was only a matter of time before he went rogue."

Jules opened his mouth, then closed it with a click, realizing he understood more than Drake had said. Drake might have been the one to kill Carter, but Jules would bet anything it had been on Eli's order. He was covering for Eli after all.

"You're not like Carter," Drake finished. "This is an aberration."

To Jules's surprise, Hannah hopped off her bed and came to sit next to him, putting her arm around his shoulders. The small gesture of solidarity felt better than it should have.

"I hate to tell you this," she said, her voice serious for once, "but it doesn't sound like you've got a whole lot of good choices here. What would you do if you didn't go back to Philly?"

He sighed. "I don't know." Once or twice, he'd tried to plan for the aftermath of his vengeance, but his mind had always balked. Besides, he figured when it all played out, he would either be dead, or in such a different place in his life that it was pointless to try to plan for it.

Bitter as the realization was, he knew now he had to go back. Maybe Eli really would forgive him. And if he didn't . . . Well, death at Eli's hands would no doubt be quick and merciful. Certainly nothing like what Ian had planned for him.

Jules shoved that thought away. If he let himself think about what had almost happened, he'd fall apart—something he wasn't about to do in front of Hannah or Drake.

Hannah's trim little body was a comforting warmth by his side. He wanted to lean into that warmth, put his arms around her and let her dispel the chill that had settled over his soul. Of course, he did no such thing, shrugging out from under her arm and giving her a stern look.

"I thought I left you nice and snug in the hotel room," he said, eliciting a cheeky smile.

"You did your best, sport. But I'm a slippery little devil."

He picked up the two ties she'd bound him with and saw the other—the one he'd used to gag her—crumpled on the floor. He frowned as fiercely as he could manage when he felt more tempted to laugh or pull out his hair. "So I ruined three perfectly good ties for no reason."

She reached up to ruffle his hair, but he managed to dodge her hand. "Stop that!" he said, but his lips were twitching into a smile in spite of himself.

Drake's cell phone rang, shattering the moment of ease. Drake unclipped the phone from his belt and scowled when he checked the phone number.

"Camille," he said, shaking his head. "Not good." But he answered anyway.

The expression on Drake's face was hardly promising as he listened to whatever the Master of Baltimore had to say. Hannah tucked her hand into Jules's elbow. He didn't know whether she was seeking comfort or trying to comfort him. But no matter how annoying she was, she'd risked her life to come help him when he'd been too stupid to help himself. Gratitude warmed his heart. He covered her hand with his own and gave her a rueful smile.

Drake seemed to be having trouble getting a word in edgewise, and a fierce frown had taken permanent hold of his face. Finally, he snapped the phone closed and swore colorfully. Jules couldn't remember the last time he'd heard Drake swear. Or look so worried, for that matter.

"What's the matter?" he asked, not at all sure he wanted to know.

"Camille has decided she would like to speak with you about whatever happened with Ian tonight."

Not a prospect Jules was terribly keen on, but it hardly seemed worth Drake's level of concern.

"She wants us to come to the house in three hours." Drake clenched his fists. "I was hoping to be long gone by then."

"So we'll be here a little longer than you'd hoped," Jules said. "It's not the end of the world."

Drake stood up from his chair, pacing the length of the room. "There's more." He stopped in his pacing and looked back and forth between Jules and Hannah. "She wants *all* of us to come."

Jules shot to his feet. "No fucking way!"

"Jules . . ." Hannah said in a warning tone.

"I am *not* taking a mortal into that creature's house!" he continued, more forcefully.

"I don't like it either," Drake countered, "but we don't have much choice."

"Like hell we don't! I say we head out of town full speed immediately."

"We can't. She's set her fledglings to keep a watch on the hotel and make sure we don't leave."

"Why would she do that? Why does she care?"

"I don't know," Drake said, looking frustrated and angry.

"I don't know how strong the rest of Camille's fledglings are, but I know Gabriel by himself is enough to take all three of us together without breaking a sweat. We're not going anywhere if she doesn't want us to."

"*Marde!*" What had he brought Hannah into? Not that he'd meant to, of course, but it was still his fault she was here. "We can't just take Hannah into a house full of Killers!"

Drake chewed his lip. "We don't have a choice. Camille doesn't kill every mortal who crosses her path. She's got a mortal working as a butler in her house. Hannah will probably be safe enough."

"Oh, I'll *probably* be safe enough. Gee, Drake, that makes me feel *so* much better. You guys are just tons of fun to hang around with, let me tell you."

"I'll go reconnoiter," Drake said. "See how many fledglings are out there and see if I can find a hole in their perimeter we can sneak out through."

He didn't sound very hopeful, but Jules and Hannah had to agree it was worth a try.

But when the door closed behind Drake, Jules realized that his troubles were just beginning. For he was alone with Hannah now, and she'd heard too much, and already he knew her too well to think she'd just let things be.

He turned to find her looking at him with narrowed eyes and cocked head. The interrogation was soon to begin.

✌

DRAKE RODE THE ELEVATOR down to the lobby, then found a secluded corner where he could lurk in the shadows and keep an eye out. Then he flipped open his phone and speed-dialed Eli's number.

"We have a problem," he said as soon as Eli answered the phone.

"We already had a problem," Eli said. "What's happened now?"

"There was a confrontation between Jules and Ian tonight. No," he said, before Eli could come to the wrong conclusion, "Jules didn't kill him. And Jules is all right. But it seems Carolyn's friend Hannah followed him down here too. And now Camille wants to talk to all of us."

"And the reason you're not already in your car speeding toward Philadelphia is . . ."

Drake sighed. "She *really* wants us to stay. What is she holding over your head, Eli? I get the feeling it's more than just your feeding habits." No, Camille had been far too sure that Eli would order them to stay in Baltimore. Eli's secrets ran deeper than Drake had imagined. "I told Jules and Hannah that she'd set her fledglings to watch us. For all I know, it's true. At least one of them is incredibly strong and could keep track of us from far enough away that I couldn't sense him.

"But I told a lot of lies tonight, Eli. And if we all go chat with Camille, I'm going to get caught in some of them." He'd thought himself clever, taking all the responsibility on himself, claiming it was he who knew Camille. And if they'd gotten out of the city tonight, then he'd probably be happy with that decision.

"I'll talk to Camille," Eli said after a long pause. "I'll tell her what you've told the others. As long as the three of you do what she wants, she'll keep up the illusion."

Drake shivered, not liking the sound of that at all. "What is she to you, Eli? Why would she do you favors?"

Not surprisingly, Eli ignored the question. "Gabriel might be a problem."

Drake liked the sound of that even less. "So, you know Gabriel, too?"

Eli snorted. "Of course I know him. It's impossible to know Camille and not know Gabriel. He's a troublemaker. Camille can probably keep him under control during your interview with her. But you've got to keep him away from Jules and Hannah when she's not around to hold his leash."

Drake laughed bitterly. "And just how do you suggest I do that? He gave me a little demonstration today of how easily he can knock me on my ass."

"Just . . . do whatever you can. I'm sorry to put all of this on your shoulders, but . . ."

"It's okay, Eli. If I didn't understand and agree, I wouldn't be doing it."

"One more thing."

"Yes?"

"Don't lie for me anymore. I don't want you putting yourself in that position."

Drake smiled a little sadly. "You have a reputation to protect. Mine sucks already. What do a few more stains matter?"

"It matters."

"So should I take a page from your book? If I can't answer truthfully, I don't answer at all?"

Eli chuckled. "It's a practice that's served me well for a long, long time. Try it. It's easier than trying to keep the lies you've told straight."

"All right. I'd better get back upstairs before Jules decides to do something stupid like sneak Hannah out of the hotel behind my back. He doesn't much like the idea of taking her to see Camille."

"Camille won't hurt her. I'll let her know Hannah is under my protection just like you and Jules."

He had a feeling he didn't *want* to know why Camille would do Eli any favors while threatening him with exposure.

Drake swallowed another mouthful of questions he knew Eli wouldn't answer. The undercurrents here were deep and strong, and he didn't want to get washed away by them.

8

So," HANNAH SAID, AND Jules flinched at the curiosity in her voice, "what's the deal with you and Squires anyway?"

How much of their conversation had she heard? And had she known what to make of it? He mentally reviewed what Ian had said to him, wondering if an outsider would be able to read between all the lines.

He turned away from Hannah's inquisitive gaze, busying himself with picking up his scattered ties. "The deal is he's a sick son of a bitch," he said, snatching one of the ties off the floor.

"Details, Jules. Inquiring minds want to know."

He tossed the handful of ruined ties into the waste basket. "I'm not up for a game of twenty questions."

"Oh, I'm *way* too nosy to stop at just twenty."

He looked for something else to occupy his attention, something to keep him from having to face her, but the room offered no distractions. Crossing his arms over his chest, he put on his most repressive frown and turned to her.

"Do you think you could take it easy on me for just a little while? This has been a rotten night already, and it's not going to get better anytime soon."

Her hawk-like stare softened, and she stepped closer to him. He had to fight the ridiculous instinct to back away.

"Take a load off," she said, putting a hand on his shoulder and pushing gently.

Reluctantly, he sat on the edge of the bed. Hannah sat beside him, close, but not too close. She bowed her head a bit, and her riot of dark curls obscured her face.

"I know guys don't like all this touchy-feely talk, but sometimes you've just got to share the load. There's a lot of water under the bridge with you and Ian, and it's obviously some pretty toxic stuff."

Toxic didn't begin to describe it. Maybe if he told her a little, she'd be satisfied and shut up. Probably wishful thinking, but it was worth a shot.

"It's pretty simple, really," he said. "There's nothing that hurts as much as being betrayed by someone you thought was a friend, and that's what Ian did to me.

"We went to Penn together. The guy was a natural-born loser, and in my arrogance I thought I could help him. I made him into my own special pet project." He tried to rein in some of the bitterness that had seeped into his voice, without much success. "I thought he was just socially awkward, so when he said mean-spirited, shitty things to people, I made excuses for him. I took him with me to parties he wasn't invited to. I loaned him money. I introduced him to girls.

"He was a wannabe-rake, but he didn't get that you actually have to be *nice* to your date to get laid. He acted like he was granting these girls a supreme privilege just to let them be near him." Jules shook his head, amazed at how much bad behavior he'd overlooked in his naïveté.

"Sometimes, we'd go out drinking and gambling together, and we'd end up in places where Ian could buy female companionship—with my money, of course, because he was always broke. He was into some things that made me uncomfortable, but since the women were willing professionals, I figured it was none of my business." He grimaced. "What kind of idiot doesn't realize that a guy who pays prostitutes to pretend he's raping them is pretty damn twisted?"

Hannah looked at him, her head tilted. "How old were you at the time?"

He shrugged. "I don't know. Twenty, twenty-one. I met him my sophomore year."

She nodded sagely. "If there's a creature on the planet stupider than a twenty-year-old guy, I don't want to meet it."

He couldn't help chuckling, despite the memories that haunted him. "You have a lot of experience with twenty-year-old guys? I didn't take you for a cradle-robber."

She slapped his arm with the back of her hand. "I have three older brothers. Each one of them was twenty for a really long, really miserable year." She frowned. "Actually, it was probably more like *five* years for them. But you get the picture. They were hormones on two legs, with maybe one fully functioning brain between the three of them."

Her pert little nose wrinkled with distaste, sending her glasses sliding, but he heard the undertone of affection nonetheless.

"Three brothers, eh?" he teased. "That explains a lot."

She narrowed her eyes. "Don't change the subject. If you're beating yourself up because as a twenty-year-old kid you weren't sophisticated enough to figure out Ian was a creep, then I officially give you permission to forgive yourself."

Once again, she surprised a laugh out of him. Nothing ever seemed to quell this woman's spirit. "Thank you. I'm all better now."

"Hmpf! You're still not telling me everything."

He heaved an exasperated sigh. "Since when am I obligated to tell you everything?"

He'd expected Hannah to respond with another light-hearted quip, but instead she laid her hand on his arm and peered up at him.

"Look" she said, "I may be a tomboy, but I'm still enough of a woman to want to help when I see someone in pain. And you're in a lot more pain than you're willing to admit."

A hint of resentment stirred in his center, then quickly subsided. How could he be angry with someone who so clearly meant well? He took her hand and raised it to his lips, meaning only to thank her for caring. It should have been a courtly, but gently dismissive, gesture. But the moment his lips touched her bare skin, the room seemed to hold its breath around them.

There was a warm, slightly earthy scent to her skin, and he tasted a faint hint of salt on his lips. He heard rather than saw Hannah lick her lips. A nervous gesture, he thought. He stared at the small, olive-skinned hand in his and found himself unable to let go. He raised her hand to his lips again, this time turning it over so he could brush a kiss over her vulnerable palm. She shivered and sucked in a quick, startled breath. But she didn't pull her hand away.

He shouldn't be doing this, he knew, as he pressed another kiss to the underside of her wrist, where he could feel her pulse throbbing steadily. He inhaled her ·scent—not clouded by perfumes or lotions—and told himself to stop immediately. After tonight's dramatics, he was not in his right mind, and neither was Hannah. Hell, he wasn't even sure he *liked* the little spitfire. He had no business kissing her.

His body couldn't have cared less about his logical arguments. His pulse kicked up and his gums tingled in a prelude to his fangs descending. Hannah moved closer to him, so that her body was tucked neatly up against his side. Her scent changed, a musky hint of arousal adding to her enticing bouquet. That scent shot straight to his groin.

When he raised his eyes to hers, he took in her expression of stunned desire and briefly battled with himself. This was some kind of freaky aberration, a reaction to the stress of the night, a mindless desire for pleasure to ward off pain. And yet, even knowing this, he couldn't help bending his head forward, wrapping one arm around her back and drawing her even closer.

When he brushed his lips over hers, they both gasped. Jules pulled away a moment, overwhelmed by the power of that simple kiss. His fangs were fully descended, his cock fully hard, a lightning-fast arousal that shocked him to his core. With a little groan, he moved in for another kiss.

Then jumped backward when he heard the distinctive click of a card key in the door.

"*Marde,*" he muttered, glancing at Hannah's flushed cheeks and darkened eyes, then glancing at the noticeable bulge in his pants. He willed the fangs to recede as he heard the door swing open.

Biting her lip, Hannah moved to sit on the bed across from him instead of beside him. She wouldn't meet his eyes, though the flush of desire remained in her cheeks. He crossed his legs in an effort to camouflage his state of arousal as Drake walked into the room.

Drake's nostrils flared briefly, and Jules realized that no amount of playing innocent would fool his superior senses, for the scent of arousal lingered in the air, a scent that would not escape a vampire's nose. Drake gave him a faintly disapproving look, but otherwise pretended not to notice.

"As I suspected, we're surrounded," he said. "We'll just have to brazen our way through this interview with Camille." He shook his head. "I'll be glad to put this cursed city behind me."

For a fraction of a second, Jules actually agreed with him, until he remembered that putting this city behind him meant leaving Ian alive and well and killing. Somehow, he was going to have to find a way to resign himself to that fact. He just didn't know how.

⚬

HANNAH WISHED SHE WERE as brave about this as she was pretending to be. She held her chin up high and tucked her hands in her jacket pockets so she wouldn't fidget as she walked. Drake walked on one side of her, Jules on the other. She sneaked a peek at Jules from under her lashes and wondered what he was thinking.

She'd gotten him to talk some in the hotel, but not enough. Whatever it was that caused his pain was still buried deep, hidden from the light of day. If only she hadn't let her stupid hormones take over, he might have let it out.

Speaking of hormones—how many times did she have to learn by experience that alpha males and her were not a good combo? She wasn't the type to let some guy dominate her just because of that Y chromosome, and they couldn't stand being with a woman who was just as insistent on getting her way as they were on getting theirs. And yet, every time she was attracted to a guy, wouldn't you know it, he was one of those alpha males?

For a year and a half now she'd gone cold turkey on men of any type, sick of the struggle. What was the point of playing these silly games, anyway? She'd never come close to falling in love—whatever, exactly, that meant—and as for the physical pleasure a man could give her . . . Well, that's what vibrators were for.

Now, suddenly, she found herself faced with the ultimate temptation—a sexy, wounded, alpha male in deep trouble. And she forgot all her resolutions and promises to herself.

He reminded her so much of the men in her family—except for the vampire part, of course. Her policeman brothers and fireman father were all quintessential, testosterone-laden alpha males, and all of them adhered to a strict I-don't-need-help-from-anyone policy. Which she couldn't help thinking had something to do with why her father was twice divorced, her two oldest brothers drank too much, and her youngest brother suffered from what she felt sure was clinical depression. Not that he would see a shrink about it or take Prozac or anything. *Real men don't take Prozac*, he'd told her when she'd gently suggested he might feel better on medication. He'd made it into a joke, but it had been a brush-off all the same.

She should have learned her lesson about trying to help this particular brand of male long ago. But some hopelessly romantic part of her, a part she wished she could exorcize once and for all, kept hoping that *this* time would be different. Which was no doubt why she was letting herself get all hot and bothered over a guy like Jules. He was probably even more fucked up than her father or brothers. Sternly, she ordered herself to keep her distance from now on.

Drake called a halt a few yards away from an impressive-looking columned doorway, looking down his nose at Hannah repressively. "I would ask you to please not say anything unless you absolutely have to. I doubt Camille would appreciate your sense of humor, and Jules and I aren't strong enough to protect you in there."

She forced out a nervous laugh. "Oh, goody. Sounds like fun." The corners of her mouth were lifted into something that was supposed to be a smile, but she didn't think the expression was very convincing.

Looking satisfied with himself, Drake started forward again.

"*Enculé*," Jules muttered under his breath. He gave Hannah's arm a squeeze. She didn't want to know how intimidated she must look if Jules thought she needed the comfort.

"What does that mean?" she asked in a whisper, figuring it was okay to encourage his habit as long as she wasn't the one being insulted.

Jules bent his head close to hers, his voice so low she could barely hear him. "Loosely translated, it means 'fucker'."

"Hmm," she said with a frown. "I was imagining something more colorful."

He chuckled. "Well, it actually means *he's* being fucked, but there's no exact English equivalent."

"How about 'fuckee'?"

He made a sound somewhere between a cough and a laugh, covering his mouth with his fist as Drake gave them a narrow-eyed look over his shoulder. The twinkle in Jules's eyes ruined his "I was just coughing" act.

Hannah smiled, glad to see that sparkle back in his eyes when his expression had been so miserable before. When he smiled with genuine good humor, his whole face came alive and he looked so damn good her pulse hiccupped. She averted her gaze before her hormones could go into overdrive again.

The momentarily playful mood evaporated when they climbed the steps and rang the bell. Hannah's palms went distinctly clammy and she cursed herself for being such a chicken. She swallowed past her fear and stiffened her spine. She would *not* disgrace the Moore family name by acting like some faint-hearted female. She could just *hear* her brothers' playground taunts ringing through her head—*afraid of heights, little girl? You gonna scream like a girl? Who wears the panties in your family?* These were the taunts they'd thrown at *each other*, and Hannah had learned her lesson well. To show fear was to be girlie, and to be girlie was bad.

None of this stopped her heart from pounding as she walked through the foyer of the palatial house of the Master of Baltimore. When the butler ushered them into the living room,

Hannah swore she could actually *feel* the power in the air. The door closed behind them, and Hannah felt like the Christian who'd just been thrown into the coliseum with a lion.

The Master of Baltimore sat in a regal chair, staring at the three of them without speaking. She was, as Drake had described her, a handsome woman. Her dress and bearing screamed of old money—it wasn't just the opulence of the house—and Hannah felt grubby by comparison.

Camille's face held little expression past a certain curiosity as she examined them. However, her son, whom Drake had aptly described as a young-looking punk—but a very dangerous punk—wore a very definite expression. Seething resentment, Hannah would label it. He was leaning over a chair, his elbows resting on the back, his hands clasped in front of him. His eyes pierced them one by one, and it took all of her willpower not to cower under that chilling, malevolent gaze.

"So," Camille said, drawing everyone's attention to her, "please introduce me to your companions, Drake." Her voice had a slightly sing-song quality to it, fluid and melodic. Pleasant, even, though Hannah doubted the woman was anything like pleasant.

Drake made the introductions, and there followed another short period of staring and assessing.

Gabriel rose from his slouch and came around the front of his chair, his stare as frightening as before. "I hear you're a Guardian," he said to Jules. His lip curled up in a sneer at the word. "And you've never felt the pleasure of a kill."

"That's right."

Hannah was surprised at how level and calm Jules's voice came out. The sneer on Gabriel's face and in his voice would usually have roused Jules's temper. But perhaps even *he* was too smart to let his temper go at a time like this.

Gabriel looked disgusted. "Pathetic."

"Gabriel." Camille's voice held a distinct tone of command, and Gabriel shut up. But his eyes still shot daggers at the three of them, and his body language said he was on the verge of attack.

Why? Hannah wondered. As far as she knew, they hadn't done anything to him.

"I hear you were on the verge of killing my fledgling," Camille said, directing the words at Hannah.

Hannah shoved her fear aside and met Camille's eyes boldly. "Well *he* was on the verge of killing my friend." The word felt odd on her tongue. Was that what Jules really was to her? A friend?

"So why didn't you pull the trigger?"

"I'm not used to murdering people." Oops. That was probably the wrong thing to say. Or at least the wrong way of saying it. Beside her, she felt both Jules and Drake tensing.

Luckily for her, Camille didn't seem particularly insulted. "Well, it's a good thing for you that you didn't. My son would have greatly enjoyed punishing Drake and Jules for that death." She glanced over at Gabriel, whose sudden wolfish smile revealed wicked-looking fangs. Maybe she was just imagining it, but Hannah thought those fangs looked bigger than the ones she'd seen on other vamps.

Gabriel's disturbing gaze settled on Hannah. "And my mother would have enjoyed punishing *you*," he said.

Unwilling to seem daunted by him—no matter how daunted she actually was—Hannah planted her fists on her hips. "What's the matter? Don't think you could take me your-self?"

Drake groaned softly, and Jules elbowed her, but though she knew it was dangerous to provoke these two, she also knew that with certain kinds of people it was better not to show your fear. She thought she might have guessed right when she saw the hint of a smile briefly cross Gabriel's face.

"Gabriel has a strange squeamishness about hurting mortals," Camille explained.

Gabriel looked offended. "I'm not squeamish! It's just that they break so easily there's no fun in it."

"I have no such problem myself," Camille continued as though he hadn't spoken.

Hannah nodded to acknowledge that she got the message loud and clear, and Camille turned her attention to Jules. "You must hate Ian a great deal to have ventured this far for revenge."

Jules said nothing, but his face spoke for him.

"And he must hate *you* a great deal to defy me by seeking his own revenge."

So Ian's attack had been an act of defiance? Hannah salted that little tidbit away for further examination later.

"Why should he hate you so bitterly?" Camille asked, an expression of polite inquiry on her face.

Jules visibly fought for calm, but the strain showed in his voice. "I suppose he's blaming me for getting him hounded out of Philadelphia."

A tiny frown furrowed Camille's brow, then vanished. "So he tells me. And *you* hate *him* because . . ."

"He made me what I am," Jules answered from behind gritted teeth.

Hannah cut a quick glance in his direction, then looked away. Admittedly, she didn't know him very well, but she'd never gotten the impression he much minded being a vampire. Any fool could see there was more to it than that. And Camille was not a fool.

"I should think you would thank him for the honor he did you," she said. Jules's Adam's apple bobbed, but he said nothing and Camille continued. "My mortals scratch and claw at each other for the privilege of my bite."

"Ian might have been eager to become a Killer. I wasn't." Jules's fists were clenched at his sides, his knuckles white.

Gabriel raised a white-blond eyebrow. "Is that all?" he asked. "It should be water under the bridge, shouldn't it? Sounds to me as if you haven't *earned* your hate. You've gotten the best of both worlds. Ian gave you eternal life, and you are spared the distasteful need to kill thanks to—"

Camille hissed—just like a snake, Hannah thought—and Gabriel fell silent. His face took on a sullen cast, but his eyes still glittered with danger. Hannah was impressed that Jules was able to drag his eyes away from the menace that stood so close, but he turned his attention to Camille once more.

"Ian has earned my hatred," he said, sounding calmer than he looked. "A great deal of that is . . . personal."

"Oh, do share. I'm eager to hear what my fledgling was up to for the brief time he wasn't tucked firmly under my wing."

But Jules shook his head. "As I said, it's personal."

Gabriel made an ugly snorting sound. "Personal," he mocked. "But we here in this room keep no secrets from one another."

"Gabriel, behave," Camille warned.

Gabriel whirled on her. "Why?" he cried, throwing up his hands. "Why shouldn't the truth flow like wine?"

Camille stood up and Hannah shivered with a sudden chill. Jules and Drake must have felt it too, for both of them moved a little closer to her and, as if by some silent agreement, put themselves between her and the squabbling pair.

"We've discussed this," Camille said, her voice low and soothing.

Discussed what? Hannah wondered. It was like they were talking in code, and she desperately wanted to break it. What was Camille trying to hide? And why did Gabriel not want to hide it?

Gabriel snorted. "We *discussed* nothing. You ordered. And this once, I don't feel inclined to obey, not when the request comes from Daddy Dearest."

From a good ten feet away, Camille swung her arm. Gabriel flew across the room, going ass-over-teakettle over the chair he'd once been leaning on. He landed with a thud and a grunt of pain, but quickly rose. The flush of his pale face made the scar on his cheek stand out like a white lightning bolt in contrast. He was breathing hard, showing his fangs, though his posture was defensive as Camille stepped closer and he backed away.

"Why do you protect him?" Gabriel asked as he continued to back up, his body visibly tensed for another blow.

"My son, don't make me—"

"Why should you do anything *Eli* asks?"

He flew through the air again, this time all the way across the room and out the door. As he lay on the floor, looking stunned, the door slammed shut.

Silence, fraught with tension, fell on the room. Camille stared at the door through which she had thrown her son. Jules and Drake both stood with open mouths, too stunned to mask their expressions.

Hannah's impression of Eli hadn't been so great to start with, but this just put the cherry on the sundae. Still, she felt bad for Drake and Jules, who so obviously looked up to their Founder. Or used to, at least.

Eventually, Camille's posture relaxed, and she sighed. "He's gone," she said, turning back to them. The corners of her mouth were tight with displeasure. "Your presence in Baltimore is having an unpleasant influence on my dear son."

"Your son by Eli," Drake said, as if he couldn't possibly have heard right.

Camille fixed him with an arctic stare. "Perhaps you now understand our non-interference pact. A pact that you and your friends may well destroy.

"I want you out of my city. All of you. If you cause any more trouble before you go, I will give you to Gabriel and allow him to take out his anger with Eli on you."

She turned her gaze to Hannah. "My son might be . . . sentimental enough to make a quick meal of you, but you can be sure your friends will not be so lucky."

Hannah suspected her face was about the color of Gabriel's hair right now. "Okay, I think we got the message."

"We were just leaving anyway," Drake said, flashing Jules a quelling look when it seemed he might argue.

"Yeah," Hannah said, "this is a nice place to visit, but I wouldn't want to die here." No one seemed to think that was funny, and Hannah couldn't blame them. Jules gave her a withering glare, and she grinned feebly. "Sorry. I make jokes when I'm nervous. I'm all for leaving, but what if Gabriel's waiting for us? He doesn't seem too keen on this whole non-interference thing you've got going."

Camille's eyes glittered dangerously. "He would not dare defy me."

Hannah refrained from pointing out that he just had. Somehow, she didn't think Camille would appreciate the reminder.

God, would she ever be glad to get home. And she promised herself that once she did, she would never, ever get involved with vampire hunting again.

9

Jules cautiously entered his hotel room, making Hannah wait in the hall while he confirmed there were no intruders. Like he could do anything about it if Ian or Gabriel were hiding out here. He got the distinct impression she was humoring him by letting him go in first. What he wouldn't do to be alone for just a little while! But Hannah gave him about twenty seconds before she decided the coast was clear and came in. Cheerful as ever—though he thought he saw a hint of strain around the corners of her eyes—she sat cross-legged on one of the beds while he opened one of his suitcases on the other.

"So," she said, "what do you think the story is with Eli and this Camille chick? I'm guessing they still have a bit of a thing for each other."

He grunted irritably as he jerked open a drawer with unnecessary force. He shouldn't be so surprised that Eli had secrets. Hell, *everyone* knew he had secrets. But no doubt about it, this particular one left a bad taste in Jules's mouth. How could Eli have taken someone so vastly, obviously evil into his bed? How could a viper like Gabriel actually be his son?

"Vamps can't have kids, right?" Hannah asked.

Jules paused in the act of folding a sweater and frowned. "Right."

"Which means they had Gabe when they were still mortal. Whenever that was."

Of course. Jules was surprised at how relieved he felt by the realization. "I suspect Camille had a somewhat more appealing personality when she was mortal."

Hannah raised her eyebrows. "Does going vamp really change someone that much? I mean, I knew Gray before and after. He's changed some, but I'd say he's still basically the same person underneath."

Jules shook his head. "It's not that you necessarily change that much. It's just that you lose a lot of your inhibitions. So, if deep down inside you're a real selfish bastard, but you've been hiding it because that's not an acceptable way to behave, then you become a real selfish bastard of a vampire."

She grinned at him. "So if you're a mortal with a short fuse, but you keep it under control to be polite, you become a vamp with a temper problem?"

He didn't dignify that with an answer.

Undaunted, Hannah stuck out her lip and looked lost in thought. "Hmm. I wonder what *I'd* be like as a vamp."

Jules pretended to give that some serious thought, then nodded sagely. "I doubt you'd change a bit, since you have no inhibitions that I've been able to detect."

For that little pearl of wisdom, she gave him the finger.

"Shouldn't you be packing?" he asked, glancing at the bedside clock. "We've only got forty-five minutes before Drake gets here."

They were all going to have to ride in the car Drake had rented. When they'd checked on Hannah's car, they'd discovered it had been towed. No doubt that would cause her some major headaches, but they didn't dare hang around to straighten things out.

She laughed. "I barely *un*packed, remember? So anyway, we never did finish our conversation about what happened between you and Ian."

Jules rolled his eyes. "For God's sake, Hannah. Give it a rest. I can't even hear myself think with you around." If she'd just shut up for a few minutes, maybe he'd be able to digest the evening's unpleasant revelations.

"Hey, I'm just helping you think out loud is all."

He stuffed a shirt carelessly into his suitcase, too irritated to worry about wrinkles. "Do I have to kiss you again to get you to be quiet?"

Idiot! Why did he have to go and say a thing like that? He leaned his hands on the edges of the suitcase, staring sightlessly at the contents. He didn't want to know what expression Hannah was wearing just now. The springs on her bed squeaked as she moved.

"Is that why you kissed me the first time?" she asked. Her voice was oddly subdued. She barely sounded like herself.

Reluctantly, he turned to face her. A frown puckered her forehead, and he thought he detected a shadow of hurt in her eyes. But surely she couldn't have taken that kiss seriously! She was a mature adult, she knew that stress could make people do stupid things.

"Well it does seem like the only time you don't talk is when your mouth is otherwise occupied," he said. He fought against the vision of Hannah's overactive mouth occupied with something other than kissing. It was a stubborn, tempting vision.

She grinned at him, and the hint of hurt left her eyes. "I have to admit, I like your way of shutting me up better than some of the other ways guys have tried."

He cocked his head. "Like what?"

"Like the guy who thought slapping me around would teach me a lesson."

He winced in sympathy even as he felt his temper stirring once more. He hated bullies. Always had, though he supposed he'd been blind where Ian was concerned. He'd never realized someone could be physically weak and still be the worst kind of bully.

"Oh, don't feel too sorry for me," Hannah said, her grin reappearing. "Remember, I know karate. And judo. And tae kwon do. And I firmly believe giving is better than receiving. I literally kicked him out on his ass."

He shifted awkwardly, sympathy still hovering in the forefront. However, he and Hannah were enough alike that he knew she wouldn't appreciate the sympathy. So . . . "I guess you tend to bring out the worst in people. I know *I've* wanted to strangle you at least ten times since last night."

She grabbed a pillow from her bed and hurled it at him. He ducked easily, laughing. She reached for another pillow, then stopped, shaking her head.

"Damn, you're good," she said.

He blinked. "Huh?"

"I've never met anyone as good at changing the subject as you are. First, you change the subject away from Ian by mentioning the kiss, then you change the subject away from the kiss by insulting me. And I just go right along for the ride."

Jules groaned. "You know, Gray always says how stubborn Carolyn is, but I bet you could give her a run for her money."

Hannah made a haughty face. "Carolyn's stubborn. I'm persistent. And you're trying to change the subject again."

A knock on the door saved Jules from having to answer. He glanced at the clock, but they still had more than a half hour before Drake was supposed to show up. A brief psychic survey confirmed that a vampire lurked in the hallway outside.

"Drake?" he called out as he neared the door. Sensing his alarm, Hannah grabbed for her gun.

"No," a voice said from the other side of the door. Gabriel's voice.

Jules looked around frantically, but there was no other way out of this room. Hannah moved up beside him, her gun pointed at the door, her face pale with renewed fear.

"I haven't come to hurt you," Gabriel said, drawing twin snorts of disbelief.

"That's very reassuring," Jules said. He reached out to lock the deadbolt. Not that it would do much good. "What do you want?"

"Just to talk. I thought you might want to hear the rest. What my mother wouldn't allow me to say."

The idea that there might be more sat uneasily in his stomach, but Jules told himself only a fool would believe anything Gabriel said right now. Of course, if Gabriel was even close to as powerful as Eli, there would be nothing Jules could do to stop the bastard from killing him. And Hannah.

"We can do this one of two ways," Gabriel continued. "I can overcome the two of you with glamour and force you to open the door. Or you can open the door of your own free will. If I have to use force, I'll be . . . annoyed."

Once again, Jules glanced around the room, wishing he could at least get Hannah out of here. But there was no way out.

To his surprise, Hannah lowered her gun. "Let him in," she said.

"What?" he cried, unable to believe his ears. "Are you nuts?"

She shrugged. "Like the man said, if he wants in, he's getting in. It's actually kind of polite of him to ask."

She started to walk past him, her obvious intent to open the door. Though she was right and Gabriel could get in with or without their cooperation, Jules still wasn't ready to give up without a fight. If they stalled for a little while, maybe Drake would get here to help even the odds. Not that the odds would be much better with Drake here—Gabriel had obviously overpowered him before. Jules put a hand on Hannah's arm to stop her from going to the door. Then, he froze, trapped by Gabriel's glamour. How old did Gabriel have to be for his glamour to work through a closed door?

"Damn," Hannah muttered under her breath, then pried his unresisting fingers loose. He couldn't even move his tongue to tell her once again not to let Gabriel in.

Hannah opened the door.

❧

"THERE'S BEEN A CHANGE of plans," Ian told Harvey Fisher. He drove with one hand while holding the cell phone he'd stolen from a pretty young coed who would have been Camille's dinner tonight, if Ian hadn't decided it was time for a strategic retreat. The coed had been a delicious diversion, though he'd been in too much of a hurry to enjoy her as thoroughly as he might have liked.

"What kind of change?" Fisher asked suspiciously.

He was one of Camille's "initiates," mortals she was grooming to be her fledglings. She used to make them serve her for two years before turning them. After Ian's desertion, she'd upped the waiting period to five years. Some she just killed. It had been easy enough for Ian to buy Fisher's loyalty with a promise of immediate transformation once Camille and Gabriel were dead.

"My idiotic fledgling came to Baltimore alone. It's only a matter of time now before Camille figures out what I'm up to."

Harvey started to curse, his voice a mixture of anger and terror.

"Calm down," Ian said. Fisher was way too volatile for Ian's taste. And Ian was no more going to transform him than Camille was. Still, Fisher served a purpose and Ian could still use him when his cover was blown. "She doesn't know anything yet, and even when she finds out what I was planning for her, she won't know that I have an accomplice. And contingency plans."

"What kind of plans?" Fisher demanded to know.

"If the subtle approach doesn't work, then you go for the bold one."

"Yeah? What does that mean?"

Fisher wasn't too bright. "It means I'll bring my fledglings into the city and attack her." The bitch would figure out Ian had been lying to her before the night was out. But there was no way she'd find out about his fledglings.

"She'll eat them alive! How old is your oldest?"

"It doesn't matter." Which was a good thing, seeing as Ian's oldest fledgling besides Jules was only two years old. A veritable baby. "Even the strongest vampire can be overcome with sheer numbers. And I've been stepping up production lately."

Fisher grumbled. "Then why haven't you turned me?"

"Because I need you on the inside," Ian explained with exaggerated patience. "I need you to tell me when Camille is unprotected." Even Ian's dozen fledglings couldn't take on both Camille and Gabriel at the same time. Hell, he wasn't even sure they could take Camille, otherwise he wouldn't have bothered trying to get the Guardians to take care of her for him.

Fisher was silent for a long time. Ian held his breath. He'd taken a huge risk recruiting this mortal—Harvey knew way too much about Ian's plans for comfort. But Ian needed a spy, and it wasn't like any of Camille's other fledglings, slavishly loyal, would help him.

"She's alone right now," Harvey said. "I just came from there. She and Gabriel had a fight."

Hope surged in Ian's chest, but it was too late to launch an attack tonight. "If they keep fighting, we're home free." An exaggeration, to be sure, but if Fisher began to doubt him, he might be stupid enough to tell Gabriel or Camille the truth.

"The other initiates and me are supposed to take her to the opera tomorrow night. Gabriel never goes."

True, but Ian could hardly set his fledglings on her and

her mortals in the middle of the street. The fledglings didn't have the power to hide the fight from prying mortal eyes. Maybe they could manage it with Ian's help, but he couldn't afford to be anywhere near the fight for fear of what Camille could make him do.

Gabriel might not go to the opera, but chances were he'd be hanging around the house beforehand anyway, keeping Mommy nice and safe. Unless they were still fighting.

"Call me at this number if Gabriel isn't at the house to-morrow night," he instructed Fisher. "If she's alone, we can take her out right in the comfort of her own home." He smiled at the images in his head. "Then when Gabriel finally comes to kiss and make up, he'll be in for a big surprise."

"This isn't your normal cell phone number."

"No, I 'borrowed' a cell phone. I don't want to leave any unnecessary evidence lying about. But this phone should be good for tomorrow still." Surely the authorities wouldn't find the body that soon, if at all. Ian had gotten very, very good at hiding bodies.

"All right, then. I'll let you know."

Ian closed the phone and tossed it onto the passenger seat. If he got lucky—for once in his life!—by this time tomorrow night, Camille and Gabriel would be dead, and he would be the Master of Baltimore.

⁊⊙

GABRIEL STRUTTED INTO THE room, all pride and attitude. He closed the door behind him, then turned to Jules. He sniffed the air, then wrinkled his nose.

"You *stink* of Eli," he said, releasing Jules from his glamour.

"What's that supposed to mean?" Jules asked, unable to

keep a hint of challenge out of his voice. Gabriel's very existence tweaked his nerves, set his teeth on edge.

Gabriel opened his mouth to answer, but Hannah—surprise, surprise—interrupted before he could get a word out.

"So, Gabe, you said you had something to tell us?"

Jules almost laughed at the look on Gabriel's face as he blinked at Hannah.

"*Gabe*?" he asked, sounding appalled.

Hannah's face wore another of her irrepressible grins, and Jules had to admire her pluck even while he cursed it. Luckily, Gabriel seemed more amused than angered.

"You should learn to treat your betters with respect," he said, his voice holding a hint of a growl, though his expression showed grudging admiration.

"When I find my betters, I'll respect them just fine," Hannah quipped back.

Jules groaned. "Hannah, please, for once in your life—"

"I haven't dined yet tonight," Gabriel said, stalking closer to Hannah, who held her ground though she had to look up to meet his gaze.

"Is that what you came here to do?" she asked. She oozed bravado, but Jules knew she couldn't possibly be as unintimidated as she was pretending to be.

"Perhaps." Gabriel reached out with his index finger, his obvious intent to touch her face. She jerked away from the touch, and Gabriel smiled.

"I thought you didn't like to pick on mortals," Jules said, hoping to draw Gabriel's attention away from Hannah.

It worked. Gabriel turned to him, sneering. "True enough. Were I to dine on your little mortal, she would not suffer."

"I'm not his little mortal!" Hannah said indignantly, but Gabriel ignored her.

"Would *you* suffer, Guardian?"

Jules hoped he didn't flinch at the thought. "Whatever you want, leave her out of this," he said. "She doesn't work for Eli. She's never even *met* Eli."

"But *you* work for Eli," Gabriel said, his lip curled in distaste as if even mentioning his father's name pained him.

"I do." Or did.

"And you hunt vampires and kill them."

"Yes." There was no point in denying it.

"You're a traitor to your own kind."

"Your mother seems to think you've killed your fair share of vampires yourself."

Gabriel shrugged. "We all have our foibles. And those I've killed have richly deserved every torment they suffered at my hands."

Jules bristled. "And the Killers the Guardians destroy deserve to die!"

"Don't give yourself airs. You're but a step removed from the rest of us. Had my mother made you, you would have hundreds of kills to your name by now. It was only chance that gave you a choice not to kill. A chance that was denied to the rest of us, the ones you so self-righteously murder."

Something akin to guilt stirred in Jules. In truth, he *was* lucky. If Ian had had his way, if it hadn't been for the Guardians, Jules himself would be a Killer right now.

"Oh, yeah, you seem real unhappy with the situation," Hannah said. "I can tell killing people just breaks your heart. I feel really sorry for you."

A weird light shone in Gabriel's eyes as he started to turn toward her. Jules caught a glimpse of his fangs and his heart nearly stopped.

"Hannah, please," he said. "Shut up before you get us both killed. Gabriel, if you have any quarrel, it's with me. Leave her out of it."

Power crackled in the air. Even Hannah seemed to feel it, the starch going out of her spine. She took a step backward, then came to a stop with a visible effort. Jules wondered if he should use his glamour to keep her from getting them in any more trouble, but from the look on her face he guessed she was out of quips.

Relief flooded Jules's system when Gabriel turned away from her. Anger still simmered in those gray-green eyes—eyes Jules now realized were the exact same color as Eli's—but it was a controlled anger.

"Finding out I'm Eli's son must have poked some holes in the halo you've given him. Yes, Saint Eli practices preferential treatment for Killers who are of *sentimental* value to him." Gabriel's voice seethed with scorn and contempt. "My dear Da gave me this," he said, tracing the jagged scar that marred his cheek, "but when it came right down to it, he didn't have the balls to kill me. Would you like to know why?"

Jules felt as if his very soul cringed. No, he didn't want to know. But Gabriel was going to tell him anyway.

"Because if it weren't for Eli, I wouldn't be what I am."

The shock of those words stole the breath from Jules's lungs. He shook his head. "No," he said, the word weak and unconvincing. "I'll never believe that Eli made you."

"How about my mother? Will you believe he made her?

Because he did, you know. That's why she still feels inclined to do what he tells her to. Being his fledgling—"

"No!" Jules shouted, lunging at Gabriel. His fangs had descended and his fury reigned supreme. Hannah screamed a warning, but he didn't care what happened as long as he stopped the words flowing from Gabriel's mouth.

The next thing he knew, Jules was lying face down on the floor, a heavy, booted foot pressing on the back of his neck. He blinked away a haze of confusion, wondering how much time had passed since Gabriel's glamour had taken him.

"Shall I snap your neck and put you out of your misery?" Gabriel asked, pressing down harder with his boot.

Jules had no doubt the older vampire was capable of carrying out his threat. Considering how heavy his heart felt, perhaps that wouldn't be so bad.

"Eli came by his sainthood relatively recently," Gabriel said. "It was very inconvenient for him that he happened to be the Master of Philadelphia when he changed his stripes. He killed his fledglings one by one, but in his sentimentality, he spared my mother and me. Instead of killing us, he merely banished us forever from our home. A sure sign of his great mercy."

"You're lying," Jules ground out, the words barely audible with his face mashed against the carpet.

"Tell yourself that if it makes you feel better."

The pressure on the back of his neck let up, and Jules sprang to his feet, whirling around. But Gabriel was gone.

10

Jules stood staring at the door through which Gabriel had disappeared. Every predatory instinct in his body urged him to charge out in pursuit, even though he knew he couldn't catch him and couldn't hurt him even if he did.

"God, I hate vampires," Hannah muttered under her breath.

Right now, Jules shared that opinion. How could Eli have created a Killer like Camille? How could he have created a vampire at all? He billed himself as a defender of the human race, and he had unleashed that creature and her son.

"You okay?" Hannah asked.

His breaths came quick and shallow, his fists clenched at his sides as his fangs descended. There was no one here he could vent his rage on, but how he wished to kill right now.

Hannah snapped her fingers in front of his face. "Earth to Jules. Come in, Jules."

He drew his lips away from his fangs and glared at her. The *last* thing he needed right now was to have her poking at him. One wrong word out of her, and the walls around his temper might crumble.

"I know you're pissed," she said, "but let's not go off the deep end. You don't want to give Gabriel that much satisfaction, do you?"

He just continued staring at her, letting her glimpse the beast that always hovered just below his civilized surface. Letting her see just how dangerous he was.

Her eyes widened. "Jules, you're scaring me." Her voice quavered ever so slightly. "You look like you want to hurt me."

Paradoxically, now that he'd scared her—just as he'd meant to—a hint of remorse crept in to mingle with the anger.

"There are a lot of people I'd like to hurt right now," he said. His voice held a hint of a growl, and he doubted his expression was much less intimidating. "You're not one of them. At the moment."

She held up both her hands. "Okay, I hear the warning loud and clear. I'll behave like a perfect angel."

A little more of the rage drained out of him. "That'll be the day."

She wrinkled her nose. "Yeah, I know, I'm not really angel material. But I'll try really hard."

"Good idea. And before you ask, no, I don't want to talk about it."

"Got it. Bottling it up inside you is really a much better idea anyway."

"Hannah . . ." The growl was back in his voice.

She raised her eyebrows. "What? I was agreeing with you."

Without another word, he turned to his suitcase and began violently stuffing his clothes into it. Hannah took the none-too-subtle hint, ducking into the bathroom to pack her own meager bag. He'd have had an easier time fitting everything in the suitcases if he slowed down and folded things, but it felt good to take some of his fury out on inanimate objects.

After a quick trip to the ice machine to restock his cooler, he was ready to go. When Hannah emerged from the bathroom, he had the cooler slung over his shoulder and a suitcase in each hand. She eyed him warily.

"We've still got twenty minutes before Drake gets here," she said.

"I'm not going with Drake." Which he had a feeling she'd known damn well before she spoke.

"Think this through, Jules."

"I'm not going back to Philadelphia, I'm not going back to Eli, and if you argue with me I might not be able to keep my temper under control anymore."

"Okay. I won't argue. Where are we going instead?"

"*We* aren't going anywhere. You're going back to Philly with Drake." It was far too dangerous for Hannah to remain anywhere near him. He doubted she would give in easily, but one thing was for sure: she was *not* going with him.

He tried to make eye contact, but she quickly ducked her head and stared at her feet.

"I'm on a job here, you know," she said. "I was hired to keep an eye on you, and I plan on doing it. Until you're safely out of Baltimore, you're stuck with me."

He reached out with his glamour, urging her to raise her chin and meet his eyes. Once he had eye contact, she wouldn't be able to fight it. She squeezed her eyes tightly shut.

"Stop it, Jules," she said. "You can use your damn glamour

if you absolutely have to, but then I'll have to chase you through the city. I really don't want to chase you through this city at night."

"Then don't!" God, this woman was impossible! And she just might be stupid and stubborn enough to do as she threatened. Gabriel might not harm her—though Jules had serious doubts about that—but Ian certainly had an axe to grind. The thought of what Ian would do if he got his hands on her . . .

He *had* to get rid of her.

"I'm not leaving," she insisted. "We'll both be a lot safer if you just let me come with you instead of making me chase you."

Boldly, she raised her eyes and met his gaze. The temptation to seize her with glamour was almost overwhelming. But obviously, using glamour to get away from her wasn't enough. He had to keep her from following him.

"I can see why men have hit you in the past," he snarled, "though I can't imagine how they put up with you long enough to have a relationship in the first place!"

It was a low blow, and she flinched. Guilt stirred in his center, but he didn't take the words back. He couldn't soften his stance, had to stay strong even if that meant being an asshole.

Of course, Hannah wasn't one to take a blow like that without fighting back. "What's the matter, Jules? Not man enough to handle a woman who has a mind of her own?"

Jules ground his teeth, pulling back on the reins of his temper. This impossible female was going to get herself killed! How the hell could he get rid of her?

Suddenly, he remembered the day Hannah had killed the

Banger. After all the excitement was over, Gray had decided to chase Carolyn away from him for her own good. He'd pretended to go mad with bloodlust and attacked her, knowing full well Jules and Drake wouldn't let him hurt her.

The tactic had worked for Gray, but Hannah would never believe Jules was mad with bloodlust. However, he might just know of a way to make her so pissed off at him that she'd wash her hands of him for good . . .

He dropped his suitcases and cooler. The bottles rattled loudly, and he hoped none of them broke.

He took a moment to gather up his rage. Then, he rushed her.

༂ઝ

THE AIR WHOOSHED OUT of Hannah's lungs as Jules flung himself on top of her, knocking her flat on her back onto the bed. Furious herself now, she tried to punch him, but he grabbed both of her wrists in one of his hands and pinned them above her head. Then his mouth came down hard on hers.

It was an angry, brutal kiss, and everything in Hannah rebelled against it. She struggled and squirmed, keeping her mouth tightly closed as his tongue demanded entrance.

He was way too strong for her. Probably would have been even if he were human. A little whimper of fear escaped her, and her heart suddenly leapt into her throat. She was helpless against him. A weak, helpless female. He could do anything he wanted right now, even without his glamour, and she wouldn't be able to stop him. His body pressing down on hers, trapping her, stealing her air, her space, her light. Her lungs tightened until she could hardly breathe, and another whimper rose in her throat. A tremor shook her whole body.

Jules's mouth left hers, though he kept his hold on her wrists, and his body still pinned hers to the bed. She closed her eyes tightly, fighting the panic, but it wouldn't go away. Her breaths came fast and shallow. A hot trickle leaked from her eye and slid down toward her ear.

"Hannah?" Jules asked, letting go of her wrists. His finger traced the tear track. Then he rolled off of her and she curled into a ball and hugged her knees.

His hand gently brushed over her hair, a touch so gentle in contrast to his recent roughness that it wrung another tear from her, no matter how hard she clamped her jaws shut and tried to force herself to calm down.

"I'm sorry, Hannah," Jules said, his voice subdued and quiet. "I was trying to get you pissed off enough that you'd decide not to follow me. I didn't mean to hurt you."

She concentrated on breathing slowly, steadily. She hated, hated, *hated* feeling helpless. That's why she'd taken all those martial arts classes. She'd spent her entire childhood learning that her brothers were bigger, stronger, and faster than she was, could overpower her whenever they wanted. It wasn't that they'd ever really *hurt* her, but they'd damaged her pride many a time. She'd determined she'd never be helpless again. And then she'd had to go and get mixed up with vampires. Life had a sick sense of humor.

It was far too late to pretend his little show of dominance hadn't scared the crap out of her, but she tried her best.

"It wouldn't have mattered how pissed you made me," she said, her voice hoarse and scratchy sounding. "I'd have followed you either to keep you safe or to kill you myself."

He groaned loudly. "You are the most impossible female I've ever met."

She surreptitiously wiped away the last traces of her tears. "We're wasting time. If you don't want Drake too close on our tail, we'd better get out of here now."

Jules sighed. "Whatever you say. Apparently, you're the boss."

She couldn't even muster a hint of a forced smile.

~

DRAKE DIDN'T BOTHER TO go up to Jules and Hannah's room. As soon as he'd reached the hotel, he'd scanned the area, hoping that Jules's would be the only vampire psychic footprint he picked up. Instead, he'd sensed none. With a curse and a groan, he parked, then slapped the steering wheel for good measure.

Had Gabriel or Ian gotten to Jules? Or had the fool changed his mind about going home?

He dialed Jules's cell phone. When he heard the connection going through, he breathed a quick sigh of relief. Then the anger was back.

"I'm not in the mood to talk right this moment, Drake," Jules said.

"You idiot! Where are you? Stop playing games and let's get out of here." Not that he expected Jules to listen to reason, but he had to at least try.

"I'm not going back to Philly, and nothing you say is going to change my mind."

"Why? I thought—"

"I had a visit from Gabriel." Even with the poor reception on his phone, Drake could hear Jules's anger. "Give Eli a call,

Drake. Ask him who made Camille and Gabriel. Then maybe you'll understand why I'm not coming."

Jules cut the connection, leaving Drake to stare at his phone in amazement and disgust. Jules was quite a piece of work. Didn't the idiot know that Gabriel meant them all harm? Couldn't he extrapolate from that that Gabriel might have been lying through his pointy teeth?

Knowing it was useless, he tried Jules's cell again. Not surprisingly, he got his voice mail. "Call me when you've come to your senses," he said, doubting that Jules would do it even if he *did* come to his senses.

Leaving his car in a no-parking zone, Drake ducked into the hotel to see if by chance Hannah was waiting for him, but of course she was gone too. She and Jules made quite a pair—stubborn, willful, and apparently suicidal.

Now what? he wondered. The sensible thing to do was abandon Jules and Hannah to their fate. But while he might have been able to stomach leaving Jules here, it was much harder to imagine leaving Hannah. As a mortal, she no doubt had less of a grasp on what she was up against, and she was following her protective instincts. But she was highly likely to end up dead—or worse—if she hung around with Jules. Drake would rather not have that on his conscience.

Slipping back into his car, which thankfully hadn't been towed or ticketed, Drake dialed Eli's number. Eli answered on the second ring.

"Jules and Hannah have flown the coop," Drake said.

Eli muttered something that might have been a curse. "I thought you said—"

"Yeah, they were planning to come back with me. But Gabriel got to them before we could get out of town. He's convinced them that you made him and Camille, so now Jules is throwing another of his temper tantrums."

There was an eerie silence on the other end of the line. A chill snaked down Drake's spine. He shook his head slowly.

"Gabriel was lying. Wasn't he?" His heart thudded as the silence stretched. "Eli?"

"He's not lying," Eli said, and Drake had never heard the Founder's voice so subdued. "I was not always what I am now. I made Camille, a long time ago."

"Jesus, Eli."

"You understand now why I was so adamant Jules not go to Baltimore."

Drake couldn't seem to swallow, nor could he find his voice to speak. But why should this shock him so? He already knew Eli was a Killer. Why should discovering he'd made another Killer be so much worse?

And yet, it was. Immeasurably so.

"I'm very old, Drake," Eli said. "Old enough to have changed a great deal. I'm not proud of my past, but I can't make it go away. All I can do is try to make amends."

Drake cleared his throat, hoping that would loosen his vocal cords. His voice still came out tight and strained. "And that's why you founded the Guardians? To make amends?"

"Yes."

How many fledglings had he made? How many people had he killed? How many people had his *fledglings* killed? He had a lot to make amends for.

"What about Gabriel?" Drake asked. He'd always assumed he was Camille's fledgling, but if Eli had made Camille . . . "Did you make him too? Your own son?"

"Not exactly."

Drake had to fight down a surge of his own temper. "What does that mean?"

"It means that contrary to popular opinion, vampires *can* have children. It's just very rare, and it seems we can only have them with each other, not with mortals. Before Camille became pregnant, I'd never heard of a vampire less than five hundred years old recovering their fertility. Camille was only a little more than three hundred. Her pregnancy was unexpected. She barely survived the birth."

Drake was too stunned for words. A pregnant vampire? In all his hundred and ten years as a vampire, he'd never heard of such a thing. But then, before Eli, the oldest vampire he'd ever known had been about two hundred and fifty years old. And Eli never shared a drop more information than necessary, so it wasn't surprising he'd failed to mention this little tidbit.

"The truth is," Eli continued, "unlike you or me or Camille, Gabriel never was human. So while Camille and I can claim joint responsibility for him, neither of us is his maker."

Drake's head throbbed. He wished he hadn't had to hear any of this. Blissful ignorance would have been ever so much better.

"You see, Drake—there's a reason I keep secrets. It's not just an old man's whim. It would have been far better for everyone if neither you nor Jules had learned any of this. I hope I can count on your discretion. You can see what such knowledge has done to Jules. Just imagine how some of the younger Guardians would take it."

Oh, they would take it very badly indeed. "And what about me?" Drake asked, his voice rough. "Does it matter how *I* take it?"

"I know how you're taking it," Eli said quietly. "You're angry and disillusioned and maybe even a little sad. But given time, you'll be able to accept the truth about me. You're too practical to let emotions rule for long."

Drake mulled that over. "I might be able to accept it. And I won't betray your secret because I know you're right and it could destroy the Guardians. But I'll never be able to forgive you for creating a creature like Camille."

Eli sighed. "As I will never be able to forgive myself."

The hurt and sadness in Eli's voice was almost enough to trigger Drake's sympathy. Almost.

"What do you want me to do now?" Drake asked, wondering if he had enough respect left for Eli to do as he ordered.

"I'll leave that up to you. Jules and Hannah have put themselves in great danger, but I'm not sure how much you'll be able to help them. Especially if they don't want to be helped."

That was unquestionably true. And yet, if Drake left town now, not only would he have to deal with his conscience, he'd also have to go back to Philadelphia and deal with Eli. He wasn't sure he could do that right now.

"I'll find them. And I'll do what I can to help them. But don't get your hopes up—I don't see Jules coming to terms with what he's learned about you."

"I don't either," Eli admitted. "But people are still capable of surprising me once in a while. Perhaps Jules will too."

Drake hung up without another word.

JULES COULDN'T STAY IN Baltimore—at least, not indefinitely—and he couldn't go back to Philadelphia. Honestly, he didn't know where that left him. Where did he want to spend the rest of his long, long life? And how could he be sure his chosen residence wasn't already "taken" by a master vampire?

One thing he *did* know—he wasn't making that decision in the middle of the night while his head was spinning and his heart aching. The best he could do was find a relatively safe place to lay low until he figured out what to do.

The Harborside Inn was not exactly the sort of establishment Jules was used to patronizing. Despite the name, it was nowhere near the harbor or the scenic, historic streets lined with brick row houses. Instead, it was tucked into the shadow of a seedy alley, across the street from a strip club and an X-rated video store. The man at the desk hadn't batted an eyelash when Jules had paid in cash, hadn't even asked for a credit card or ID of any kind. And the place rented by the hour.

The elevator was out of order, so he and Hannah trudged up a flight of grimy stairs to the second floor. The hall was dimly lit, but not dimly enough that he couldn't see the walls had needed a new paint job about ten years ago. And no carpet cleaner in the world would get the stains out of the worn floor coverings. A faint disinfectant smell wafted in the air. He was beginning to think he'd rather sleep out in the street.

Hannah opened the door to their new home sweet home

and gestured him in. He maneuvered the suitcases through the narrow doorway, then stood rooted in place as he inspected the room.

There was only one queen-sized bed, covered in a faded floral bedspread with frayed edges. The center of the bed sagged visibly. The walls and carpet were as dingy as those in the hallway, and the disinfectant smell was stronger. He hated to think what the place would smell like without it.

"Okay, so it's not the Ritz," Hannah said. "But you've got to admit, Drake would never think to look for you in a place like this."

Her voice was bright and chipper as always, but he thought even *she* was affected by the squalor of this place. Reluctantly, he put his bags down. They'd stay here for a night or two at most. Just until he figured out where to go from here. Tonight's only agenda had been to avoid being dragged back to Philly by Drake, and Hannah was right—Drake wouldn't look for them here.

Hannah yawned, not bothering to cover her mouth. It was after four in the morning, so she must be exhausted. Jules wasn't feeling too alert himself.

"Dibs on the bathroom," she said, and he wasn't about to fight her for the honors.

He continued to examine his distasteful surroundings as Hannah prepared for bed. A gentle push on the edge of the bed showed that the mattress was as soft as cement and the springs squeaked. There was no couch he could sleep on. Perhaps the floor would be more comfortable, but this not being the Ritz, as Hannah pointed out, there didn't appear to be any extra blankets or pillows. If he slept on the floor, he'd have to have all the blankets to himself to keep himself protected from the sunlight.

Perhaps Hannah wouldn't mind sharing the bed. It wasn't like he was capable of staying awake for much longer anyway. Shortly after dawn, the lure of sleep would be too strong for him, and she wouldn't—

A shrill scream from the bathroom cut off his line of thought. Jules leapt toward the bathroom door, heart in his throat. Halfway there, he collided with Hannah, who'd flung herself through the door as if fleeing for her life. He wrapped his arms around her and swung her around so that he was between her and whatever had frightened her in the bathroom. She trembled in his arms, and he held her tighter.

"What is it?" he gasped. Anything that actually frightened Hannah must be terrible indeed. He had visions of dead bodies or dismembered body parts.

"R-roach," she panted between frantic gulps of air. She was clinging to him now, her fingers digging painfully into his arms.

He frowned. "Roach? You mean as in a bug?"

He felt her head nodding against his chest. She was still shaking. Her skin was clammy with fear-sweat and her pulse drummed a palpable rhythm against his fingers. If she weren't so terrified, he'd have laughed himself sick over this. As it was, he still had to struggle against amusement.

"Let me get this straight," he said. "You have no qualms about antagonizing powerful Killers, but a bug can send you screaming from a room?"

Her fingers dug in a little harder. "I can't help it! It's a phobia. I *hate* roaches. *Hate* 'em!"

This was twice in one night he'd seen a chink in Hannah's impressive armor. There was some satisfaction in knowing she had weaknesses too. He gave her another squeeze, then gently extracted himself from her grip. Her face was pale, and she was biting her lip hard.

"Relax, Hannah," he said, dropping his voice to a soothing croon. "I'll take care of it for you."

She nodded, but didn't look much more relaxed. He briefly considered using a touch of glamour to calm her but decided against it. She would *not* have appreciated the thought.

He slipped into the bathroom, looking for the offending creature. He found it soon enough, skulking in the shadow of the toilet. His lip curled in distaste, though this was just the kind of place where he'd expect to find roaches in the bathroom. At least it wasn't a rat, though it practically rivaled a rat in sheer size. One quick stomp sent it to its maker, and he flushed the remains. He hoped there weren't too many more scuttling about in the walls.

When he returned to the bedroom, he found Hannah huddled in the middle of the bed, her arms wrapped around her knees. She glanced up at him briefly, but her eyes slid away almost immediately.

"Your nemesis is no more, milady," he told her, trying not to grin. "Verily I have vanquished the creature with my trusty shoe."

She lowered her head to her knees and groaned. "Oh, God. I'll *never* live this down."

He instantly regretted teasing her and joined her on the bed, the mattress sagging enough to tilt her body toward his. He rubbed his hand up and down her back, noting that her blouse was damp from the remains of her fear.

"Don't worry about it," he said. "Like you said, it's a phobia."

She shuddered. "Yeah, the ultimate girlie-girl phobia." She sounded positively disgusted with herself.

"Maybe your mother was attacked by a giant cockroach while you were in the womb," he suggested, grinning at her. She raised her head to give him one of her fierce glowers. Now, he couldn't help laughing. Her glower grew darker.

"It's so easy to push your buttons," he teased. "You're almost as easy as Gray."

She snorted. "Oh, now you're going to add insult to injury." She tried to sound as if she'd completely gotten over her discomfort, but he heard the lingering traces of disgust under her light words.

"It's really not a big deal, Hannah. Lots of people are scared of roaches. They certainly aren't the most attractive of God's creatures."

She sighed heavily. "Yeah, but they're completely and utterly harmless. If I had to be afraid of something, couldn't it be something more ominous? I mean, take spiders. At least some of them bite, so it's not completely ridiculous to be afraid of them."

He shrugged. "If it were something you're *supposed* to be afraid of—like, say, vampires—then it wouldn't be a phobia, now would it?"

She inclined her head in a shadow of a nod, but still something unhappy hovered behind her eyes. Jules frowned and cocked his head at her.

"Why does this bother you so much?" he asked. "So you have a phobia. So what?"

"Try living in a household with three older brothers when you've got a phobia."

Jules himself was an only child, but one of his childhood friends had had older brothers. He well remembered the cruelties of older siblings. "Ouch," he said with genuine sympathy.

"Yeah. To this day, they give me hell about it. Doesn't matter how tough I am, doesn't matter that I can kick their butts in a fight—well, sometimes anyway—they still fixate on that one little thing, and they stick me right back in my place. The helpless little girl, the damsel in distress." She looked like the words tasted sour in her mouth.

He cleared his throat. At last, an insight into what made Hannah tick. "I've made the mistake of calling you a helpless mortal in the past. You've made me eat my words. You're not a damsel in distress."

She quirked a grin at him. "Well, good thing, because you're not exactly a knight in shining armor."

He met her grin with one of his own. The grin faded as he met her eyes and desire kicked him in the gut. He remembered suddenly how her body had felt beneath his earlier this evening, the soft, warm curves of her that camouflaged the woman warrior beneath. He remembered the scent of her skin, the taste of her lips. He'd been dead wrong to go after her like that, but that didn't stop him from lusting after her right now.

Hannah licked her lips, making him harden to an almost painful extent.

"May I ask you a personal question?" she asked, her voice husky. "One I have no right to ask and shouldn't even be *thinking* about at the moment."

He couldn't help but be intrigued. "You can ask. I may or may not choose to answer."

She dropped her gaze down to her lap. "Why do you have condoms in your toiletries bag? I mean, if vamps can't have kids, then . . ."

He shifted uncomfortably. "When you said a personal question, you really meant it."

"Never mind. You don't have to answer. I'm just being too nosy for my own good."

Of course, she was right, and he didn't have to answer. But he found himself answering anyway. "I found it easier to use condoms than to explain to women why I didn't need them."

She nodded sagely. "Women in general, or is there someone special?"

He raised an eyebrow, amused and curious about her sudden interest in his love life. "Trying to find out if the coast is clear?"

She grunted. "You wish! I'm just trying to understand you."

Usually, Jules was quite confident in his ability to fathom the female mind. But with Hannah, he wasn't so sure. Perhaps there really *had* been no ulterior motive to her question. Was that a good thing, or a bad thing? He wished he knew.

"I try to avoid having 'someone special' as a general rule," he said. "Relationships get awkward when you're immortal."

"But you had a girlfriend last year, right? A girl the Banger killed?"

Remembered pain stabbed through him. "Yes. Courtney was special." He hadn't loved her, but he'd been very fond of her. He'd never met another woman who so closely matched his ideal—pretty, sweet, devoted, and not too bright. The last being a requirement because it would be hard to hide the truth about himself from an overly bright woman.

"So over this last year, you've lost a special girl, and a son, and now you've lost your respect for your mentor. You might want to consider that you aren't in the right state of mind to make radical decisions about your future."

He glared at her, wishing he'd been able to figure out how to get her to go with Drake. "If I needed a shrink, I'd go to one who actually had a degree in psychology."

"Just wanted to plant that thought in your brain. Now, I'm over my fit of hysterics, so you can use the bathroom and then we can both get some rest."

Glad for any chance to escape Hannah's probing questions, he hurried to the bathroom.

11

Hᴀɴɴᴀʜ ᴡᴏᴋᴇ ᴜᴘ ᴡʜᴇɴ the couple in the room next door started going at it.

She'd started off the night . . . day . . . whatever, sharing the bed with Jules. His chivalrous sensibilities hadn't allowed her to sleep on the floor, nor had he been willing to sleep on the floor himself when it meant having to hog all the covers. She'd been tired enough to give in to him, but as soon as he'd fallen asleep, she'd gotten out of bed. After all, she didn't want to toss in her sleep and suddenly drag the covers off of him. The drapes in this flea-bag barely kept out any light at all, and he'd burn to a crisp if he didn't keep entirely covered.

She'd made a relatively comfortable nest for herself, stealing one of Jules's cashmere sweaters for a pillow and trying not to wonder how many more roaches were lurking around. When the rhythmic knocking sound woke her, she guessed she might have had two or three hours of sleep.

At first, she tried to tune the sound out and go back to sleep, but the walls were paper thin, and the lovers next door were growing steadily more enthusiastic, banging the headboard against the wall. Hannah could actually feel the vibrations in the floor.

Groaning, she sat up, wondering if it would be rude to knock on the wall to let them know they had an audience.

Pleasured moans soon joined the drum beat of the headboard against the wall, and the woman started encouraging her lover with such pithy sayings as "oh, yes," and "fuck me, baby." The walls were so damn thin, Hannah could hear the guy's heavy breathing.

"Oh, brother," she grumbled in disgust as the noise went on and on. But as irritating as the noise was, the suggestive rhythm triggered some very unwelcome images in Hannah's mind. She tried covering her ears with her hands, but the sound penetrated easily.

It had been far longer than she wanted to admit since she'd had sex, but the sounds from next door evoked memories of skin sliding against naked skin, of tongues battling for supremacy, of hands stroking and teasing. She pressed her thighs together, trying to deny the moisture that gathered there. And trying desperately not to picture Jules, gloriously naked as he thrust into her.

"Stop it, Hannah!" she ordered herself sternly. The *last* thing she wanted was to have sex with Jules! Even though he was sexy as sin. This sudden lust attack of hers was just the power of suggestion paired with abstinence. Yeah, that was it.

Next door, the woman howled in climax, her cries so loud they just *had* to be fake. Didn't seem to matter to her man, who soon roared his own release. Hannah sighed in relief, wiping a thin sheen of sweat from her forehead. Maybe now she'd be able to go back to sleep.

But her mind had latched onto an image of naked Jules and refused to let go. She bet he'd be absolutely spectacular in bed. Most of the men she'd been with had managed to turn sex into a power struggle. At the slightest sign that she was taking control of her own pleasure—for instance, if she offered the tiniest suggestion of what she wanted—they'd set out to let her know that they were running the show. She wanted to be on top? They used their superior weight to make doubly sure she stayed on the bottom. She wanted to touch herself to help herself along? They pinned her wrists.

Instinct told her Jules wouldn't be like that. He was as dominant and opinionated as any alpha male she'd known, but he was far too vain to let himself be bad in bed. He'd try his best to run the show, but if that wasn't working for her, he'd adapt.

Hannah slapped herself on the head, telling herself to stop thinking about sex. It might even have worked if the couple next door hadn't decided to have another go.

She decided she was better off trying to distract herself while waiting it out, so she rose from her improvised bed, meaning to boot up her laptop and do a little surfing. The hotel didn't have wireless access, but the phone line would do in a pinch.

Unfortunately, she made the mistake of glancing over at the bed to make sure Jules was fully covered first.

The covers had settled around him like a shroud, outlining every contour of his body. He was lying on his back, his hands clasped over his abdomen, his chest rising and falling steadily with his breaths. But that wasn't what had caught her attention.

There was an unmistakable tent in the covers right at groin

level. Unmistakable, and mouth-wateringly impressive. Next door, the woman began talking dirty, encouraging her lover—or john, as was beginning to seem more likely—to fuck her harder.

"It's a freakin' conspiracy," Hannah muttered under her breath. Her cheeks felt like they were glowing with repressed heat, and her eyes were riveted on the super-sized tent. She swallowed hard. "Jules? You awake under there?"

There was no answer, nor any hint of movement. Which was a damn good thing. What would she have done if he'd said yes? She had a sneaking suspicion she might have slid under those covers and impaled herself. Which would have been oh so wrong. And which she suddenly wished with all her might she could do.

Knowing she would have no peace—and no sleep—if she didn't find release, she lay down on the bed on top of the covers, careful that Jules remained safely under wraps. Then, staring at the evidence of his massive hard-on and listening to the couple next door, she slipped her hand into her panties.

Climax came almost before she'd had a chance to really get started. The physical pleasure almost drew a cry from her throat, but she managed to swallow it down. But no amount of lying to herself would make her believe that the self-induced orgasm was a hundred percent satisfying. Yes, her physical desire had been quenched. But something deep inside of her wanted more than just physical release.

Too bad she wasn't about to get it.

⊰⊱

JULES AWOKE SHORTLY BEFORE sunset to find himself alone on the bed. He pushed the covers away from his face and turned to glance over the edge of the bed. As he'd suspected, Hannah was fast asleep on the floor, using one of his jackets as a blanket and a sweater as a pillow. He shook his head at her. Had she feared he would jump her in his sleep?

A memory stirred, blurry and surreal like a dream. Hannah lying beside him on the bed while in the room next door a couple fucked loudly. His nostrils flared with the remembered scent of Hannah's arousal, and he rose to full mast when he remembered what she'd been doing. His daytime lethargy had been too powerful to overcome, but as hazy as the memory remained, Jules had no doubt it had really happened.

He let out a long, slow breath. If there'd been any doubt in his mind that Hannah was attracted to him, this morning's little indulgence effectively banished it. And his own current state of painful arousal suggested the attraction wasn't one-sided.

Propping his head on his elbow, he gazed down at her sleeping form and wondered what it was about her that triggered his desire. She wasn't at all his type. Sure, she was pretty enough, in a kind of tough-girl, no-nonsense way. But he'd never describe her as "sweet," or "docile." Adjectives that would describe practically every other woman he'd been with for the better part of a century. Even *before* he'd become a vampire, he'd preferred meek women, though perhaps he was merely a product of his times.

Hannah was everything he *didn't* want. Bold. Willful. Stubborn. Smart. So why did he seem to have a constant hard-on in her presence? It made no sense whatsoever. Maybe he'd just gone without too long. A little bar-hopping ought to find him a playmate for the night, relieve some of the pressure building within him . . .

But no. That would be far too awkward with Hannah sharing his room. And of course, awkwardness was the reason he felt so uninterested in his half-baked plan. It had nothing to do with him wanting Hannah in particular, rather than just any warm, willing body.

Irritated with himself, he flung back the covers and slid out of bed, meaning to take advantage of the rare opportunity to have first dibs on the shower. But some unseen force, call it fate, or call it his subconscious, decided it would be better for his foot to get tangled in the covers and for him to take a nosedive. Directly onto Hannah.

Jules caught himself on his arms and twisted to avoid hurting her, but he still bumped her pretty hard.

Hannah came awake with a shriek. Before Jules had a chance to utter an apology, she jerked her knee up in an attempt to unman him. Instinct allowed him to block her knee with his upper thigh, but as he protected his most vulnerable spot, he unknowingly gave Hannah another opening.

With a snarl, she twisted out from under him, the suddenness of her move leaving him even more off balance. Instead of retreating, she proceeded to roll him over onto his back and sit on him, her hand pulled back in a way that suggested a karate chop was on its way.

"Take it easy, Hannah," he said, though with her sitting on his stomach he was a little short of breath. "It's just me!"

Her eyes still blazed, and she didn't lower her hand. But she didn't hit him, either. "What the fuck did you think you were doing?"

He almost allowed himself to answer her anger with anger of his own. Then he remembered that he'd pretty much attacked her last night, so it wasn't entirely crazy of her to think he was doing the same now.

"I think I was tripping over my own feet and fell," he said. And suddenly it became too funny for words, so he started laughing.

"Prick!" Hannah said, slapping his chest. "You scared the shit out of me."

She made to hit him again, but he grabbed her wrist to stop her. Not that she was really hurting him or anything, but still . . . For a split second, she struggled against his grip. Then, she relaxed, resting her palm gently against his chest.

After her less-than-flattering assessment of his sleep wear, Jules had decided to forego the pajama top, so her hand lay against the bare skin of his chest. He saw the moment that fact sank in when a flush of rosy color warmed her cheeks. She tried to jerk her hand away, but some devil made him hold on to her wrist. He liked her hand just where it was.

He wasn't sure if his erection had ever flagged even during their brief struggle, but if it had, it was back with a vengeance. Blood throbbed in his groin. His gums tingled, and he didn't even try to stop the fangs from descending.

Sitting on him as she was, Hannah couldn't fail to notice the effect she was having on him. Her eyes darkened and her scent changed to that delicious, womanly musk that was becoming imprinted on his senses.

"I should get off of you now," she said, her voice husky. She didn't move.

"That would probably be a good idea," he agreed, but he didn't let go of her wrist, instead holding her hand tightly against his chest so she could feel the hammering of his heart.

She cleared her throat and squirmed. He doubted she'd meant to do it, but her squirming landed his cock right in the valley between her legs. He couldn't help raising his hips, pressing a little harder against her heat. She gasped and her lower lip trembled.

Lust and logic battled for supremacy in his brain. He wanted her. Badly. But sleeping with her would be a major mistake. It wasn't like he didn't have enough troubles already without having some kind of weird, complicated relationship with a woman on top of it all. And he doubted very much there would be any such thing as uncomplicated sex with a woman like Hannah.

"This is a really bad idea," she whispered.

"I know," he agreed. But he reached up to cup her breasts anyway. She'd slept in an oversized nightshirt that left her looking almost shapeless, but his hands found generous curves beneath, topped with pebbly nipples. He wanted to tear the shirt from her body and take one of those nipples into his mouth. He could almost taste her skin on his tongue.

To hell with all the reasons he should leave well enough alone!

With an embarrassing sense of urgency, he slid his hands down her sides, reaching for the hem of her nightshirt. To his surprise, Hannah pulled away. She practically jumped to her feet and took two hasty steps backward.

Lust pounded through his veins, and it was all Jules could do to resist the urge to dive after her. Instead, he propped himself on his elbows and stared at her, his heart still pounding, his cock still throbbing. Hannah held up her hands as if to ward him off.

"This is a really bad idea," she said again, shaking her head.

He looked pointedly at the bulge in his pajama bottoms. "At this moment, I don't much care."

"Yeah, but you will in ten minutes or so."

He laughed. "Ten minutes? The lady underestimates me. Again."

She didn't crack a smile. "I'm serious, Jules. We can't do this. We'll both regret it before the night is out."

Keeping a careful eye on her—she did tend to be jumpy, and he didn't want her coming to the wrong conclusion and decking him—he rose slowly to his feet. She took another step backward, but didn't seem to be going on the offensive.

He honestly didn't know what to say to her right now. Every instinct told him she was right. But his body didn't seem to give a shit what his instincts said.

"I get this feeling we're fighting the inevitable," he said. "And that maybe it's not worth fighting."

Her eyes narrowed. "I hate to burst your bubble, Jules, babe, but getting me in your bed is *not* inevitable."

He knew he was acting like an arrogant, cocky bastard, but he just couldn't help it. He looked her over slowly from head to toe, taking in the flush of her cheeks, the darkness of her eyes, the way her nightshirt clung to the contours of her beaded nipples. She crossed her arms over her chest and glared at him. He grinned back.

"You realize, of course, that you just issued me a challenge no red-blooded male could refuse," he said.

She groaned. "Let it go, Jules. I know you're probably used to dealing with air-headed floozies who swoon at your feet if you smile at them, but in case you haven't noticed, I'm not like that."

"Perhaps that's part of your charm."

Hannah stiffened, and he knew he'd put his foot in his mouth big time.

"So *that's* what this is all about?" she cried. "You're looking for a new challenge, like some kind of goddamn trophy hunter?"

"That's not—"

"Well screw you, buddy! I'm no one's trophy! Touch me again, and you might lose some body parts you'll miss."

She stormed into the bathroom and slammed the door shut behind her. Jules was pleasantly surprised the force of that slam didn't bring the hotel crumbling down around their ears.

He sat on the edge of the bed, bemused and remorseful. He hadn't meant to make it sound like she was some kind of trophy he was intent on bagging, but he could see how she'd take his words that way. Once upon a time, he'd thought of himself as something of a smooth-talker, but either he'd been fooling himself or Hannah was immune to his charms.

Of course, both he and Hannah agreed it was better for everyone involved if they didn't sleep together. So, while he might not be what you'd call thrilled with what had happened, it had no doubt saved both of them a lot of awkwardness and discomfort.

Telling himself repeatedly that it was all for the best, he opened one of his suitcases and picked out the least wrinkled of his shirts to wear for the night.

12

DRAKE HAD THOUGHT HE'D been reluctant the *last* time he'd come to Camille's house. He hadn't known what reluctant was.

But he couldn't remain in Baltimore without informing her of his intentions. Not if he wanted to live, that is. He left his hotel at nightfall, reaching out with his senses and hoping not to find any vampires lurking nearby. He was only mildly relieved to find himself the only vampire in the area. His senses could stretch over about a three-block radius, but a vampire as strong as Gabriel could cover three blocks in very little time.

When he neared Camille's house, another reconnaissance survey revealed two vampires in residence. Was one of them Gabriel? Drake hoped so. It seemed likely Camille was the only person who could control him, so it was best for all involved he stay directly under her nose. Unfortunately, Drake also sensed a total of five mortals in the house. One of them was no doubt the butler, but who were the rest?

He hesitated just short of the doorstep, then decided he

had no other choice but to continue on, unless he was going to tuck his tail and run back to Philadelphia. And Eli.

He rang the bell and waited.

Shortly afterward, the butler answered the door and ushered Drake into the opulent living room. Camille sat in the same chair she'd occupied last night, with Gabriel slouched in the armchair. Drake suffered a moment of deja-vu, but although Gabriel wore an outfit almost identical to last night's, Camille most definitely had a new look. Her glorious blonde hair was piled onto her head in an elegant up-do, and a choker of diamonds circled her neck. A strapless black evening gown clung to her every curve, revealing and concealing in equal measure. Black satin gloves reached over her elbows, and another cluster of diamonds circled one thin wrist.

Her lips, painted a glossy red, curved into a slight smile, and she rose to her feet, turning to give him a view from all sides. Perhaps, he thought to himself, he could understand Eli's attraction to the woman after all. He offered a courtly bow of appreciation, and Gabriel snorted softly.

"What an unexpected pleasure," Camille purred. "I'd expected you to get out of town last night. As I think I made quite clear."

Drake flicked a glance at Gabriel, who was inspecting his fingernails with great concentration. Had the little shit told his mother what he'd been up to last night? Somehow, Drake doubted it. Getting between the two of them seemed like a very bad idea, but Drake wasn't sure how to avoid it.

"That was my plan. But apparently your son had other ideas."

Gabriel tore his attention from his manicure and pierced

Drake with one of his unnerving stares. "I'd be happy to be rid of you, old son," he said.

"Then perhaps you should have kept your mouth shut last night." Out of the corner of his eye, Drake saw the ever-so-slight dip of Camille's shoulders. So, she hadn't known.

Gabriel shrugged. "I can't imagine what you mean." He wasn't even *trying* to sound sincere. Why he bothered with the words, Drake couldn't guess.

The countenance Camille turned on her son would have scared Attila the Hun. Certainly it wiped the smugness from Gabriel's face. He rose slowly, eyes fixed on Camille as though she might strike if he looked away for an instant. Maybe she would have.

Power crackled in the air, raising the fine hairs on Drake's arms. Instinct screamed at him to get the hell out before something exploded, but he fought against it and stayed put.

It was rare indeed to find a master vampire who would allow a fledgling not her own to be part of her "family." The tie between mother and son was based on affection, duty, and respect—all of which could be denied. The tie between a master and her fledgling was based on pure power, which could not.

Camille was older than Gabriel, so she could probably take him in a fight, but it would be a *fair* fight. The kind of fight no master vampire would willingly engage in. It seemed with strength came an inherent affinity for bullying.

Camille bared her fangs in silent threat. For a long, tense moment, Gabriel met her gaze head on. The temperature in the room dropped sharply, the chill deeper than anything Drake had experienced in Eli's presence. Drake actually shivered in the cold.

Finally, Gabriel broke the eye contact, his gaze dropping to the ground. Anger and rebellion still sparked in his eyes. He was backing down, but not gracefully. Did he know he was one false step away from being killed by his own mother?

"Don't disobey me again," Camille said.

The rebellion flared higher in Gabriel's eyes, but he kept his gaze focused downward.

"Go now," Camille continued. "Come back to me when you are ready to take your discipline."

Gabriel gave a curt bow, then whirled toward the door, striding out with anger riding in his wake. The room still had not warmed, and Drake was not overly pleased to have Camille's attention turn to him. She seemed very much the type to make a habit of killing the messenger.

"Once again, you and your friends have proven to have an unwholesome influence," she said. Her face had gone still and inhuman, an expression reminiscent of Eli's, except for the rage that brewed behind her eyes.

"Gabriel's hatred isn't our fault."

"I could kill you with little more than a thought."

Yes, she could. But *would* she? Drake remained silent. What could he possibly say?

She shook her head. "But I promised Eli I wouldn't. Not without provocation." She smiled, an expression both beautiful and icy. "It takes little to provoke me, however. And as Ian failed to return to me last night as I'd ordered, I could assume that your friends have killed him. Even Eli wouldn't intervene on your behalf if they have."

Drake's stomach dropped. Surely Jules wasn't *that* stupid.

He knew that Hannah would suffer if he killed Squires. Besides, Squires was more than he could handle.

"I highly doubt that they've gone after Ian," he said with more confidence than he felt. "And even if they have, surely they wouldn't have caught him and managed to kill him in so little time. Squires is Jules's maker."

Camille looked vaguely disappointed. "True. Perhaps there is some other explanation. But I will require you to remain as my . . . guest until I can discover my fledgling's fate."

He should have just left town. To hell with Jules, and even Hannah. No one was forcing them to stay here, in danger.

"I won't have much success hunting down Jules and Hannah if I'm serving as your hostage," he pointed out, without much hope of success.

Camille smiled that cold smile again. "I said you would be my guest, not my hostage. I don't as a general rule keep my guests confined to my house."

An ornate grandfather clock chimed the hour. Camille pursed her lips. "This has all been most inconvenient timing," she said. "I had plans for dinner and the opera this evening, and you've made me late."

Drake had to bite his tongue to keep from saying something stupid. He paused just long enough to get his distaste under control, then said, "I had best be off, then. I'll get Jules and Hannah out of your hair as soon as I can."

"I didn't mean to rush you," Camille said, and there was something ugly about her voice despite the blandness of her words. "Please, stay for dinner."

His stomach turned. "Kind of you to offer, but I'm not

hungry." He could go about ten days without feeding, so he had a full week left before the need would be upon him.

"Perhaps I can tempt you into indulgence." She picked up a delicate brass bell and rang it, the sound incongruously sweet and cheerful.

"I expect our tastes run in opposite directions," Drake said, wishing he could get out of this room immediately. Better to *know* Camille was killing some innocent victim than to *see* it. Or be forced to participate.

One of the side doors opened and a cluster of mortals stepped into the room. Three men, dressed in tuxedos, and one lone woman. A girl, really, no more than eighteen or nineteen years old. A gag had been stuffed in her mouth, and tears streamed from her terrified eyes. Drake's nose wrinkled as he scented her fear. His temper stirred when he picked out another scent. The girl had been raped, no doubt by one or more of the tuxedo-clad men. Drake clenched his fists against a swell of impotent fury. There was nothing he could do for this poor girl, not with Camille determined to hurt her.

Camille smiled at him and licked her full lips. "Are you sure you're not tempted?"

Oh, he was tempted all right. Just not in the way she thought. Had she not been in the room, he would have happily fed—on the mortal men who seemed to be so enjoying the girl's pointless struggles.

Camille turned to the girl and bared her fangs. A muffled scream rose in the girl's throat, but the gag wouldn't let her give full voice to it. Camille glided closer, eyes aglow with anticipation. She didn't even use her glamour. The girl was fully conscious and terrified. Drake could hear the frantic hammering of her heart from across the room.

In her desperate search for rescue, the girl's eyes locked on Drake's. He held her gaze, reaching out with his glamour. Her eyes went dull and she stopped struggling.

Camille put her hands on her hips and turned to Drake. "Release her. I want her to feel herself die."

It was all he could do not to charge across the room and seize Camille by the throat. But attacking her would do no one any good. He had to find some other way to help the poor girl.

"Don't take out your anger with us on an innocent," he said. "I won't interfere with your feeding, but—"

Camille laughed. "Why, how *generous* of you to *allow* me to feed. I'm glad to know it will bother you to see her suffer. You've caused me no end of grief already. Now, I would like to cause you some as well." She stepped back and gestured at the girl, who stood unresisting in the arms of one of her captors, her eyes glazed over. "If you hadn't come to call and chased my son away, he'd have argued for a merciful kill, and I would have granted it. No matter what he says, he *is* squeamish about hurting mortals, especially females. A lesson he learned from his father and has never been able to set aside. So in a way, you are personally responsible for her suffering."

Camille licked her lips and gazed at him eagerly. "Unless you'd care to kill her yourself. I think I'd very much enjoy that."

Drake's heart sank. If he kept the girl protected by his glamour, he could kill her painlessly and she wouldn't even be afraid. He'd never killed an innocent, and he wasn't sure how his conscience would absorb the sin.

He took one step toward the girl, then stopped and shook his head to clear it. What was he thinking? If he killed this girl, he'd succeed in making her death painless, but Camille would simply find another victim for her evening meal. Two would die instead of one.

Camille laughed. "Poor fool. You really do have an excess of conscience. Either kill her or release her from your glamour. Those are your choices. Now hurry up. I'm going to be late for the opera as it is."

He glared at the beautiful, inhuman creature and wished with all his might that Eli hadn't sent him down here. If he could turn the clock back twenty-four hours and erase all his newfound knowledge, he would gladly do it. But that wasn't an option. He cursed Camille for her cruelty, and he cursed Eli for making her. Then he dropped his gaze to the floor and released the girl from his glamour.

❧

HANNAH WAS HUNGRY ENOUGH to eat a horse, but the Harborside Inn didn't exactly do room service. At least, not any kind of room service she was interested in. She and Jules agreed—what a surprise!—that wandering into a restaurant for a casual dinner wasn't the brightest idea, so she settled for a lukewarm hotdog on a stale bun from some no-name convenience store. Given the neighborhood, she attracted way more attention than she would have liked and was very glad to have Jules at her side.

Even so, when they left the convenience store, she noticed a couple of thuggish teens peel away from the shadows and amble in their direction. She could almost feel their hostile eyes boring through her back. She glanced over at Jules, who was as usual wearing a full-length cashmere coat and a rakish black felt hat. He looked good enough to eat. But he also looked like a tempting target. Not good. Her gun was a solid, comforting weight in her coat pocket, but she sure as hell didn't want to have to use it.

A police car cruised slowly down the street. Hannah glanced at it from the corner of her eye and saw one of the cops giving her and Jules the once over. Great. They were drawing attention from all corners. Perhaps this wasn't the best part of town for them to go incognito after all.

Jules's face was closed and shuttered, his eyes strangely distant. She didn't think he could afford to be lost in thought just this moment, so she gave him a gentle poke with her elbow.

"Carolyn called this afternoon," she said. That got his attention. He blinked and came back from la-la land.

"What did you tell her?"

Hannah sighed. "I didn't tell her Eli's little secret, if that's what you're asking." She hadn't liked keeping secrets from her best friend, but she figured she couldn't drop a bombshell like that over the phone. "She asked me what you're planning to do next, and I told her it beat the hell out of me. So, what's your grand plan? Or are we still making this up as we go along?"

"I'm working on it."

"Well work fast. I don't think hanging around this neighborhood has good long-term prospects." Not unless Jules planned to go on a killing spree. The two punks from the convenience store were still shadowing them, no doubt waiting for the right opportunity to attack. They'd get a rude surprise if they did.

Jules glanced over his shoulder, making no attempt to be subtle. "You're not afraid of those two, are you?"

So he hadn't been completely oblivious to his surroundings after all. "I'm sure you could take them, but do we really need the hassle? It's not like we don't have enough problems already."

She would have loved to get out of town the moment the sun set, but they were still without wheels. She'd called the impound lot, and they'd insisted she had to pick up the car between the hours of nine and five. At the Harbor Court, she'd have felt safe enough leaving Jules alone for an hour or two while she went to the impound lot. At the Harborside Inn, she wouldn't feel safe leaving him alone for five minutes. So, no car.

"True," Jules agreed. "Let's just stay on the main street until they lose interest."

She doubted the punks were going to lose interest when the two of them looked like easy money, but she didn't say so. "Regardless, we can't stay here indefinitely. Street punks aren't the only problem. You've got to figure out where you want to go, then we'll have to figure out how to get you there." And even when they figured all that out, Jules would still have some serious issues to work through.

"Of course," she continued, "that's easier said than done. How can you pick a place to live where you won't be trespassing on a Killer's territory?"

"I don't know."

"And what about food? You've got a nice stash in that cooler of yours, but it won't last forever. And keeping the cooler iced up was a pain in the ass when we were in a nice hotel with an ice maker. How will you—"

"I don't know," he said again, more abruptly. "One problem at a time, if you please."

She swallowed about a half-dozen more questions. She already knew the answer would be "I don't know." She liked Eli less and less the more she learned about him, but he was still seeming like the lesser of about a hundred evils right this minute. Jules seemed unlikely to agree.

"We have to get your car back," Jules said. "Or can you just rent another one?"

She might be able to, if she went to a different rental company. She honestly didn't know. But she also knew she *had* to get that rental back, unless she wanted to be arrested as a car thief. "We'll just have to go by the lot and hope we can persuade someone to give us a break."

"And how will we do that?"

"I'm sure you'll think of something."

He got the hint and nodded briefly. They were almost back to the hotel. "Do you suppose we can get a cab to come pick us up at this miserable place?" she asked. It had taken a touch of Jules's glamour to persuade last night's cabbie to venture into this part of town, but it wasn't like he could use his glamour over the phone.

"I suppose there's only one way to find out."

Hannah breathed a sigh of relief when the two punks who were following them veered off. One hurdle down, nine hundred ninety-nine left to go.

&

CAMILLE LET THE GIRL'S body drop heavily to the floor. Drake tried not to wince. This death would gnaw at him more than all his own kills combined. That there had been nothing he could do to prevent it didn't ease the sting.

Her fawning mortal henchmen removed the body from the room while Camille licked the last drops of the girl's blood from her lips. She flashed Drake an evil, self-satisfied smile, then crossed the room and picked up a small evening bag that lay on a side table. He felt a renewed urge to kill her when she plucked a lipstick and a compact from that purse and proceeded to fix her makeup.

"I'll give you another three days," she said, still gazing raptly at her own reflection. Her lips glistened red, her lipstick the color of fresh blood. Drake doubted that was a coincidence. "Anyone who's still here on the fourth day is fair game." She flashed another of her unpleasant smiles. "Of course, under the circumstances, I cannot guarantee that Gabriel will give you the same three days. I'll do what I can to reel him in, but . . ." She shrugged as if it hardly mattered.

Though he knew that a wise man would keep his mouth shut, Drake couldn't resist his sudden desire to hurt her right back. "You'll never reel Gabriel in, not all the way. He's tasted rebellion, and he likes it."

An expression he might almost have labeled as worry flickered over Camille's face, then was gone. "My son is not a fool. He will come to his senses. The quicker you and your friends get out of Baltimore, the sooner things will return to normal." She sounded like she was trying to convince herself.

Drake wasn't proud of the malicious pleasure he felt at seeing her uncertainty. "Does he know that you'll kill him if he doesn't toe the line? Or does he think that as your son he's immune?"

She dropped her lipstick and compact back into her evening bag, then tossed the bag aside. Before he even had a chance to blink, she was behind him. Her hand tangled in his hair, pulling his head sharply to the side, leaving his neck exposed. He tried to twist out of her grip, but glamour held him completely immobilized. Her breath was warm and moist against the skin of his neck. He smelled the poor mortal girl's blood and hated the hint of hunger the scent evoked.

"I promised Eli not to kill you," Camille said. Her tongue flicked out to taste the skin of his throat, and he felt the prick of her fangs. "I didn't promise him I wouldn't hurt you."

A chill passed down Drake's spine as he stood statue-still. She certainly couldn't kill him by biting him, and there were far worse pains she could inflict. But some ancient instinct greatly disliked the sensation of her fangs against his throat.

She nipped lightly, fangs breaking the skin. He smelled his own blood in the air before he felt the trickle crawl down his neck. Camille's tongue was an obscene warmth against his skin as she licked away that lone droplet.

"Don't toy with me, Drake," she warned. "I can hurt you more than you've ever imagined being hurt. My son thinks he's the master of torture, but I'm far more skilled than he. I could have you begging for death in minutes, and not grant you that relief for days. Weeks, even. I'm sentimental enough to spare you for Eli's sake, but my sentimentality has its limits. Have I made myself clear?"

"Yes." Drake forced the word out, hating his own helplessness. Maybe Jules had been right all along. Maybe the Guardians *should* come down to Baltimore. Only it wasn't Ian they needed to kill. How could Eli allow this . . . creature . . . to live?

How could he retain even the slightest thread of attachment to her?

Camille released him from her glamour and stepped away. He didn't turn to look at her, didn't want to see the look in her eyes.

"Go find your friends," she said. "I have an opera to attend."

Drake couldn't have been more eager to get the hell out of her house. Even so, he reached out with his senses as he approached the door. Gabriel was still out there somewhere, and he was as great a threat as Camille. Perhaps more so, for Camille's control over her son *was* slipping, whether she wanted to believe it or not. Open rebellion seemed an almost foregone conclusion.

Drake halted in the doorway. He'd been searching for a hint of Gabriel's presence. Instead, he felt something even more disturbing. He turned to the butler who was waiting for him to leave.

"Is Camille expecting visitors?" he asked.

"Visitors, sir?"

"Yes, visitors. As in about a dozen vampires who are heading in this direction."

The butler blanched, giving Drake his answer. He tried to dart out the door, wanting no part of whatever was to come next, but Camille must have sensed the approaching vampires. She appeared in the hallway, her smug, malicious smile a thing of the distant past.

"Stay here!" she ordered, her glamour yanking Drake back in the door.

It was Drake's turn to smile, though he refrained from

gloating. Even a vampire as strong as Camille would have a hard time fighting off a dozen foes. Especially if one of those foes was Gabriel himself.

"Stand with me and I will give you a full week to find your friends," she said. She was scared. He could feel her fear in the air, though her face showed nothing and her voice was calm.

"If I stand with you, you'll give me as much time as I need." It didn't matter what she offered him—he'd decide to stand with or against her when he saw who was leading this attack. If he had hopes for his own survival and for that of Jules and Hannah, he had to pick the winning side.

"As much time as you need," Camille agreed. She turned to her butler. "You may wish to go to the back for the duration, Roger."

Almost as pale as a vampire, Roger nodded and beat a hasty retreat. Camille stepped up to the door and opened it wide, ignoring the chill air that swept into the house. Wishing he could be anywhere but here, Drake stood behind her, his nostrils flaring, his pulse racing, and his eyes straining into the night.

13

Strangely, all the cab companies seemed to be "busy" tonight. Hannah glared at the phone as she hung up. They tended not to notice how strained their schedule was until she told them the address. Then, suddenly, the nearest available cab was in freakin' Idaho.

After the third phone call, she lost any semblance of patience. "It's a lovely night for a walk," she grumbled. Jules snorted. They could both hear the patter of rain. And according to the map Jules had picked up, the impound lot was a hell of a long way away.

Jules stepped to the window and pushed the curtain aside. "I don't suppose you brought an umbrella."

Hannah laughed. "You mean you practically packed your whole house in those suitcases, but you forgot an umbrella?"

"Well, did you?"

"No." For half a second, she tried to resist yanking his chain. But she didn't try very hard. "What's the matter? Afraid a little rain will ruin your coat?"

He glanced at his coat with a look of horror on his face. "I'd never *dream* of wearing that out in the rain."

She thought he was joking, but it was hard to be sure. "Well, let's hit the road before the rain gets any worse."

Jules rummaged through his luggage until he found a heavy sweater in the perfect shade of green to complement his auburn hair. Hannah smothered a laugh. He really was serious—he wouldn't wear his cashmere coat out in the rain.

Her own down-stuffed parka had been through far worse than a little rain, and she put it on with no hesitation. Jules frowned at her.

"What?" she asked. "Does my coat violate the sensibilities of the fashion police?"

He chuckled. "Yes, but that's beside the point. I'm just wondering if it's waterproof."

In a light drizzle, she'd stay dry. In a steady rain, she'd be soaked through in five minutes. "Hey, I won't melt if I get wet. And I bet that sweater isn't waterproof either."

"True, but since vampires don't catch cold I'm not overly concerned."

Something warm glowed in her chest, even as she waved away his concern. "I hardly ever get sick." What was the matter with her, that his concern would make her feel good? Her usual reaction to male protective instincts was to give the chauvinist pig a piece of her mind.

Jules shrugged. He perched his hat on his head at a jaunty angle, then opened the door and motioned Hannah through.

As soon as they stepped out of the protection of the hotel and into the rain, Hannah regretted the decision to walk. The rain fell short of a torrential downpour, but only just. And the temperature was barely above freezing. Icy water trickled down the back of her neck, making her shiver, and though she kept her head down, her glasses needed windshield wipers. She took them off and stuck them in a coat pocket.

"Can you see without those?" Jules asked.

She squinted at him in the dim light of a street lamp. Her vision wasn't that bad, as long as no one expected her to read street signs from a hundred yards away. Water dripped from her lashes like tears, stinging her eyes. Great. Acid rain.

"I can see just fine." She made a show of groping for his arm, as if she couldn't see it.

He chuckled, then shocked the hell out of her by taking off his hat and sticking it on her head. It was too big for her— what a surprise! Jules had a big head—and came to rest just above her eyebrows. It was still warm from his body heat. The warmth caused a paradoxical shiver. Jules's auburn hair was transformed almost instantly into stringy, bedraggled locks that clung to his skin.

"There," he said, patting the hat down a little farther. "That ought to keep your glasses dry."

"Thanks." She fished her glasses back out of her pocket and did her best to wipe away the water droplets. Jules was staring straight ahead, the look on his face suggesting that he was embarrassed by his own gallantry. And once again, she felt that little glow of warmth in her center. She was beginning to think there was a good heart buried beneath that façade of vanity and arrogance.

Not to mention, he looked damn good when he wasn't quite so perfect.

Hannah rolled her eyes at herself and forced her attention

away from Mr. Beautiful. She had perfectly good things to think about other than what he would look like after she'd thoroughly mussed him up in bed. Like, for instance, she could think about how the cold rain had already soaked through her coat and clothes and was now trying to soak through her skin. Or how her shoes squished with every step. Or how the wind was picking up, dropping the wind chill to somewhere around absolute zero. She hunched her shoulders and lowered her head, wishing she could fast-forward about half an hour.

The blocks passed in a blur of misery, eighteen of them in all. Toward the end, pellets of ice joined the raindrops, like tiny stinging bullets. Hannah's teeth were chattering and she was about as miserable as she could ever remember being. She glanced over at Jules, who didn't look much better. His sweater had the look of good, close-knit wool, but it was no more waterproof than her coat. His lips were tinged with blue, and he was visibly shivering.

"Whose bright idea was this?" she grumped, drawing a reluctant smile from him.

"Yours. And if we can't persuade them to let you have your car, I'm going to have to kill you."

She crossed her arms over her chest and tucked her hands under her armpits. "I might thank you for it."

When the impound lot came into view, she gave a little cry of relief. She and Jules both hurried their footsteps. Maybe even if they couldn't get her car out, they could at least stand out of the rain for a little while.

Jules's long legs put him at a distinct advantage in the speed department, and he quickly outpaced her. When he came to an abrupt halt, she collided with him, grabbing his arm to keep herself from falling face-first onto the pavement.

"*Marde!*" he said.

"What does that mean?" Hannah asked, looking ahead to the impound lot and seeing nothing that should have triggered his ire.

"It means 'shit'."

"I thought that was 'merde'."

"It is. We just pronounce it differently in Quebec."

"And the last time you were in Quebec was . . . ?"

He put his hands on her shoulders and turned her body slightly, and she finally saw what had drawn him up short.

There was her car, parked across the street instead of in the impound lot. And there was Gabriel, clad in a heavy raincoat and an Orioles baseball cap, leaning against the hood and staring at them.

༼ఌ

DRAKE AND CAMILLE RETREATED deep into the foyer. The doorway would have made a good choke point, but it wouldn't do to wage battle in plain view of all the neighbors and passersby.

As they waited in the back of the foyer for the enemy to appear, Drake sensed a strange . . . stirring . . . in the air. Was that the sensation of power gathering for the attack, or just his imagination? He glanced over at Camille, who stood very still beside him.

She had slipped off her high heels and peeled away her gloves. Her fangs protruded, messing up her lipstick again. She was so still she might almost not have been breathing. Her eyes seemed unfocused, and again Drake had that sense of power filling the room.

Then, her eyes suddenly came back into focus, and she threw back her head and laughed.

Drake blinked, wondering if the woman had suddenly taken leave of her senses. The vampire horde was fast approaching, would be at the doorway in a minute or less.

"Care to share the joke?" he asked.

Genuine humor warred with malice on her face. "They are new fledglings. All of them. *Infants!* And they think they can harm the Master of Baltimore?"

"You can tell how old they are?" When Gabriel had guessed his age, Drake had assumed Camille had told him. Perhaps that wasn't the case after all.

She smirked at him, but before she had a chance to answer—if, indeed, she planned to—the first fledglings charged up the stairs and into the foyer.

Drake had no chance to size up his options and choose sides. The fledglings poured through the door, practically pushing each other out of the way in their eagerness to get in. Most of them rushed directly at Camille, but a handful came after Drake, fangs bared, snarling.

A quick impression told Drake these fledglings had been chosen for a definite purpose. All were young, male, and built like football players, muscle layered upon muscle. They would have been strong as mortals, and now were even stronger as vampires.

One of them swung a meaty fist at Drake's head. A very human form of attack, for even if he connected he was unlikely to do more than annoy Drake.

Drake ducked easily and came up snarling, showing his fangs, giving the idiot one chance and one chance only to make the right decision and retreat. The fledgling lowered his shoulder and rammed into Drake's chest, knocking him to the floor and landing on top of him. He must have weighed over two hundred pounds, but Drake had little trouble tossing him off.

Another fledgling came at him while he was still on the ground. He bit at Drake's neck, but missed his target, fangs sinking into the flesh of Drake's shoulder.

For the second time tonight, Drake smelled his own blood in the air, and it pissed him off. Someone screamed shrilly, and the scent of blood grew stronger. Ignoring his own pain, Drake grabbed the head of the fledgling whose teeth were still embedded in his shoulder, and pushed him away, his flesh tearing as the fledgling refused to release his grip.

When the fledgling's fangs finally tore free, Drake gave his head a hard, sharp jerk, snapping his neck with a loud crack. Drake pushed him off and leapt to his feet, braced for the next attack.

What he saw was a bloody rout.

The fledglings were in full retreat, practically stampeding out the door, eyes wide with terror. Camille howled and grabbed the one closest to her, pulling him toward her even as he screamed for his friends to help. She lifted him easily into the air, then threw him against the wall. The plaster cracked at the impact.

At her feet lay three of the attackers. Their blood soaked the carpet. Two of them had their throats torn out. There was no sign of any healing, so she must have snapped their necks in the process. The third fledgling's head lay about two feet from its body, dead eyes wide with horror, mouth open in a silent scream.

Camille stalked the remaining fledgling, who was fighting to his feet, using the wall for support. Her face and hair were slick with blood, as were both her hands. As the fledgling cowered, she licked blood from her lips and smiled. It was a terrifying sight.

"Who made you?" she asked as she glided closer. "Tell me, and I'll kill you quickly. Don't tell me, and I'll make the agony last for many, many days."

The fledgling swallowed convulsively, his eyes bulging with terror. Drake felt briefly sorry for the man, then dismissed his own pity. This was a fledgling Killer, not a man. He'd prefer Camille not torment her victim, but he would be just as dead either way.

The fledgling, trembling violently, pressed his back to the wall. Camille bracketed his head with both her hands.

"Speak now," she said, tonguing her fangs. "Who made you?"

"G-Gabriel," he stuttered.

Camille's shriek was so loud and piercing Drake had to cover his ears.

When she finally stopped screaming, the fledgling lay in pieces on the floor. Blood soaked her from head to toe. The walls and floor were spattered with it. Her chest heaved with heavy breaths. Drake's stomach roiled. He'd seen gruesome kills before, but never anything like this. The room stank of blood and other bodily fluids.

When Camille's mortal henchmen tentatively entered the

foyer, two of them immediately vomited, adding another layer of foulness to the smell.

Camille's eyes glittered with madness. A single tear marked a path through the blood on her cheek.

"Clean up this mess," she ordered her henchmen, her voice hoarse and choked. She turned her gaze to Drake. "You'll help them. And you won't set foot outside this house until I give you leave."

Her back straight, her head held high, Camille swept from the room.

❧

"WELL," HANNAH SAID, PEERING up at Jules from under the brim of his hat, "I guess we have two choices."

The corner of his mouth twitched in a hint of a grin. The expression was ruined by the wariness in his eyes. "Those are?"

"Go have a nice chat with our friend Gabe, or run like hell." Gabriel was still leaning against her car, arms crossed over his chest, legs crossed at the ankles. The pose would have looked a lot more natural and relaxed if little pellets of sleet weren't bouncing off the brim of his cap. Of course, no matter how relaxed he looked, he could no doubt catch them if they decided to run for it. Where could they go where his vamp-dar wouldn't home in on Jules?

Jules brushed a lock of wet hair off his face and gave her a penetrating look. "If I tell you to wait here, will you do it?"

"Babe, I wouldn't wait here even if you *asked* and said pretty please." She doubted she could do much to help Jules if Gabriel had plans to kill him, but she wasn't about to be left behind. She could tell from Jules's tone of voice, and by his lack of surprise at her answer, that he was coming to know her.

He made a little sound that was either exasperation or resignation, then shook his head. "All right, then. Let's go. But please let me do the talking. You really don't want to stick your pins in this guy."

Hannah shrugged in a way she hoped Jules would take as agreement. He gave her a suspicious look, then took her arm and guided her across the street toward Gabriel.

Camille's son should have looked distinctly less intimidating in his raincoat and ball cap. But apparently, whatever it was that leant him his aura had nothing to do with the tough-guy clothes or hairdo, because Hannah felt a distinct chill in her spine—a chill that had nothing to do with the miserable weather—as they approached. She really hoped she and Jules weren't about to die.

"Should I thank you for getting my car out of impound," she asked, drawing a faint groan from Jules, "or are you about to do something that makes thanking you really low on my priority list?"

Gabriel blinked, then cracked an almost human-looking grin. "You have quite a mouth on you."

She could feel Jules's disapproving glare, but she did her best to ignore it. So far, she figured she had a pretty good read on how to act around Gabriel, and cowering in fear wasn't it. She returned Gabriel's grin, though it was hard to look too perky when her teeth were chattering. "Yeah, so I've been told."

"It doesn't seem to have quite sunk in."

"Why don't you just answer my question?"

"I'd like a word with your boyfriend."

"He's not—" Hannah started, at the same time Jules said "I'm not—" They glanced at each other, then away. Despite the cold, Hannah's cheeks warmed. They had both protested way too vehemently.

Gabriel laughed. "How precious," he mocked.

"Let's just get on with it," Jules said. "What do you want?"

The laughter died on Gabriel's lips, replaced with that familiar, ugly sneer. "I want many things, Guardian." He spat the word like an insult. "You'd better pray I don't get them all."

Obviously, Hannah's technique was better than Jules's. Which of course didn't stop Jules from being his normal, prickly self. His eyes hardened, and he opened his mouth to say something stupid.

"Hey, Gabe," she interrupted before Jules got a word out, "why don't you just talk to me. You and Jules seem to rub each other the wrong way, so I think it's better for everyone if you don't talk to each other."

"Oh for God's sake, Hannah!" Jules snapped. He clearly had more to say, but the life suddenly drained out of his eyes and he stood there with his mouth gaping open.

Hannah shivered again, thinking she'd probably never get warm if she lived to be a thousand. Gabriel's glamour was scary-strong.

"There," he said, sounding terribly pleased with himself. "Now I don't have to tear his liver out through his ass in front of you."

Hannah crossed her arms over her chest, a defensive gesture she just couldn't help. "I'd kind of prefer you not do that behind my back either," she said. She hoped she didn't sound as scared as she felt. "He's not my boyfriend, but he's a pretty decent guy, and I like him alive."

Gabriel seemed to think that one over before he answered. "I try not to make promises I can't keep."

She swallowed hard. "Jules has never done anything to you. Why can't you just leave him alone?" If Gabriel was going to kill them, why didn't he just get on with it? Not that she was complaining, mind you.

He straightened, coming to stand nose to nose with Jules. Hannah noticed that Jules's eyes tracked his motion. So, he couldn't move, but there still seemed to be somebody home. Was that a good thing, or a bad thing?

"He's a *Guardian*," Gabriel said, once again imbuing the word with disgust. His lip even curled. "Eli's pet. Eli's slave." He spoke those words into Jules's face, almost like he'd forgotten Hannah was here.

With a little jolt, Hannah heard the words Gabriel *didn't* say. "Someone your dad likes better than you."

Gabriel whirled on her, a hint of madness in his eyes. She couldn't help taking two stumbling steps backward. Her foot landed on the curb, which was now coated with ice. With a startled squeak, she started to fall. Headlights seared her eyeballs and a car's horn deafened her.

If Gabriel hadn't crossed the small distance between them at blinding speed and grabbed hold of the collar of her coat, she'd have been road kill. He yanked her back onto the pavement, and the cab that had almost hit her roared by, the driver still leaning heavily on his horn.

Hannah's knees threatened to give out and her breaths

came in short, frantic gasps. For a few seconds, all she could think about was the close call she'd just had. Then it occurred to her that Gabriel had just saved her life.

"Well, damn," she said, her voice shaking. "I guess now I have to thank you after all."

Once again, Gabriel looked taken aback, then laughed. "I'm sorry to have inconvenienced you." The deadly rage, the near madness she'd just seen on his face was wiped away. "You're much more entertaining alive than you would be as a hood ornament."

Hannah'd never seen anyone whose moods changed as quickly as Gabriel's. And his mood swung again before she even had a chance to continue that thought, his jaunty grin replaced with a marrow-freezing glare.

"But don't ever taunt me about Eli again. I *will* kill you. And your boyfriend."

"He's not my boyfriend. And I didn't mean to taunt you. You may have noticed that whatever goes through my head comes out my mouth."

The rain finished its transition into sleet, which made little clinking sounds as it bounced off the parked cars. Hannah's feet had gone numb from cold, as had her nose and ears.

"Look, I'm freezing my ass off out here," she said. "Why don't you just tell me what you want."

Gabe's smile turned sly as his gaze shifted to Jules. "I want to know more about my dear old dad. What he's up to these days. How many Guardians he has working for him. Who they are. How old they are. Who matters to them. That kind of thing."

Oh, that didn't sound good at all. Was Gabriel thinking of taking a field trip to Philadelphia?

Jules moved slightly, and Hannah realized Gabriel had released him from the glamour. At the same moment, Jules's cell phone started ringing. He ignored it, facing off against Gabriel.

"Why should I tell you anything?" Jules asked.

Gabriel snorted. "Perhaps because you'd like to live? Besides, I was under the impression you'd split with Eli. Why should you want to protect him?"

"Eli can rot in hell for all I care. But I don't think you'd be a big improvement."

Hannah's cell phone chirped. She figured now wasn't a good time to answer.

"Perhaps I'm not making myself clear," Gabriel said. "You're going to tell me what I want to know. I'm content to let you and Hannah walk away without a scratch if you answer my questions. But frankly, I'm extremely pissed off right now and I wouldn't mind working off my frustrations."

Hannah slipped her hand into her pocket, wrapping her fingers around the comforting weight of her gun. She suspected it would be of little use against someone as powerful as Gabriel—he didn't seem to require any eye contact for his glamour—but she'd have to try. Jules's cell phone rang again.

"Shut that damn thing off," Gabriel snapped.

Jules made no move to obey. "I have no personal loyalty to Eli anymore," he said, speaking slowly, choosing his words carefully. "But I am loyal to the Guardians and our cause. I can't answer your questions."

It was Hannah's phone's turn to ring. It sure seemed like someone was very, very anxious to get in touch with them right this moment. Keeping her right hand clasped around the butt of her gun, she pulled out her cell phone with her left hand and answered.

"This isn't a good time," she said in lieu of a greeting. Both Jules and Gabriel turned to look at her like she was nuts for answering the phone at a time like this. But hey, she could stall with the best of them.

"Too bad," Drake said over the tenuous phone connection. "Gabriel's apparently more twisted than we knew. He had a band of a dozen fledglings attack Camille's house tonight. You and Jules have to get out of town. If he's still obsessing over Guardians—"

"Drake, he's right here in front of us. I believe he was in the middle of threatening to torture Jules." She lowered the phone away from her mouth. "Was that about right, Gabe?"

"Oh, shit," Drake said.

"Maybe I ought to start my persuasion by cutting your tongue out," Gabriel said, but as usual when he threatened her, there was a flicker of humor in his eyes that suggested he didn't mean it.

"So Drake says you sent a band of fledglings to attack your mother this evening." Instinct told her that was bullshit. Gabriel had plenty of anger to spread around, but he was way more focused on his daddy. He wouldn't have wasted the energy attacking Camille, even if they had been fighting.

The expression on Gabriel's face—a combination of horror, shock, and outrage—suggested her guess was correct. "The hell I did!" He did another one of those lightning-speed moves of his and snatched the phone out of her hand. "What the fuck are you talking about?" he shouted into the phone.

Gabriel fell eerily silent, listening. He ducked his head as he did, hiding his face behind the shadow of his ball cap. Hannah wondered if she and Jules should make a run for it right about now, but she figured Gabriel could easily catch them.

"Tell my mother it wasn't me," he said finally. Gone was the growling menace. He sounded shaken and . . . hurt? His Adam's apple bobbed as he swallowed hard. "I'll find the bastard who's responsible. And he'll pay for what he did. Dearly."

He flipped the phone closed and tossed it at Hannah. Her hands were so numb she barely managed to save it from landing in an icy puddle.

She didn't have a hell of a lot of information, but little bits and pieces started lining up in her mind. Ian Squires had lured Jules to Baltimore. Supposedly because he wanted revenge for Jules getting him kicked out of Philadelphia. It had always sounded like a flimsy motivation. And on paper, it looked like the house Camille lived in was Ian's. Gabriel and his mother had fought—a friction that apparently was unusual for them. Then suddenly, Camille was attacked by a band of unknown fledglings who claimed to be working for Gabriel. What better way to make sure mother and son stayed apart, unable to defend one another?

"Squires wants to take over the city," Hannah said, sure she was right. Both Jules and Gabriel turned to her. "That's why he lured you down here, Jules. He thought you'd sic the Guardians on him, and Camille is living in his house."

Gabriel's eyes glittered in the darkness. "That traitorous, conniving dog! I told Mother we should have killed him the moment he came slinking back to Baltimore." His voice was deadly quiet. "Ian thinks he's suffered at my hands. He has no idea what suffering is. But I'll show him." He turned to Jules. "This isn't over between us, Guardian."

Then, he disappeared.

14

THE RIDE BACK TO the Harborside Inn was a tense and quiet one, the silence broken only by the plinking sound of sleet on the windshield and the chatter of Hannah's teeth. She had the heat on full blast, but it did nothing to warm her.

Beside her, Jules brooded. Storms brewed in his eyes. The muscles of his jaw stood out in sharp relief as he ground his teeth.

"Penny for your thoughts?" she tried as they waited at a red light. Jules ignored her.

What was going on in that handsome head of his? She doubted it was anything good. If only she knew how to reach him . . .

She sighed and focused her attention on driving. The roads were slick as hell, and she didn't want to end up wrapped around a lamppost.

Back at the hotel, she found a parking space—legal, this time—and she and Jules skated down the sidewalk toward the doorway. The icy weather had chased all the predators inside, leaving the streets almost deserted. The fresh dousing left Hannah shivering even more violently. She'd never been this cold in all her life.

By the time they entered their room, Jules still hadn't spoken a word, but Hannah was too damn cold to care.

"I'm getting out of these wet clothes," she said, yanking open a drawer and pulling out dry clothes at random. Jules nodded mutely.

Never had it felt so good to get out of her clothes! Hannah draped each dripping item over the shower rail, then rubbed herself all over with one of the sandpaper-rough off-white towels the hotel provided. But even when she tucked herself into her warm, soft sweater and fleecy sweatpants, the shivering didn't stop. She was chilled to the goddamn bone.

Clenching her teeth to stop the chattering, she exited the bathroom to find a shocking sight: Jules had already changed, leaving his wet clothes piled in a heap on the floor. Man, he must really be in bad shape! He was standing in front of the window, back turned to her, staring out at nothing. Feeling like a bit of a dork, but unable to help herself, she picked up his wet clothes and carried them to the bathroom, making room on the shower rail for them. She was caught somewhere between arousal and amusement when she found the Speedo-sized black briefs. The image of him in those briefs brought a flush of warmth. Oh brother. She was incorrigible.

He was still standing in front of the window when she returned. She couldn't resist walking up behind him and laying a hand on his shoulder.

"You all right?" she asked, not entirely sure what was bugging him.

He nodded briskly but didn't answer. He was giving off an unmistakable leave-me-alone vibe. If he were any other man, she would have let him stew, but every once in a while, she thought she was actually reaching him, and that meant she had to keep trying.

"Come on, Jules. Talk to me. What's eating you?"

He licked his lips. A nervous gesture she found disturbingly erotic. "I'm thinking Ian is fair game now."

She groaned. That was the *last* thing she was expecting him to say. "Don't be an idiot. Again."

He didn't look at her. "I came here to kill Ian. Now he's not under Camille and Gabriel's protection anymore."

She put her hand on his back, feeling the solid, tense muscles under his crisp cotton shirt. He closed his eyes at her touch. Pleasure, she guessed, though he didn't relax any. She pressed harder against one of the knots in his shoulder. He hissed softly, but she didn't think it was an unhappy sound. She put both hands into action, trying without spectacular success to knead the tension out of his muscles. Her body warmed in that telltale way again, but right this moment, she didn't care. She met Jules's gaze, reflected back at her from the window.

"Why don't you come sit down," she suggested, her voice low. "I'll be able to get more leverage if I don't have to reach up so high."

His shoulders rose and fell with a sigh, then he gently pulled away and turned around. "You don't have to take care of me, Hannah." Despite his words, his expression was soft and warm.

Without realizing she was going to do it, without *meaning* to do it, she reached out with both hands and laid them tentatively against his chest. The wall of solid male muscle that met her touch dispelled the last of her chill. When she explored the breadth of his chest, her fingers brushed over hardened nipples.

"Hannah—"

"Shh," she said, reaching up to lay a finger over his lips. His eyes were huge and dark, their warm cinnamon color hidden by the black of his pupils. His lips parted under her finger, and she caught a glimpse of his fangs. Her heart stuttered.

Jules opened his mouth and enveloped her finger, his tongue stroking the tip. Warmth turned to heat. He sucked her finger deeper into his mouth, his head moving back and forth so she felt the delicate prick of his fangs. A chill of fear, followed by another rush of heat.

He released her finger. She was unable to tear her eyes away from his, but it wasn't glamour that kept their eyes locked. He pressed his body close to hers. A gasp of desire escaped her when she felt the flaming hot length of his erection against her. His lips came down on hers. For the span of several heartbeats, she felt him trying to keep the kiss light, holding back. She wriggled her body against the length of his, and his tenuous self-control snapped.

The gentle kiss turned into a savage one, his lips pressed bruisingly hard against hers. His tongue thrust into her mouth. He buried one hand in her hair and tugged her head back so he could get a better angle. She groaned as desires warred within her, the desire to escape his rough handling beaten down by the desire to stay right where she was. Her arms wrapped around him and she sucked hard on his tongue.

When his tongue started thrusting rhythmically in and out of her mouth, she thought for a moment she was going to come from nothing more than a kiss.

Jules tore his mouth from hers, releasing his grip on her hair and shoving her away from him hard enough to make her stumble. Her breath came in frantic gasps and her mouth dropped open in shock as she wondered how he could possibly stop.

The answer was simple: he couldn't.

His hands shook as he started unbuttoning his shirt, his eyes still locked with hers. Halfway through the task, he muttered a curse and tore the rest of the buttons free. She dropped her eyes to drink in the sight of his sculpted chest, lightly dusted with auburn hair. She wanted to touch him, wanted to taste him, but her feet were rooted to the floor and she could only stand and watch as he whipped his belt open.

What was the matter with her? If she was about to go to bed with him, she should at least be taking her clothes off. Doing *something*, not just standing here gaping like an idiot. And yet gape was what she did when he shoved his trousers and briefs down and stepped out of them.

He was so hard the tip of his penis strained upward toward his belly. He was so large, she knew there would be some pain as she stretched to accommodate him.

He took a step toward her and she tore her eyes away from his erection. What she saw on his face scared the shit out of her.

He wasn't just walking toward her. He was *stalking* her, a predator chasing down his prey. His fangs were bared, his eyes black with desire. Hannah heard her own breath sawing in and out of her lungs, felt how her body trembled in reaction to the threat. But for all that, moisture pooled between her legs, and deep inside she knew she was perfectly safe. Even so, she took a step backward, a futile attempt at retreat.

Jules smiled broadly, a feral smile that chilled and warmed in equal measure. Then, he was on her.

He moved so fast she didn't even have a chance to get her hands up in a defensive gesture. His body crashed into hers and he propelled them both onto the bed. She landed with a startled squeak, Jules on top of her, though he caught most of his weight on his elbows to keep from crushing her.

Another bruising kiss as with one hand he wrestled with the knot on her sweatpants. Her heart thudded against her breastbone, and Hannah realized with a jolt of near-terror that once again he was holding her completely helpless.

The knot slipped open, and Jules yanked her sweatpants and panties down. With a little cry of distress, she tried to hold him off. Pointless. He grabbed her wrists and pinned them. She whimpered as he kissed her again, sure he was about to plunge into her, no longer so sure she wanted him to.

No matter her doubts, when his tongue demanded entrance, she opened her mouth. She couldn't help it. It just felt too damn good, whether she appreciated his technique or not.

The kiss seemed to last for hours, his tongue exploring every millimeter of her mouth in great detail. His erection rubbed and pressed on her wet, achy core, but he didn't push in, merely tormented her with his exquisite strokes. Her hips strained upward toward him, yearning for the completion he denied her. He positioned himself at her entrance, then tore his mouth away from hers. She cried out in protest.

"I want to watch your face when I take you," he growled, his words made indistinct by his fangs.

A tremor passed through her entire body. This was so wrong. He was holding her down, had her wrists pinned to the mattress. He was being rough and brutish, threatening her with his fangs. She should be telling him to get the hell off of her. Adrenaline surged through her veins, the fear mixing with her desire in an intoxicating, confusing cocktail.

Then, he filled her with one hard thrust.

A cry ripped from her throat, and her back arched. There was a tingle of pain as he stretched her, but her desire softened it and she lifted her legs to wrap them around his hips.

His eyes devoured her face as he pounded into her. No slow buildup, not now, not with him. He growled deep in his throat, a strangely inhuman sound, raising the hairs on the back of her neck even as she moaned in pleasure. When his tongue started playing with one of his fangs, her paradoxical fear peaked.

"You're not going to bite me, right?" she gasped.

A frown briefly puckered his brow. "Of course not."

That small reassurance was all she needed. She gave in to the pleasure, let the sensations overwhelm her until even his hold on her wrists felt good. Walls cracked, a seismic shift inside her. She surrendered. Jules filled her mouth with his tongue just in time to swallow her scream of release.

The aftershocks of her orgasm were still shaking her when Jules came, his face a mask of pleasure that looked almost like pain. His hips continued to thrust slowly, languidly afterward as he lowered his forehead to touch hers. His breath was hot against her face, and she closed her eyes, inhaling the scent of him and the musk of their lovemaking.

It wasn't until he let go of her wrists that she came back to herself. The thought of what he'd just done to her, what she'd *let* him do to her, brought a shiver. His body still weighed hers down, kept her trapped. Fighting a wave of panic, she put her hands on his chest and pushed.

"Give me some air," she gasped, hoping he thought her breathlessness was just from the sex.

Jules obliged, rolling off of her with a satisfied sigh. She quickly turned her back to him, clenching her teeth hard as another wave of panic crashed over her.

She *hated* men who were dominant in bed. She hated feeling helpless, trapped, out of control. She rubbed one aching wrist. He'd been rough with her, and she hadn't uttered a word of protest. But, damn it, she wasn't some meek little woman who let a man do whatever he wanted to in bed for his own pleasure! Sex was supposed to be an equal partnership, *shared* pleasure.

Yeah, Hannah, you just hated every minute of that.

To her shame, tears stung her eyes. She clenched her teeth harder, willing the tears not to spill. What did it mean about her that she'd let Jules dominate her? That she'd *liked* it?

The mattress shifted as Jules rolled over behind her, his spectacular body spooning hers. His arm snaked around her waist, pulling her closer.

And suddenly, Hannah couldn't bear to be held for another minute. She struggled out from under his arm, trying for an orderly retreat when her body demanded headlong flight.

Jules grumbled a protest but let go. She practically leapt out of bed and had to force herself not to sprint for the bathroom.

"Hannah?" Jules asked, his voice full of concern.

But she couldn't think of a single thing to say to him, couldn't even turn to face him or he'd see the tears that trickled down her cheeks despite her best efforts. She rushed through the bathroom door and slammed it behind her, locking it and plastering her back against it. She slid down until her butt hit the cold tile, then wrapped her arms around her knees and really cried for the first time in years.

⋐ॐ

APPARENTLY A HUNDRED YEARS, give or take, wasn't enough time for a man to understand women, Jules mused as he swung his legs out of bed.

Hannah had given him every indication that she'd enjoyed what he was doing, even though he was rather shocked at his own behavior. He'd never been like that with a woman before, always priding himself on his ability to inflict slow, sensual torment on his partners. Tonight, he'd been out of control, wild with lust, the beast within him taking charge.

That's what I get for being celibate for so damn long, he thought. No question about it, he and celibacy were not meant for each other.

He approached the bathroom door tentatively. Maybe Hannah knew what was best for herself and needed a little time alone. Certainly he could understand her feeling a bit overwhelmed by what had just happened. Or maybe she needed a little tenderness, some proof that he truly was a man and not a beast. He honestly didn't know.

A sharp pain stabbed through his chest when he heard the

sound of muffled tears. Hannah was *crying?* Guilt swamped him and he laid both hands against the door, a knot tightening in his throat.

"Hannah?" he said, his voice showing the strain. "Hannah, are you all right?"

"I'm fine!" she called, but there was no missing the lie.

"I'm sorry. I didn't mean to be such a brute. Did I hurt you?" If he had, she sure as hell hadn't given him any indication of it.

"I'm fine, Jules," she repeated, her voice a little steadier.

"Why don't you come out so we can talk?"

"I don't need a nursemaid. Just leave me alone for a bit."

He swallowed hard, her rebuff hurting more than it had any right to. She'd never been too thrilled about the obvious chemistry between them. Obviously, she was shaken because the chemistry had overruled her conviction that sleeping with him would be a bad idea.

Understanding didn't make the pain go away. He wanted her in his arms, wanted to revel in the pleasure they'd shared and not think about the consequences. But right now, it wasn't just the closed door that separated them.

"You don't need to hide out in the bathroom," he said, sounding far calmer than he felt. "I'll go take a walk so you can have the room to yourself."

He expected her to protest, remind him that it was sleeting out and that they were in a dangerous neighborhood. She said nothing.

Stung once again, Jules pulled on his clothes and left the room, slamming the door behind him.

❧

[217]

FOR THE HUNDREDTH TIME, Drake wished he'd gotten out of Baltimore when he'd had the chance. He paced the length of the "guest room" where Camille had ensconced him for the night while she prepared a plan to hunt down and kill her own son. The door and the windows were reinforced with iron, keeping him thoroughly trapped despite his strength.

He wasn't sure why she was keeping him here anymore, but he supposed it was some way of striking back at Eli. As Gabriel had requested, Drake had delivered his plea of "not guilty," but Camille had instantly dismissed it. No doubt she was blaming Eli and the Guardians for her son's desertion. Which was wishful thinking, for if Gabriel really was the culprit, he had obviously created his fledgling army long before Drake and Jules had set foot in Baltimore. Something Camille no doubt didn't wish to accept.

Drake's phone rang. When he checked the caller ID and saw that it was Eli, he debated whether to answer or not. He still needed more time to absorb the distasteful truth about the man he had once admired so greatly. But he wasn't ready to give up all that the Guardians and Eli had given him in a fit of anger, so he answered.

"Things have gone to hell down here, Eli," he said, skipping the polite greeting.

"Tell me."

Drake recounted the harrowing events of the evening, concluding with the cheerful news that he was now Camille's prisoner.

"One thing's for certain," Eli said when Drake was finished, "whoever made those fledglings, it wasn't Gabriel."

"Oh? How do you know that?"

"I know Gabriel. He's very loyal. Camille would have to provoke him beyond endurance to make him turn on her."

Drake thought about that a moment. "You mean, like you did?"

He could almost hear Eli's wince. "I can't blame him for hating me."

"What exactly happened between you two?" Drake didn't expect the usually closed-mouthed Eli to answer, nor was he sure he wanted him to.

"I tried to kill him. When I decided to found the Guardians, I knew I had to start by destroying my own fledglings. Gabriel wasn't my fledgling exactly, but he was just as much a Killer as the rest of them. I captured him with my glamour and I meant to behead him with my old sword."

Drake shuddered, wishing he hadn't asked.

"In the end," Eli continued, "I found I couldn't do it. I forced myself to swing, but I pulled up at the last moment."

"The scar on his face . . ."

"Yes."

Drake frowned. "But he was a vampire when he was wounded!" And vampires don't scar.

"I can come up with any number of explanations for that scar. Perhaps it was because of the iron sword. Perhaps it's because he's never been human that he's vulnerable to scarring. Or maybe it had something to do with my own power."

All of this gave Drake a little more insight into Gabriel's state of mind, but didn't really convince him that he wouldn't turn on his mother. No one who carried that much rage around on his shoulders could truly be predictable.

"Perhaps given a little time to calm down, Camille will

realize he couldn't have been the one to order the attack," Eli concluded.

"You would mourn him if he died."

"Yes, Drake. I would. Though no doubt he deserves to die." Eli's voice sounded a bit husky, and he cleared his throat.

Under other circumstances, Drake might have felt sorry for Eli, for the burden of pain and guilt he carried. And maybe he would take the time to do so, once he got out of here. *If* he got out of here.

"What are the chances you can get Camille to release me?" Drake's phone beeped to let him know its battery was running low.

"Not very good, I'm afraid. I can only assume she's detaining you to punish me. But I'll do what I can. Maybe once she realizes it wasn't Gabriel who attacked her, she'll calm down."

The phone beeped again, then went dead.

"Dammit!" Drake said. What condition was he going to be in if and when Camille decided Gabriel wasn't guilty? Right now, she was too busy planning her hunt to spare him much attention, but eventually she'd remember she had a whipping boy available to take her frustrations out on.

If by some miracle they both lived through this, Drake was going to make Jules very, very sorry he'd started this mess.

15

THE FIRST LIGHT OF dawn was trying to struggle through the heavy clouds when Jules finally returned to the hotel. He hadn't meant to be gone so long. He'd originally figured he'd give Hannah an hour of solitude. But when a quick psychic scan of the area told him there was another vampire nearby, he'd gone in pursuit.

Stupid, probably. One-on-one, he was no match for the Baltimore vampires. But at least this one had fled at Jules's approach. He greatly preferred to keep any and all vampires—save himself—as far from Hannah as possible.

The vampire had led him on quite a chase, continually trying to circle back toward the hotel. No question about it, he and Hannah were going to have to change residences again. If only he could get her to leave him alone, go back to Philly where she'd be safe! Never mind that the thought of her leaving made his chest ache. He hated putting her in danger, and he would never forgive himself if something happened to her.

Shortly before dawn, his quarry eluded him, and Jules

was left to return to the hotel, feeling like he was being watched the whole way.

He entered the room to find Hannah fast asleep on the bed, her knees curled to her chest in what looked like a defensive posture. He sat on the bed beside her, careful not to wake her, and softly stroked the cascade of curls that draped the pillow. Her cheeks showed no lingering trace of tears, and she had that freshly washed smell that said she'd showered very recently. Even so, Jules's sensitive nose picked up the lingering scent of sex that bathed the room.

His throat knotted up, and he wondered if he should wake her after all so he could ask her what had happened. He still wasn't entirely sure what had gone wrong, but he suspected it had something to do with how she'd opened herself up to him. She was not a woman who was comfortable with feminine vulnerability, and he suspected last night's events had left her feeling vulnerable. Certainly it had left *him* that way.

Jules yawned and glanced at the window, where the feeble light was strengthening. Better to let Hannah sleep. He wouldn't be able to stay awake much longer, and he didn't think this was a conversation they could finish in such a short time.

Not wanting to disturb Hannah, he lay on the floor between the bed and the wall and covered himself with his coat and a couple of sport jackets. It made for a stifling, uncomfortable bed, but the double layer increased the chances he could survive if he tossed and turned in his sleep.

If he'd been human, he'd have been *far* too uncomfortable to sleep. As it was, his mind started its drift into nothingness within seconds of his lying down.

HANNAH WOKE TO A subtle feeling of wrongness. She lay still, fighting the urge to yawn or stretch, and tried to figure out where that feeling came from. That was when she realized from the bright glow behind her closed eyes that there was way too much light in the room.

With a gasp, she sat up. "Jules!" she cried, flinging herself to the edge of the bed to see the impromptu second bed on the floor. She let out a huge sigh of relief when she saw the man-shaped lump, covered from head to toe with his cashmere coat and a couple of jackets.

Another burst of adrenaline shot through her system. *She* certainly hadn't opened the curtains to let that much light in, and Jules wouldn't have done it either. The hairs on the back of her neck prickling, she slowly turned to the windows.

Gabriel stood directly in a shaft of sunlight, arms folded over his chest as he regarded her with a distinctly amused expression. She swallowed hard. She hadn't liked seeing him last night. She liked seeing him now, during the day, much less.

"Are you wearing SPF sixty or what?" she asked, folding her legs to sit Indian style in the middle of the bed. She could make a dash for her gun, but the effort seemed futile. Besides, if he wanted to kill her—or Jules—he probably would have done so by now.

Gabriel smiled, an expression that didn't reach his icy eyes. She noted that while he had fixed his hair after its encounter with the baseball cap, he was wearing the same clothes as yesterday. She supposed he couldn't go home and change without running into Camille.

"Always ready with a quip, aren't you?" he asked.

She shrugged. "Guess so." She didn't want to know how

old he was to be able to tolerate direct sunlight like that. "What are you doing here?"

"If you remember, I had some questions for your boy-friend."

"He's not my boyfriend," she said, an automatic, knee-jerk response she wished she could swallow back. Could she sound more defensive?

Gabriel's nostrils flared, and he gave her a knowing look. Suddenly, she remembered that vamps had really good senses of smell. She hated the blush that crawled up her cheeks, but there was nothing she could do to stop it.

Trying to ignore her embarrassment, she glanced at her watch and frowned. "It's four o'clock in the afternoon. You have to know Jules won't be awake for at least another hour."

"Indeed I do." Another one of those weird smiles of his. Hannah didn't like it one bit. "I could have waited until sun-down to do what I'm going to do," he said. "I'm easily strong enough to keep both you and Jules under control. But if I did it in front of him, I'd feel obliged to be a hard-ass about it or it would spoil the effect."

Fear congealed in her belly and the remnants of the blush vanished with all the other blood in her face. She bit her tongue to keep from saying anything, sure her voice would shake if she spoke. What was the freak planning to do? She didn't want to know. Unfortunately, she was sure to find out.

"Don't be afraid," Gabriel said, his voice surprisingly gen-tle. "I won't hurt you." He took a step toward her, and she scooted backward until his glamour seized her and wouldn't let her move. Panic clawed at her and her breath came in short little gasps that didn't seem to bring enough oxygen into her lungs. She hated it when Jules used glamour against her, but at least when *he* did it, she spaced out for the duration. Being fully aware and yet unable to move sucked.

Suddenly, Gabriel released his hold on her. She breathed easier, even though her situation hadn't in truth improved.

"Don't run away from me," he said, "and I won't immobilize you." He sat on the edge of the bed, then reached out to grab her wrist. The grip was gentle, but unbreakable. "I won't hurt you," he repeated, then drew his lips back in a smile that revealed his fangs.

Hannah wasn't able to stop the frightened whimper that escaped her throat, but she did her best to fight the fear. "As a Killer who's showing fang, you lack a certain credibility." Despite the smart-mouth words, her voice shook.

"I only kill mortals I don't like. So far, you don't fall into that category. I'll let you know if and when that changes."

That wasn't particularly comforting at the moment. "What are you going to do?"

"I'm going to bite you."

She practically screamed. Her attempt to free her wrist from his grip was as fruitless as she'd suspected.

"Shh," he said. "There's nothing to be afraid of. It won't hurt. And I won't feed, since I'd have to kill you to do that."

She shivered. "Your bedside manner could use a little work."

"I'm just going to leave a mark, a little something to remind Jules what's at stake."

She figured he probably meant that, but in her experience so far, vampires weren't famous for their restraint. She reflexively put her hand to her throat, wanting to keep his mouth as far away from it as possible. She looked at those long, sharp fangs of his and shuddered. Who was he kidding, it wouldn't hurt?

"Glamour," he said, as if reading her mind. "You won't feel a thing." He pulled on her wrist, drawing her toward him. She couldn't help resisting. "If you don't struggle, I'll leave your mind alone except for the glamour to mask the pain."

He had enough of a read on her to know how much she hated the mind games, and she didn't like it. Battling her instincts to fight like hell, she moved to the edge of the bed and swung her legs around so she was sitting next to him.

"Get it over with." She gritted her teeth, wishing that would quell her trembling. Her stomach roiled, and she wondered if he would mind if she barfed on him when he bit her.

He brushed her hair out of the way, then tilted her head to the angle he liked. Sweat trickled down the small of her back and soaked her palms. In contrast, her mouth was Sahara-dry.

"Take a deep breath," Gabriel said. "Truly, there's nothing to fear."

She had some instructions she'd like to give *him* right now, but antagonizing a vamp who was about to bite her probably wasn't the brightest idea in the world. She ignored his advice.

He moved in quickly, and Hannah lost the fight against her nerves. She tried to pull away, but he held her head tight as his mouth came to rest on her neck. She felt the brush of his lips, hot and wet, then a stroke of his tongue. Before she even had a chance to shudder at the violation, he'd released her. Something warm trickled down the side of her neck. Without comment, Gabriel pulled the pillowcase off the pillow, then wadded it up and placed it against her neck.

"Hold this and put pressure on it."

Numbly, she obeyed. As he'd promised, she hadn't felt even the slightest twinge of pain. The fact that his glamour had been mucking with her mind without her feeling any awareness of it made her stomach churn a little more.

"Now," Gabriel said, sounding terribly satisfied with himself, "we wait until Jules wakes up, and he sees just how vulnerable the two of you are."

৵

JULES AWAKENED WITH A nasty crick in his neck from having slept on it wrong. He rolled onto his back and stretched, working the crick out before he pushed his suffocating coat off his face.

Hannah was sitting on the edge of the bed, watching him. She looked scared, which was all wrong for Hannah. Surely she had to know she was in no danger from him. He sat up slowly, trying to find the perfect words to set things straight after last night's fiasco.

Hannah looked away from him, over her shoulder. He followed her gaze and saw Gabriel, standing in the middle of the room and looking smug.

"*Marde!*" he cried, struggling out from under his makeshift blanket. His instincts spurred him to put himself between Gabriel and Hannah, to protect her, even though he was of little use against the older, stronger vampire.

"Relax, Jules," Hannah said. She didn't sound particularly relaxed herself. "He's been here for over an hour, and he hasn't killed either one of us yet."

"Over an hour?" Jules asked. He glanced at the windows, where the curtains were drawn back to reveal the failing light. It had taken him almost a century to be able to move about before sunset. How many centuries would it have taken Gabriel to withstand the full light of day?

"Daylight won't protect you," Gabriel said. "Nor will it protect your lady." He moved Hannah's hair away from her neck, revealing a pair of neat puncture wounds.

He'd bitten Hannah! He'd scared her, *hurt* her.

All rational thought fled Jules's brain. With a primal roar, he launched himself at Gabriel, fangs lowered. A red haze clouded his vision. Blood thundered in his ears, muting all other sounds. Pain blossomed in his stomach, but he ignored it. He couldn't see Gabriel through the haze, but he could *feel* him. He charged once more.

More pain, this time from the region of his kidneys. Although he was aware of it, it hardly seemed important. He snapped his jaws, hoping to taste blood as his fangs sank into flesh, but his teeth closed on empty air.

A crushing weight crashed into his back and he fell. His head collided with the floor and he tasted blood. Still the pain was as nothing and he tried to thrash. But something heavy was sitting on his back, knee digging hard into his already wounded kidney. The pain seemed a little more real, more urgent. An arm snaked under his chin. He tried to bite it, but failed. Then, that arm pressed hard on his windpipe and he couldn't breathe. The red faded from his vision as he struggled for breath. Then, his vision went entirely dark.

&

HE CAME TO LYING on his stomach on the floor. His lower back throbbed. His chin ached. And every gasped breath hurt on its way down his throat. He groaned and turned his head slightly, his eyes coming to rest on a pair of black motorcycle boots.

"Are you in there, Guardian?" Gabriel asked. "Or are you still berserk?"

Jules blinked away a haze of confusion and pushed himself up to his knees. Hannah, her face ashen-pale, came to squat beside him.

"Are you all right?" she asked.

"Yeah," he answered hoarsely, not at all sure he was. He'd always had a volatile temper, had lost control of it before. But *never* like that. It was . . . disconcerting.

Hannah helped him to his feet. The pain that had seemed distant not so long ago now assailed him full force. He winced and hissed, but he would only have to bear it for a little while as his body healed. Clinging to his arm, whether for his support or her own, Hannah fixed Gabriel with a fierce glare.

"You didn't have to hurt him! I know your glamour is strong enough to stop him."

Gabriel held up both hands, fingers splayed. "Glamour is a trick of the mind. There has to be a mind there for it to work."

If Jules didn't know better, he would swear that Gabriel was as shaken as he was. Then he remembered what had set him off in the first place, and for a moment he teetered on the brink once more.

"Well," Gabriel said, "I suppose I more than made my point. I did Hannah no harm, so calm down."

"You touch her again and I'll kill you," Jules snarled, the beast within him straining against the leash.

Gabriel looked unimpressed. "If you're finished pounding your chest, I have a proposal for you."

Jules's temper subsided, for now, and he regarded Gabriel warily. "What kind of proposal?"

"You tell me everything you know about Eli and about the Guardians."

"We already had this conversation," Jules retorted. "What makes you think I'm going to change my mind now?"

Gabriel's smile was slow and wicked. "Because in return, I'll give you Ian Squires."

❧

IAN'S PLANS HAD PRETTY much gone to shit. The attack against Camille had been a total disaster. He'd known she was powerful, of course, but he'd thought a dozen fledglings ought to at least have a chance against her. Perhaps they would have, if that interfering Guardian hadn't gotten in the way. But as he looked over his remaining "children," most of whom were still shell-shocked, he realized they'd probably never stood a chance. He should have waited until they were older and stronger before attacking. It was all Jules's fault. Again. If only he'd brought the Guardians with him as he was supposed to . . .

At least one thing had gone right—Camille had swallowed the story about Gabriel being responsible. Ian smiled secretly to himself. Gabriel was going to die at Camille's hands. How Ian wished he could be there to see it!

"What do we do now?" one of the fledglings asked, and they all looked at him with blank eyes.

"Don't pester me," he muttered, sweeping them all with a look that had each of them hanging his head. He'd picked his fledglings carefully. Camille had made a dreadful mistake in transforming a man of his intelligence and expecting him to bow to her will at all times. He refused to make the same mistake.

Yes, he'd learned much from his maker, and his fledglings were too stupid—and too scared of him—to challenge him in anything. Now, all he had to do was use his hard-earned education to bury her. Because he was not about to settle for being the Master of Nowheresville. No, only Baltimore would do.

The farmhouse had been the perfect hideout, up until now. Only thirty minutes outside of Baltimore, it afforded him easy access to the city while being far enough away that Camille and Gabriel knew nothing of it. He'd visited regularly, bringing food for his fledglings while he trained their powers.

The property had been abandoned for years, the house crumbling from neglect, on its way to being reclaimed by nature. None of the neighboring houses was close enough for anyone to hear the screams.

One of Ian's favorite games had been to release a mortal in the darkened house and let his fledglings hunt it down. In headlong flight, one of those mortals had actually fallen through the floor and into the basement. She'd broken her ankle in the process, making her easy prey. Now, his fledglings liked to herd mortals to that hole in the floor—covered by a rug—so they could enjoy the despair of their trapped victim. Even now, Ian could hear the muffled sobs of the hitchhiker they'd caught earlier.

As perfect as the house was for hiding a dozen fledgling vampires, it was not a place Ian himself would like to live. He preferred more creature comforts. And fewer creatures. He wrinkled his nose. The house stank of bat guano, and had no electricity or running water.

No, before he figured out what to do about Camille and Gabriel, he had to find a more comfortable base of operations. One that couldn't be traced to him, for if Gabriel managed to survive, he'd surely come hunting for Ian.

Surveying his remaining fledglings once more, Ian's eyes came to rest on Tommy Monroe. Tommy seemed to shrink in on himself, trying to hide in plain sight. Not an easy thing to do when you were an overweight linebacker. He'd only been a junior in high school when Ian had taken him, but he was most definitely big for his age. Ian smiled.

"If I remember rightly," he said, "your house is only two miles from here."

Tommy swallowed and nodded.

"It's just your mom and sister there now, right?"

Tommy's eyes widened. If he'd been mortal, his face would have paled. "Please don't . . ."

Ian waved off his concern. "Killing them would do me no good. The house would go on the market and someone else would move in. But if I convert them, I bet they'd be over-joyed to let me live there." It was perfect. The house would still be under the Monroes' names, but with them as his fledg-lings, he could take over the place. He could even send them to live in the farmhouse with their son while he lived in com-fort. Besides, Tommy's big sister was quite a tempting morsel, if memory served. And if Tommy objected to what Ian planned to do to her . . . There were plenty of other muscle-bound dim-wits available for the taking.

Tommy looked less than thrilled with the idea of Ian transforming his family. But though he was basically dumb as a post, he wasn't dumb enough to argue with his master.

"I think I'll take care of it tonight," Ian announced, happy to have at least one problem taken care of.

"Can I come with you?" Tommy asked. "Maybe they'd be less scared if . . ." His voice trailed off.

If the ignoramus thought Ian wanted his victims less scared, Ian wouldn't correct him. "I was thinking of letting you have one of the little tidbits in the basement, but if you'd rather come with me, you can." Ian hadn't had a chance to play with the girl yet, but he'd already thoroughly enjoyed the street punk he'd brought from the city last night. The punk had thought he was tough. Ian had taught him differently. There was probably enough blood left in him for Tommy.

The mere suggestion that he might feed brought Tommy's fangs down with lightning speed. He tongued them, still getting used to their feel. Then his eyes drifted to the gaping hole in the living room floor just across the hall. The hitchhiker had stopped crying, giving in to despair. No doubt Tommy would inspire her to more tears before he was through with her fellow prisoner.

"You can do whatever you want to the boy," Ian said. "But the girl is mine—no biting, no fucking. Not until I've had her."

Tommy's head bobbed up and down in a vigorous nod. Ian made a sweeping gesture with his hand, and Tommy forgot all about his dear family in his hurry to have his meal.

❧

GABRIEL'S OFFER SEEMED TO echo in the room, though that was surely Jules's imagination. With Gabriel's help, catching

Ian and killing him would actually be possible. Oh, it was a wicked, evil temptation Gabriel was offering!

"It might take us a while to catch him," Gabriel continued, "but he's too stupid to elude us for long."

Ian was many things, but stupid wasn't one of them. He'd graduated from Penn *summa cum laude*, although just because he was intellectually gifted didn't mean he had any street smarts. After all, what kind of moron would let someone like Camille turn him into a vampire? Ian must have thought that becoming a vampire would magically transform him into something other than a pathetic loser. Not even the transformation could work that kind of miracle.

Apparently, Jules was silent too long, for Hannah spoke up, looking at him with narrowed eyes. "Tell me you're not actually considering this."

Even if he *weren't* considering it, he wouldn't say so in front of Gabriel. Somehow, he didn't think good ol' Gabe would take too kindly to refusal.

Jules met Hannah's reproachful gaze. "I could probably track Ian down eventually without Gabriel's help, but what would I do then? He's already proven he can overpower me, and it's not like I can sneak up on him."

Gabriel's smile was sly in the extreme. "*I*, however, would have no trouble with him. And I'd be happy to hold him still while you killed him as slowly as you liked."

The glow in Gabriel's eyes was not a pleasant sight at all. It was all Jules could do not to shudder. "I'd settle for a quick, clean kill."

Gabriel raised an eyebrow. "After what he did to you?" His tone and the knowing look in his eye suggested he knew *exactly* what Ian had done. Humiliation flooded him, and he fought the urge to look away.

Gabriel laughed. "I persuaded him to tell me all about his little adventure in Philadelphia when he returned to the fold. I never did like the little weasel. Always looking for someone else to blame for his fuck-ups."

Yes, that was Ian all right, and Jules had paid dearly for not recognizing it.

"Would it please you to know I believe turnabout is fair play? Though I like to think I've refined his technique."

Jules's gorge rose. No, that didn't please him one bit. Because he heard the unspoken threat behind the words. If he had fed any time in the last couple of days, he might have had to make a quick dash to the bathroom. As it was he had to close his eyes and swallow hard to force the sudden nausea away.

Hannah put a hand on his arm, offering silent support. Of course, with Hannah, the support rarely stayed silent for long.

"What are you two talking about?" she asked. "What did Ian do?"

Jules opened his eyes, pleading with his gaze for Gabriel to keep his mouth shut. Gabriel inclined his head slightly in acquiescence.

"You'll have to ask Jules," he said. Then the moment of sympathy vanished as if it were never there. "So, what say you? Do we have a deal?"

"You give me Ian first, and let it be a clean kill, and you have a deal." He heard Hannah's outraged gasp, but ignored her.

Another raised eyebrow from Gabriel. "You would betray your friends so you can have your revenge?"

Of course not, but he hoped Gabriel believed he would. To that end, he couldn't sound too eager. He clenched his fists at his sides. "I don't want to. The Guardians are good people, for the most part, and they don't deserve to die for Eli's flaws. But since you can force the information out of me anyway, I might as well get something for it."

Gabriel's nod suggested he was buying it. "A very pragmatic approach. And, of course, it's Eli I want, not your Guardians. I won't kill them unless they make it necessary."

"Jules?" Hannah asked, and she sounded strangely uncertain. "Tell me you aren't really going to do this."

He turned his coldest stare on her. Maybe, just maybe, if she believed him a traitor, she'd get the hell out of Baltimore. Away from Gabriel, and Camille, and all the other dangers that lurked here. She'd hate him for it, but that couldn't be helped.

"I don't have a choice," he said.

"Bullshit! You can't just roll over like this!" She looked like she wanted to deck him.

Jules felt like the slimiest bastard ever to walk the planet. "You don't get to be a hundred years old without learning to accept some of the more distasteful realities of life. Like you've got to play the cards you've been dealt. If you want to help, run back to Philly and warn them what's coming." He turned to Gabriel. "You'll let her go, won't you? You strike me as the sort who wouldn't mind facing a challenge."

"She can warn them I'm coming," Gabriel agreed. "It won't do them a bit of good."

"We'll see."

Tears spilled down Hannah's cheeks unheeded. Her pain

was almost more than Jules could bear, but he maintained his stoic expression. Later, after she was gone, he would deal with his own pain that she would believe this of him so easily.

"Go home, Hannah," he urged. "Warn them. But leave now, while I still have business to discuss with Gabriel and he can't chase after you."

Hannah's eyes hardened and she swiped away the tears. "You lousy, despicable, asshole! I can't believe I dragged myself down here to look after you. I can't believe I saved your life. And I can't believe I—"

Her cheeks were already red with anger, but Jules had no doubt if they hadn't been, she would have blushed. Turning her back on him, she snatched her duffle bag off the floor, not even bothering to pack any of her personal belongings.

She came to stand within about a foot of him, looking him up and down with utter contempt. "You make me sick!"

She punctuated that little gem with a sharp kick in the shin. He clenched his teeth against the pain but made no effort to defend himself, either from her words or her dangerous hands and feet.

With a last shake of her head, she turned her back on him and stormed out the door.

16

"WELL, THAT WAS QUITE dramatic," Gabriel said with a sardonic grin.

"I'm so glad we entertained you. Now, where's Ian?"

"I don't know yet."

Jules gaped at him. "You don't know? That's going to make it hard for you to give him to me, don't you think?" Somehow, he'd assumed Gabriel had some idea where Ian was hiding, and it was just a matter of catching him.

"I said I don't know *yet*. I'll find him."

"If Camille doesn't find you first, you mean."

Gabriel's eyes narrowed, but though Jules's jibe obviously angered him, it was impossible to miss the hint of pain beneath the anger. "Remember, Guardian, I don't have to give you anything in return for your information. I could drag the information I want out of you by force. You would beg me to kill you before I was done."

Hannah seemed to be able to goad Gabriel with impunity, but Jules obviously lacked the knack. "I was just pointing out a fact of life. She's gunning for you now, and she's older than you."

"She'll come to her senses." He didn't sound terribly convinced. "I've just got to give her some time to think it through. I tried to tell her Ian was behind this, but she thinks I've killed him so he could be my scapegoat. I'll avoid her for now, but if we have to fight over this, she'll be in for a rude surprise."

The world would be a better place if Camille and Gabriel fought to the death, no matter who won. But it would be paradise on earth if Ian died first.

"How will you find Ian?" Jules asked. "For all you know, he's three states away by now."

Gabriel shook his head. "He wants to be the Master of Baltimore. He won't go far. If I were him, I'd start picking off Camille's other fledglings. Take away her support system."

That made sense. And in truth, Jules didn't believe Ian would have run away. Not after all he'd obviously put into trying to take over the city. According to Drake, five fledglings had died last night, but that still left Ian with seven. That they knew of. With Camille and Gabriel now at each other's throats, Ian had to feel some sense of hope.

"So you'll start monitoring Camille's fledglings?" Jules asked.

Gabriel nodded. "Ian will come for them, or will at least send his fledglings for them if he's too cowardly to come himself. When I catch one, he *will* tell me where Ian is hiding."

Jules pitied the poor fool Gabriel captured. "I suppose that's it, then. Will you want my help surveilling?"

"No." He smiled one of his unpleasant smiles. "I wouldn't want anything happening to you before I've had a chance to question you."

Jules couldn't say he was disappointed. The less time he spent in Gabriel's company, the better.

Gabriel pulled a crumpled piece of paper out of his jeans pocket, then held it out to Jules.

"What's this?" Jules asked.

"I thought you might prefer to stay somewhere other than the Roach Motel. This place is quiet and discreet, and far enough out of the way that no one should accidentally stumble across you. We frequently hunt this particular neighborhood, so it's not a good hiding place."

Jules felt like an idiot. The worst neighborhoods always made the best vampire hunting grounds. Much easier to make someone disappear here without arousing anyone's attention. He should have considered that before parking himself here. Not that he was thrilled with the idea of staying in a hotel Gabriel suggested.

He must have hesitated a little too long.

"Don't be difficult," Gabriel said. "If I don't know where you are, how am I going to tell you when I've found Ian?"

"Right," Jules agreed with a grimace. He took the paper from Gabriel's hand.

"It's been a pleasure doing business with you," Gabriel said.

The feeling was far from mutual, but Jules wasn't about to voice that thought. Gabriel paused in the doorway, his hand on the doorknob.

"By the way. In case you're lying to me and considering fleeing to Philadelphia, I thought you should know I'll be keeping an eye on you. If you run, you die. Slowly. Understand?"

Jules nodded tightly, and Gabriel slipped out the door.

HANNAH WAS NEARING THE I-95 on-ramp, tears still blurring her vision, when it struck her what an idiot she was being. She pulled into a convenience store parking lot and shut off the car, leaning her forehead against the steering wheel and taking deep, calming breaths.

Jules had been trying to get rid of her from the moment she'd set foot in Baltimore. And if last night's escapades had shaken him half as much as they had her, he'd be doubly anxious to be rid of her now. What better way to accomplish his goal than to convince her he was going to put his desire for revenge over the life of his friends?

"Jesus, Hannah. You're too stupid to live." She banged her forehead against the steering wheel. She'd chalk up her gullibility to sheer cowardice. After last night, perhaps she'd been eager to find an excuse to get away.

Still cursing herself, she turned the car around and headed back to the hotel. She was stopped at a red light a block away when she saw Jules exit the hotel, suitcases in hand. Geez! If he'd looked like a tempting target before, right now he was damn near irresistible. Just where did the damn fool think he was going, anyway? She scanned the streets for any sign of Gabriel but didn't see him. She wasn't terribly reassured.

The light turned green, and she quickly caught up with Jules. She slowed down to match his pace—which the driver behind her didn't much like—and lowered the window.

"Need a ride, stranger?" she asked, leaning over the passenger seat so she could see his face.

His groan was drowned out by the horn of the car behind her. There was an empty parking space a couple of yards away. She pulled into it, finally silencing the asshole who'd been leaning on his horn. Jules came to a stop by the open window, shaking his head at her.

"Go home, Hannah."

"Like hell." She popped the trunk. "Put your bags away and get in."

"I make you sick, remember?"

Her face heated but she did her best to brazen it out. "Can I help it if you're a good actor? Now come on, get in. You don't want to go this alone."

He leaned down to put his face to the open window. "I'm most likely going to end up dead before this is all over. And yes, *that* I very much want to go alone."

"Tough shit. You've dug yourself one hell of a deep hole, and you're going to need help climbing out of it. Especially if you want to climb out of it without betraying everyone you care about."

With a grunt of pure frustration, Jules stood up. The car rocked madly when he slammed first one suitcase, then the other into the trunk. She was rather surprised the trunk lid didn't crumple when he shut it, considering the deafening bang. He closed the car door with similar force. She locked the doors and turned to look at him, but his expression was shuttered.

"So, where were you headed?" she asked.

He pulled a crumpled piece of paper from his coat pocket. "Gabriel suggested I move to a different hotel, since he and his friends hunt this neighborhood on a regular basis."

"Uh-huh. I've got a radical counter-suggestion for you. How 'bout moving a little farther away than that. Like, say, to Philadelphia. Getting revenge on Ian can't be important enough to you to risk betraying the Guardians."

"I can't go back."

"Cut the crap, Jules! So you're pissed at Eli. So what? Just get over it already."

He shook his head. "That's not what I meant. I meant Gabriel may be watching me, waiting to see if I'll bolt. He said he would. Maybe it's an empty threat, but I'd hate to test it and be wrong. As long as he thinks I'm going to cooperate, he has no reason to try to torture the truth out of me. Or to hurt you, for that matter, since you absolutely *had* to come back and make my life more difficult."

She hated to admit it, but Jules had a point. Still, two heads were better than one. Especially when Jules was such a hothead he tended to make knee-jerk, temper-inspired decisions.

She pulled out of the parking spot and into traffic. Jules got the map out of the glove compartment and located the hotel Gabriel had suggested.

Hannah chewed her lip as she drove. "So, you go along with Gabe's plan and he gives you Ian. What then?"

"I wish I knew. I have to find a way to get out of town before he questions me. I'd love it to be after I've killed Ian, but if it has to be before, so be it." He sighed. "I just wish I knew how to do it without Gabriel catching me."

"And we've got to make sure Drake gets out of town too. If you're gone, you know Gabe'll go for him."

"True."

That seemed to end the conversation, and the rest of the

drive passed in silence. Hannah kept worrying at the problem, but she couldn't think of a foolproof solution.

The new hotel was a giant step up from the dump they'd just left. They checked in, then lugged the bags up to the room. Hannah fought a hint of panic as the door closed behind them. She *so* didn't want to be alone in a bedroom with Jules right now.

She started unpacking immediately, moving slowly. She concentrated hard on withdrawing her clothes from her bag, shaking out the wrinkles, carefully folding or hanging. When she was done, she'd take a long, hot bath. Alone. After that, she'd take a nap.

Eventually, she realized Jules was sitting on the edge of the bed staring at her. She wondered how long he'd been doing that. When her step faltered, he smiled at her.

"I was beginning to think you'd forgotten I was here," he said.

She rubbed her hands together, then cursed herself for the obviously nervous gesture. No way in hell she could forget he was in the room. "Look, about last night . . ." Her voice died. She had no idea what she'd been about to say.

Jules raised his eyebrow at her hesitation. "Yes? What about last night?"

"It was just a fluke, okay?" She avoided his eyes, tried not to think about how good he had felt inside her. On top of her.

"A fluke."

Her bag was empty already and she knew it, but Hannah fished through some side compartments anyway. Anything to keep from having to face him.

"You know, it didn't feel like a fluke to me," he said.

"Yeah, well, it was." She jerked open the closet door and flung her bag inside. Her hands were clammy.

"Are you going to tell me what went wrong?"

"Nothing went wrong." She looked around her, hoping to find something else to occupy her attention.

"Uh-huh. So you always cry in the bathroom after sex?"

She winced. Who did she think she was kidding? "Look, I don't want to talk about it, okay?"

She heard the faint creak of the bedsprings as Jules rose. Still, she didn't turn to look at him, even when she sensed his presence only inches away from her back. His hands came down on her shoulders and she closed her eyes.

"I think we *need* to talk," he said, his voice lowered to a seductive almost-whisper.

She shook her head. "Just leave it alone, Jules." Reluctantly, she pulled away, her body missing the touch of his hands as soon as she did.

Just listen to yourself, Hannah. You sound exactly like your brothers.

She tried to shut her internal voice up, but it was far too late. The thought had taken root. *Was* she acting like her brothers? That was a no-brainer. Did realizing that make her willing to spill her guts to Jules? Also a no-brainer. If only Jules were better at taking no for an answer.

For the first time since they'd entered the room, she looked up and met his eyes. Perhaps there *was* a way to make him take no for an answer. She almost smiled at her brilliant idea, but that would ruin the effect.

"Tell you what. You tell me about whatever happened between you and Ian, and I'll talk to you about why I freaked last night."

She saw her suggestion hit home. For a long moment, Jules seemed at a loss for words as he frowned fiercely at the floor. Then he squared his shoulders and met her gaze—and her challenge.

"All right," he said. "It's a deal."

Hannah's jaw dropped and her stomach lurched. Oh shit. If she'd known he'd take her up on this, she never would have offered in the first place.

Jules turned to the bed, pulling the pillows out from under the covers and propping them against the wall to make an impromptu sofa. He toed off his shoes, then climbed up, patting the place beside him.

Hannah swallowed hard. How was she going to get out of this? "I . . . Uh . . ."

"Come on, Hannah." He beckoned with his hand. "Sit and talk to me."

Geez, she'd thought her hands were clammy before. Reluctantly, she climbed onto the bed and sat beside Jules, her pulse hammering. *What's the big deal?* her saner, more rational side wondered. *Sticks and stones can break my bones but words can never hurt me. Right?* She rubbed her hands up and down her pants legs.

"You go first," she said quickly.

He reached over and grasped her chin, turning her head until she was forced to look at him. "Promise me that if I spill my guts here, you're not going to renege on me."

No doubt she'd be tempted, but she'd do her best not to be

a wuss. "I promise," she answered, fighting another wave of panic. Hey, maybe she'd get lucky and he'd chicken out first.

Jules released her chin and turned to stare straight ahead of him. Strain tightened his lips. She put her hand on his chest, feeling the rapid throb of his heart. She cuddled up against his side, and his arm slipped around her, holding her close.

"Are you sure you want to hear this?" he asked. "It's pretty ugly."

"I kinda figured that. Have you ever told anyone?"

"No."

His pulse raced a little faster under her hand, and she wished there were something she could do or say to make this easier for him. Unfortunately, he would have to find his own way. His Adam's apple bobbed. Then he started talking.

"Ian and I met my sophomore year in college. I told you the guy was a loser, but in my infinite wisdom I decided he was just misunderstood. I felt sorry for him. He always seemed to be down on his luck and people tended to snub him. Of course, they snubbed him because if you actually talked to him, he'd manage to work in a subtle insult or three within the first five minutes. He always got those verbal jabs in there at me, but if I called him on it, he'd claim he didn't mean it. And I bought it every time.

"I always thought he appreciated my friendship. He certainly wasn't reluctant to accept my help whenever I offered. He never really gave anything back, but I figured a guy who'd had such a tough time in life was entitled to be selfish every once in a while." He laughed bitterly. "Unbelievable, the excuses I made for him.

"After college, he got a job in Baltimore, and I stayed in

Philly. I met a nice girl, got married, had a son. I wrote to him occasionally. Sometimes he wrote back. I invited him to my wedding, but he didn't come. Then, when Luc was two, Ian moved back to Philly. My wife and I weren't getting along so well, so I was really glad for the excuse to get out of the house more often. Ian and I went out on the town a few times, got drunk, gambled. He must have been using glamour, because I never noticed he wasn't drinking.

"One night, I'd really overdone it and could barely walk I was so drunk. He took me back to his apartment, supposedly so he could sober me up before I had to face my wife. When I'd drunk enough coffee that I wasn't completely wasted anymore . . ."

Hannah had to bite her tongue to keep from prodding him. She held her breath and waited for him to let go of whatever secret pain he'd been hiding.

"He, um . . ." Jules let out a thunderous sigh.

Hannah reached for his hand and found it drenched in sweat. Her heart ached for him. "Talk to me, Jules," she said, squeezing his hand. "Whatever it is, you can tell me."

"Yeah." His chest rose and fell with a deep breath. "Okay." One more deep breath. "Heseducedme." The words came out in a frantic, slurred rush, and it took Hannah half a beat to make sense of them. By then, he was talking again. Fast. "Well, not really. It was just glamour but of course I was mortal then and didn't even know vampires existed so I had no idea what glamour was and I thought it was—"

Hannah reached up and put her hand over his lips to shush him. His eyes were glazed, looking into the past and seeing nothing of the present. His heart was beating so hard that if he'd been mortal, she'd have worried he would have a heart attack. He let out a shuddering breath, gently pushing her fingers away from his mouth and extricating his sweaty hand from hers. He dried his palms on his pants legs.

"I guess he always resented me," Jules said. "I thought he liked having a dependable friend who could get him out of trouble, but it must have galled him that he couldn't do it himself. He was happy enough to use me when I was convenient, but he was never really my friend. So when Camille made him, he decided to come to Philadelphia and show me who was boss."

Jules slouched forward and Hannah laid her hand on his back, feeling the need to touch him even though she didn't know what to say. What a way to repay a friendship! No wonder Jules wanted to kill the bastard.

"I've never been able to shake it," Jules said. His voice was hoarse. "I *know* it was glamour. I *know* it was force. But it didn't *feel* like it at the time, and that just makes me sick. What he did to my body was bad enough. What he did to my mind . . ." He shook his head. "Why didn't I see through him? Hell, everyone else did!"

"So what, you're like one of those rape victims who thinks if she hadn't been wearing a sexy dress she might not have been raped?"

He leaned back again and ran a hand through his hair. "Yeah, I guess I am. It's stupid, I know, but—"

"Actually, it sounds kind of normal to me. I'm sure it was exactly how he wanted you to feel. It was a sick, twisted thing to do." She tried to imagine how *she* would feel if Ian used his glamour against her like that. She shuddered. Even knowing it was glamour, and even without the sense of being betrayed by a friend, her mind balked at the idea. Better to be physically forced than to have your own body and mind betray you like that. Poor Jules.

"You'd think that after this much time, I'd have gotten over it."

She snorted. "Who thinks that? I sure don't. Especially not when you've been carrying it around inside you without telling anyone for so long."

He managed a weak, unconvincing grin. "Well, now that I've talked about it, I'm all better."

"Yeah, right."

"And it's your turn to talk."

Oops. She'd almost let herself forget about the quid-pro-quo thing. He probably had more talking he needed to do to clear the poison out of his system, but the look on his face was not promising. There was only so far she could push him.

"So, what happened last night?" Jules prompted when she showed no signs of starting to talk.

Hannah's fingers curled around the edge of the blanket that lay beneath her. "It wasn't what I expected."

Silence stretched for a long minute. "What did you expect?"

"Hell if I know."

"If this is your idea of talking it out, I'm less than impressed."

She glared at him. "I don't *want* to talk it out. I think I made that pretty damn clear."

He met her glare with one of his own. "Well I didn't *want* to talk about Ian. But I did."

"Okay. Fine." She plucked a piece of lint off the blanket,

focusing her gaze on the bedspread. "I don't like men who are bossy in bed. And you were damn bossy."

Jules processed that for a moment. "I've never been like that before," he admitted. "But then, you're not the kind of woman I usually take to bed."

She wasn't sure, but she thought she might have detected a hint of an insult in that. "What does that mean?"

"Well, I've had a preference for what you would probably call girlie-girls. You know, meek, mild-mannered."

"Submissive. Living to serve."

She could almost hear his grin, though she refused to look at him. "Something like that."

She sniffed in disdain. "So I suppose it pissed you off that I wasn't one of those shrinking violets, and you decided to put me in my place."

He reached out and brushed an errant curl away from her face. She felt the pressure of his eyes on her but kept her own gaze on the bedspread.

"I think you know perfectly well that wasn't what happened," he murmured.

Her throat tightened, but she forced herself to talk. "All right, then. If you know so much, why don't *you* tell *me* what happened?"

"I'd say I let passion take precedence over finesse. And every nuance of your reaction said you liked it that way."

She flinched, then wished she hadn't.

"So *that's* the problem!" he said as if all was settled.

"Jules . . ."

"You don't like that you liked it."

"Please shut up." Her cheeks glowed with heat. She

wondered if she could use arcane mental powers to create an interruption to get her out of this. Hell, she'd even be glad to see Gabriel right about now.

Jules crowded back into her space and laid an arm around her shoulders. His side pressed against hers. The heat in her cheeks intensified at the feel of his chest bumping the side of her breast. She tried to pull away, but her heart wasn't in the effort.

"Why is that a problem, Hannah?" His voice was warm and velvet-soft, causing heat to curl in her belly even while her mind screamed that she needed out of this conversation.

She reminded herself that she didn't have to answer him. To hell with their deal! Then again, seeing as she'd slept with him, he probably deserved an answer.

She squirmed and cursed herself for being such a wimp. If she could trade insults with Gabriel, she could talk about her feelings. Embarrassed by how hard this was, she forced words out of her mouth.

"You might have noticed I'm a bit of a control freak?"

He chuckled. "Yeah, I'd noticed. You know that old saying, takes one to know one?"

She nodded, her cheek rubbing against his shoulder. She'd never thought about it that way, but now that he mentioned it, she realized he liked control at least as much as she did. Which no doubt made what Ian had done to him hurt even worse.

"Last night, you were in control," she admitted. "And I wasn't. And I don't like that."

His hand stroked up and down her arm and he laid the top of his head against hers. "Sure you were. You could have told me to stop."

She pulled away a little, turning her head so she could see his face. "And would you have?"

"I really hope you already know the answer to that."

She heard the hint of hurt in his voice and cursed herself for lashing out at him. "Sorry. You're right. I know I could have called a stop." She smiled faintly. "But I wouldn't have. Not for a million bucks."

She met his eyes and saw rampant speculation in them. Which, naturally, put her on high alert.

"What are you thinking?" she asked.

Without a word, he slipped off the side of the bed. She frowned, wondering what he was up to. He put one of his suitcases on the luggage stand, then opened it and rummaged for a bit. When he turned back toward the bed, she saw that he was holding a couple of ties.

The blood drained from her face, and she scooted away from him, hands out in an instinctive defensive gesture. One corner of his mouth rose in a half-smile.

"Relax. These are for me, not you."

She could have sworn her heart skipped a beat. She *knew* her eyes must be cartoon-character wide.

Jules sat on the edge of the bed and laid the ties between them. He smoothed one of them out with those strong, clever fingers of his.

"Last night, you trusted me enough to give up control, even though you weren't comfortable with it. I want to return the favor."

Oh, man. Arousal overdrive! The image of this powerful predator lying helpless before her made her insides clench. Even the nervousness of his expression added to the heat in her core.

Last night, she'd abandoned herself to him. Yes, it had scared the crap out of her. But there was no question she had liked it, had liked trusting someone so much that she could let go of the reins. But for her, it had been a heat-of-the-moment thing, not requiring a conscious decision.

"Are you sure about this, Jules?" Her voice shook.

He flashed her one of his cocky, arrogant smiles, though she still saw the nervous glint in his eyes. "Don't tell me you're losing your nerve already."

She narrowed her eyes at him. "You think all you have to do is goad me to get me your way?" She tossed her head. "I'm not that easy."

His grin looked more natural now. "The hell you aren't."

She couldn't help laughing, despite the tension that radiated through her every fiber. "Okay. Obviously, you know me too well." She grabbed the ties. "Lie down."

He was still grinning when she tied his left hand to the bedpost, but he tensed up when she tied his right. She smoothed a hand over his chest, feeling the quickened beats of his heart. His hands clenched and unclenched in his bonds, and a thin sheen of sweat coated his brow. For all his bravado, this really did make him feel vulnerable. She ran her tongue over her lips, then smiled to see how his eyes darkened.

He pulled his lips away from his teeth, displaying his fangs. A shiver passed down her spine.

She might be in control now, might have tied his hands, but only because he'd let her. He would always be stronger than her, always more powerful. Hell, even if she wanted to keep him tied against his will, she wouldn't be able to. A little touch of glamour, and she'd do anything he wanted.

She forcibly wrenched her mind away from that line of thought. Counterproductive, to say the least. It was time to get down to business. She bent down and ran her tongue over his lips, dipping inside to brush lightly against his fangs. He moaned and strained upward, trying to take charge of the kiss, but she drew back. She drew her hands up and down the broad expanse of his chest, enjoying the softness of the expensive fabric of his shirt, but her libido urged her to hurry up. She plucked open the buttons one by one, then stroked his chest. His eyes slid closed and he made a little hum of contentment somewhere deep in his throat.

She smiled. Perhaps she was being too soothing. She brushed her fingers over his nipples, feeling them harden at her touch. Then she pinched them.

Jules hissed and his eyes popped open. With any other lover, she might have taken that as a protest, but not with him. Watching his face from beneath her lashes, she lowered her head until she could reach one pebbled nipple with the tip of her tongue. He hissed again, his hips thrusting upward. She raised herself so there was only the slightest of contacts, drawing a groan of pure frustration from Jules.

She tasted one nipple, then the other, licking, sucking, and occasionally nipping. His breath grew more ragged, and the bedposts groaned as he strained against the ties. With a little shiver, she realized he was probably strong enough to splinter those bedposts if he wanted to. The awareness that she was playing with fire only heightened her pleasure.

She slid downward, making sure their bodies rubbed the whole way down. Jules considerately made room for her between his legs, and she settled in, her elbows propped on either side of his hips as she regarded his impressive, straining erection.

"You're not about to blast off already, are you?" she asked.

His only answer was a low growl. She'd just have to trust his self-control. Otherwise; this would be over far sooner than either of them wanted. Her hands shook a little as she opened his belt. Okay, maybe it was *her* self-control that was in question. There was no denying the almost unbearable heat between her thighs.

A deep, steadying breath quelled the shaking—for the moment—and she managed to get his pants open. He raised his hips and allowed her to draw his pants and briefs off. Now he lay tied on the bed, naked from the waist down while she was fully clothed. A thrill coursed through her entire body. The heat between her legs intensified. She reached out and drew the tip of one finger across the silky skin of his erection, and his groan sounded like pleasure and pain combined.

"Please," he panted, "no more teasing. Can't bear it."

She nudged his legs apart, then resumed her former position, elbows braced beside his hips as she breathed in the musky scent of him. She didn't know how much more teasing she could take herself, but she was game to find out. Her tongue brushed lightly over his crown, and he made a sound rather like a muted howl. The bedposts creaked ominously, but the ties held.

"Please," he said again, his voice low and rough.

Loving the sense of power, spurious though it might be, she opened her mouth wide and took him in. His legs jerked, and his hips thrust upward desperately. His gasping breaths told her just how much he liked what she was doing as she savored him with lips and tongue. Her pulse drummed in her ears and between her legs, her own desire so strong she squirmed.

"Hannah." It was a choked, breathless sound, like nothing she'd ever heard from his throat before. And suddenly, the desire was too much to bear.

He cried out in protest when she released him, but subsided when she started frantically undressing. She was in too much of a hurry to get naked, so when she straddled him, she was still wearing her shirt and bra. She sank onto him, and they both groaned with the rightness of it.

Moving slowly, squeezing with her out-of-practice inner muscles, she rose again, feeling the delicious glide of him inside her, skin on skin. His hips rose with her as he tried to stay buried. She meant to lower herself with the same excruciating slowness she had the first time, but her body could no longer stand the teasing any more than his could. When he thrust, she matched his rhythm, to hell with her being in total control.

Her eyelids heavy, she glanced up through her lashes to see the rapture on his face. Her breaths were as ragged as his. With a little shock of recognition, she realized that not only were they thrusting in time with each other, they were *breathing* in time. Never in her life had she felt this in tune with another person. She wasn't controlling the pace anymore, but then neither was he. She strained forward until she could reach the ties, jerking the knots loose.

He didn't roll her beneath him. She'd *known* he wouldn't. Instead, his hands rose to her breasts, kneading them, pinching her nipples through shirt and bra, the touch so welcome there might as well have been nothing between them. Pressure mounted between her legs. Her eyes locked with his.

Almost there. So was he. She could see it in his eyes, hear it in his breaths. She made no attempt to time her climax to his, just let herself come when her body said it was ready. His cry of release came at the very same moment as hers, their voices blending eerily into one. She collapsed onto his chest, into his open arms, and felt the beat of his heart, exactly synchronized with hers.

Later, she would wonder about this. Later, she might even be a little freaked out. But not now. Now she lay still and quiet in Jules's arms and thought about nothing except how very right it felt.

17

Exhaustion urged Hannah to get into bed and go to sleep. Unease told her she had to *do* something, make herself useful. Unease won.

Jules lay sleeping under the covers, the light of day stronger than any sleeping pill. She almost wished *she* were a vampire so she could get some sleep. She yawned and poured another cup of coffee, then booted up her computer. At least the hotel Gabriel had sent them to had wireless access so she didn't have to fight through a pokey dial-up connection.

If she wasn't going to sleep, she had to do something to keep her mind occupied or she'd start thinking about how good the sex had been.

No. That wasn't it. She'd had good sex before. She'd just never had *great* sex. Never had sex that made her feel changed inside. She'd fallen asleep in Jules's arms, then awakened to a new world. She had an awful, sneaking suspicion she might finally be learning firsthand what it meant to be in love.

She shook her head violently. Hadn't she just told herself

she had to keep her mind occupied? With something other than Jules?

Drawing on every scrap of her willpower, she logged on to the Internet and started doing some searches. She'd learned from Carolyn how the Guardians went about finding Killers. It was a strangely mundane process of checking newspapers for suspicious-sounding murders and unexplained disappearances and finding patterns.

If Ian Squires had had a dozen fledgling Killers camped out somewhere, it seemed likely she ought to be able to find some evidence. It couldn't be in the city itself, or Camille and Gabriel would have known, but it had to be conveniently nearby. Trusting that Jules would be safe for a few minutes, she went downstairs to the concierge's desk to get a map of the state of Maryland, then started marking the locations of suspicious murders and missing persons.

It was a tedious business, to say the least. And she knew that the vast majority of the murders and missing persons reports had nothing to do with vampires. Still, after hours of staring at the screen, giving herself eye strain, she thought she might be detecting a pattern that looked interesting.

The Baltimore vampires were apparently very good at covering their kills. Other than the cluster of murders that had drawn Jules's attention, she'd been able to find no pattern in Baltimore itself. Probably the kills Jules had found were Ian's, a part of his plan to lure Jules here.

The suburbs, however, were a different story altogether. No murders that looked like they could be vamp kills, but a lot of disappearances.

They'd started about two years ago and spanned a number of small towns in Baltimore's rural outskirts—easy driving distance. To a mortal who was blissfully ignorant about vampires, most of the disappearances would look to be unrelated. The victims varied in age, sex, and social status, and the circumstances varied just as much. Some disappeared from their homes, some from their cars, some from grocery store parking lots. But most of them were last seen at night, and the number of disappearances had increased drastically in the last six months, which made sense if Ian's vampire "family" was growing. Hell, the pattern was beginning to look so obvious that even the mortal authorities would soon have to consider that the cases were related, no matter how widely disparate the MO's.

Hannah circled the area on the map, feeling relatively certain Ian and his nest of fledglings lived somewhere within the boundaries of that circle. Unfortunately, she wasn't sure how much help that information would be. It was a lot of ground to cover, and it wasn't like he'd put up a sign saying "Vampires R Us."

By two o'clock in the afternoon, she was too tired to keep her eyes open another minute. She climbed onto the bed beside Jules, making sure he was safely tucked in. Then she snuggled close to his warmth, her head resting on his shoulder, and promptly fell asleep.

⁂

SHE WOKE UP TO the sound of a door closing. At first, she assumed Jules must have gotten up and that was the sound of the bathroom door. Then she realized she was still snuggled up against his body.

She sat up, rubbing her sleep-crusted eyes and yawning.

"How did you get past the deadbolt and the safety latch?" she asked, without opening her eyes. She wanted nothing more than to collapse back onto the bed and sleep for a week. Instead, she forced her eyes open and squinted at Gabriel, who stood in the entryway.

"I didn't mean to wake you," he said.

She shook her head to clear some more cobwebs. "How did you get in?" she asked again.

"One of the advantages of age. Telekinesis. Had you never wondered how my dear mother managed to throw me across the room without touching me?"

She yawned again, sure she should be more alarmed at seeing him but unable to muster the energy to worry. "Just how old are you, anyway?"

He laughed. "Older than sin."

She rolled her eyes and climbed out of bed, glancing at the clock. It was after five, which meant Jules would rise soon. Hopefully, that meant Gabe wasn't planning any more demonstrations of his power.

Mechanically, she crossed the room to the coffee pot, then cursed when she realized she'd made the last of the coffee this afternoon. She scrubbed her eyes again, but it didn't make her feel any more awake.

"Why is your age a deep, dark secret?" she asked.

"It isn't, I suppose. On Christmas Day next year, I shall turn five hundred."

Yikes! She picked up her glasses, which she had left by the computer, and put them on, giving Gabriel the once-over. "You don't look a day over two-fifty."

He grinned, a hint of genuine humor in his usually flat eyes. "You're too kind."

When he lightened up like that, he was actually a pretty good-looking guy, never mind the scar on his face. Too young-looking for her tastes, but she imagined her oldest nieces would just drool over him.

Too bad he was a five-hundred-year-old serial murderer who wouldn't hesitate to torture Jules into betraying the Guardians.

Reflexively, she reached for the wound in her neck, fingers brushing over the scabs. The wound had never hurt, despite the purplish bruise that surrounded it, but she was very much aware it was there.

Gabriel's grin faded. "I'm sorry about that. It was a . . . miscalculation on my part."

"You're only sorry because you didn't really want to know that Jules can escape your mind control."

He didn't bother to deny it. "I've gone berserk like that once or twice in my life," Gabriel continued, "but I never realized it made one immune to glamour. An interesting phenomenon."

Gee, Gabe was a regular font of information today. Before she could formulate a carefully phrased question to learn more about this "interesting phenomenon," a rustling sound from the bed indicated that Jules was waking. They both turned to him.

Jules made one of those growling noises in the back of his throat when he caught sight of Gabriel. He sat up abruptly. The blankets fell away from his bare chest, reminding him that he was naked. Hannah gave Gabriel a sidelong glance. He grinned, but refrained from comment. Which, considering the look in Jules's eyes, was a good thing for everyone involved.

"What are you doing here?" Jules asked, tucking the covers around his hips.

Gabriel lifted one shoulder. "Just checking in." He turned to look at Hannah, an expression of intense calculation on his face. "Last I knew, you were on your way back to Philadelphia to warn them I was coming."

Oops. She'd forgotten about last night's little crisis of faith. Problem being, she couldn't exactly tell Gabriel why she'd come back, even though it was possible he already knew Jules had no intention of giving him any information. If he could help it.

"I guess I'm just in too deep to run away now," she said, trying to sound nonchalant. "Besides, I don't work for the Guardians, and my personal opinion of Eli is that he's a life form slightly below pond scum. Hell, I might even volunteer to help you kick his ass."

Once again, Gabriel laughed, as he seemed to do so often when she spoke. She figured that was *probably* a good thing. Jules was scowling darkly but didn't say a word to contradict her.

Gabe made himself at home, wandering around the room, eyes roving. When he caught sight of the map Hannah had left out, she wanted to slap herself silly. The only thing they'd had on their side had been time, and she would have preferred Gabriel have no idea she'd been researching Ian's location on her own. Unfortunately, there was approximately zero chance he'd believe any cover story she could think of to explain the markings on that map.

"You've been busy," he said, picking up the map and examining it.

Jules muttered something under his breath and shook his head.

"Sorry," she mouthed at him.

"You seem to have narrowed the search down to this area," Gabriel said, tracing the circle with the tip of his finger. "How?"

She supposed there was no point in lying. "I looked for clusters of unexplained disappearances. I figured twelve fledgling Killers would leave a pretty recognizable footprint."

The corners of Gabriel's mouth tightened. "How true. Squires is the worst kind of fool. No one with an iota of sense would create that many fledglings at one time even in the shelter of a big city. Out in the country like that . . ." He shook his head in evident disgust. "He's sure to draw attention to himself from mortal authorities. There's a reason my mother doesn't keep a legion of fledglings at her beck and call. The *last* thing we need is to have mortals believing in vampires."

Hannah didn't like the sound of that, and from the expression on Jules's face, neither did he.

Gabriel dismissed their concerns with a wave of his hand. "I didn't mean that as a threat to you," he told Hannah. "You are one mortal out of millions. But if those millions should start believing in us, we would be extinct in no time."

Despite her growing fondness for Jules, Hannah wasn't sure that would be such a bad thing. She suspected that for every Jules in this world, there were a hundred or more Gabriels.

"This is good work," he continued, nodding approvingly at the map. "We'll have to take a drive out into the country. If we cover the area methodically, I ought to be able to sense Ian and his fledglings." He smiled one of his especially chilling smiles. "I so look forward to seeing my old friend again."

"You promised me a clean kill, remember?" Jules said, though, sitting on the bed with the covers wrapped around his hips, he didn't convey much of a sense of authority.

Gabriel raised an eyebrow. "Why this insistence on a clean kill? Why would you not want Ian to suffer after all that he's done? It would only be justice." He locked gazes with Jules, and a silent battle of wills ensued.

Afraid of what Jules might decide to say—and of how Gabriel might react to it—Hannah decided to answer for him.

"Because he's not a sadist." *Like you.* The unspoken words hung in the air between them as Jules and Gabriel broke off their staring contest.

Gabriel looked amused by the silent accusation. Certainly, he saw no need to contradict it.

"I must feed so that I'll be at top strength," he said. "Be ready to leave within the hour."

Hannah's stomach flip-flopped as she realized someone was going to die soon at Gabriel's hands. And there wasn't a damn thing she could do to stop it.

"If you have any silly notions about running away while I'm gone," Gabriel continued, "I should point out that when I retrieved your car from the impound lot, I fitted it with a GPS tracking device." He smiled smugly. "That's how I found you at the Roach Motel. You can search for it, but by the time you find it it'll be too late." He looked at Jules. "If I have to come chasing after you, I'll have Hannah for dessert while you watch."

Jules's hands clenched into fists, and a muscle ticked in his jaw, but he didn't respond. Gabriel nodded, satisfied with himself, then left the room.

"He probably wouldn't do it," Hannah said, staring at the door through which he'd exited. "I think he kinda likes me." Gabriel wasn't exactly what she'd call a good guy, but she had a definite sense that he followed some code of honor. Of course, not being certain what that code was, she wasn't eager to test him.

Jules swept the covers aside and headed for the bathroom. "We're not going to find out," he said with finality.

Once upon a time, his tone would have sparked her to argue just for the sake of arguing. She wasn't sure her uncharacteristic acquiescence was an improvement.

⚭

THE DOOR TO DRAKE's room opened shortly after sundown. He'd been awake for almost an hour, pacing the length of the room, trying the door once or twice just to make sure someone hadn't unlocked it without his noticing. Apparently, Eli'd had no success talking Camille into releasing him. Not a good sign at all. He'd tried a couple of times to eke one more call out of his cell phone, to let Jules and Hannah know what was going on, but the battery refused to cooperate.

He stopped in mid-pace when Camille stepped into his guestroom-cum-prison-cell. No elegant opera dress for her tonight. No, tonight she meant business. A finely tailored, pinstriped pants suit clung appealingly to her curves, and her hair was swept up into a tight bun at the base of her neck. Even her makeup was understated, though no less perfect than usual.

"You will find my son and his fledglings for me," she said when she stepped into the room.

"Excuse me?" It wasn't exactly what he'd expected to hear from her.

"You work for the Guardians. You're an expert at tracking down Killers. My son may have been subtle about his own kills, but fledglings have little self-control. Wherever they're hiding, they will have left evidence. Find that evidence for me. Find Gabriel."

"What about my friends?" he asked quietly. "I thought you wanted me to find them and—"

"Find Gabriel." She stepped closer to him, baring her fangs, her eyes glowing with a hint of madness. "When you find him for me, I'll set you free and you can do whatever you want. Search for your friends. Go home. It doesn't matter to me. But until then, you'll do as I command or I'll send you back to Eli in bite-sized pieces."

He held up his hands in surrender. What did he care if Camille and her son fought to the death? As long as he could get out of this house, he'd be happy to hand Gabriel—or whoever the maker of those fledglings was—over to her.

"Do you have a computer with Internet access I can use?" he asked.

The blandness of his tone seemed to calm her some. She retracted her fangs and took a step backward. "Of course. This way."

She turned on her heel and strode out of the room. Drake had to hurry to keep up. Below, he sensed the presence of eight vampires and realized Camille had called her fledglings to her. She must be worried about another attack. Any faint hope he'd harbored of escaping the house died. He wasn't get-ting out of here unless Camille set him free.

She led him to a surprisingly Spartan office, considering the opulence of the rest of the house. She gestured him into the chair in front of her computer, then hovered over his shoul-der. He bit his tongue to suppress the urge to tell her to give him some space. He suspected it would take only the slightest provocation to inspire her to a fit of fury such as she'd demon-strated last night.

Trying to ignore the dangerous, unstable creature who lurked behind him, he started searching the local newspapers for clues.

ॐ

THINGS WERE HAPPENING WAY too fast for Jules's taste. He'd hoped to have another couple of days to plot strategy, to figure out how he and Hannah were going to get out of town with-out betraying the Guardians. He cast a surreptitious glance at Hannah as they nervously waited for Gabriel to show up again. Jules might have believed in his ability to withstand Gabriel's interrogation methods, except that Gabriel so clearly knew how to get to him. All he had to do was threaten Hannah, and Jules knew he'd do anything the bastard wanted. If only Hannah had kept driving last night!

It was when Hannah tucked her gun into the pocket of her coat that he realized what he had to do.

"May I have the gun please?" he asked quietly.

She blinked at him. "Why?"

Of course he should never expect Hannah to comply with-out an interrogation. "Come sit down," he said, patting the bed beside him.

He could only describe the look on her face as suspicious. But she came to sit by him anyway. "I have a feeling I'm not going to like this," she said.

He managed a faint smile. "I have to admit, I don't much like it myself. However . . ." His voice trailed off. He wished he had a better alternative to offer, but a sense of doom hovered over him.

"What is it, Jules? You're scaring me."

He swallowed hard, then forced himself to look at her. From the pallor of her face and the worry in her eyes, he suspected she knew what he was about to say.

"If we can't get out of this somehow," he said, "Gabriel's going to interrogate me. And I have a feeling that with five hundred years of experience, he'll know how to break me. I can't betray the Guardians, Hannah. No matter what my differences with Eli."

"So you want the gun . . . why?"

"Are you going to make me spell it out for you?"

She shook her head and looked away. "There has to be some other way. Gabe is powerful, but he isn't omnipotent."

"He might as well be, where we're concerned."

"We'll find a way," she insisted. "And I'm keeping the gun."

Impossible female! "I can take it from you by force."

"You do and I'll tell Gabe you have it."

He wanted to grab her by the shoulders and shake her till her teeth rattled. Somehow, he resisted the urge. "Don't take away my one and only chance to do the honorable thing."

"Call me a hopeless optimist, but I'm not buying the 'one and only chance' thing. If all else fails, I'll give you the gun. But for now, it's mine."

"By the time you've decided all else has failed, it'll be too late!"

"The subject is closed. And don't think I'm making an empty threat. I *will* tell him if you take the gun."

He suspected she meant it. She'd do it for his own good, of course, to stop him from shooting himself. But it meant that taking the gun from her wasn't an option after all. He considered telling her exactly what he thought about stubborn, foolish, willful females, but a knock on the door interrupted him before he got started. Giving up on talking sense into Hannah, he went to the door to let Gabriel in.

There was a noticeable flush to the older vampire's cheeks. Jules gritted his teeth, hating the knowledge that some poor fool had just died and he'd done nothing to prevent it. One corner of Gabriel's mouth rose in a sneer. Then he licked his lips, and it was all Jules could do not to attack.

Gabriel chuckled, his amusement just another irritant. Jules supposed he'd learned a little self-control over the last couple of days or he'd be at the bastard's throat right now.

"You might want to step aside just now," Gabriel said, smiling. When Jules didn't immediately obey, Gabriel put a hand on his shoulder and gave a little push.

It wasn't until that moment that Jules realized Hannah had her gun out and was pointing it at Gabriel's head.

What the hell did the damn fool woman think she was doing? Gabriel's glamour would never allow her to pull the trigger.

Gabriel smiled even more broadly, spreading his hands and taking a step closer to her. "Go ahead and shoot me, my dear."

The gun wavered, and Jules realized that Hannah wasn't

under the influence of glamour. His heart pounded as he silently urged her to pull the trigger and get them out of this mess.

"You couldn't shoot Ian when you had the chance," Gabriel continued. "What makes you think you can shoot me?"

She forced a grin that looked more like a grimace. "Keep goading me. That'll make it easier."

He crossed his arms over his chest. "You're not the type to commit murder. No matter what I am, no matter what I've done." He flicked a glance over at Jules. "Besides, without my protection, Ian would make short work of your lover."

"I'm sure with you out of the way, I'd be able to talk Jules into giving up the vendetta."

Gabriel shook his head, his smile fading away. "We're wasting time. Put the gun down and let's take a ride to the country."

Why wasn't the prick using his glamour? This whole standoff could have been finished before it even started.

Hannah was wavering, indecision clear in her eyes. Surely she had to know Gabriel could stop her if he wanted to. Gabriel took another step toward her. Jules wanted to go to her, shield her somehow, but Gabriel's glamour froze him in place.

Her finger flexed on the trigger, but still she didn't shoot.

Moving slowly, Gabriel reached out and put his hand on her arms, pushing downward until she lowered the gun. His smile when she did so was surprisingly gentle.

"It's not a bad thing that you can't shoot someone in cold blood," he said.

"It is when that someone is you," she grumbled, shoving the gun into her coat pocket.

He laughed and released Jules from his glamour.

"You've found yourself a remarkable woman, Guardian," Gabriel said. "I suggest you take good care of her. Now, let's go." He turned toward the door, beckoning them to follow.

Jules met Hannah's gaze and shook his head, though relief coursed through his system. Thank God Gabriel hadn't decided to punish Hannah for her nerve. He could only hope Gabriel's apparent fondness for her meant that when the final showdown came, he would leave her out of it.

Settling his arm around Hannah's shoulders, Jules followed Gabriel out the door.

18

THEY DECIDED TO BEGIN their search in the town of Fallston, which was just inside the circle Hannah had drawn on the map. The ride from Baltimore seemed to take about three hours, though with the streets deserted at this late hour Hannah was sure it wasn't more than thirty minutes. Jules sat beside her in the passenger seat, the map spread across his lap as he plotted their zig-zagging course. Gabriel sat in the back seat, his eyes closed as he concentrated on his psychic search. His range stretched over a couple of miles, which seemed like a long way until you considered how much ground they had to cover.

Why hadn't she been able to shoot him? Sure, it was hard to shoot an unarmed man in the head, but he was worse than any human serial killer in history. How many people had he killed in five hundred years? Even if he only fed once a month—and she was quite sure he fed more often than that—that would mean six thousand people had died at his hands. She shuddered.

Jules must have noticed, for he reached over and put his

hand on her thigh, giving it a firm squeeze. She glanced over and met his gaze for an instant before returning her concentration to the road. It was dark out here in the boondocks, with no streetlights. She hated not being able to see beyond the glow of her high beams. She was tired enough that she could easily drive off the road if she wasn't careful. Not to mention the deer she felt sure were lurking behind every bush, just waiting to hurl themselves into her path.

Time dragged, and Hannah's eyelids were heavy with exhaustion. She drove like a robot, turning when Jules told her to, no longer having any sense of where they were or how far they'd come. Everything looked the same out here in the dark of the night. Sleepy farmland and even sleepier little towns, with the occasional lighted window or lone car the only signs of life. Hours passed in excruciating tedium, and still Gabe sensed nothing. She'd have thought he'd fallen asleep, sitting back there with his head resting against the back of the seat and his eyes closed, but a creepy sense of danger lurking behind her told her he was wide awake.

"Maybe I got it all wrong," she said, stifling a yawn.

"We've still got a lot of territory to cover," Jules said, holding the map close to his face. "I'd say we've only covered about half the circle so far."

Hannah glanced at the dashboard clock. It was almost five already. "It won't be long before the sun comes up. Maybe we should call it a night and get you back to the hotel."

"No," Gabriel said. "I'm sensing something up ahead."

"Bully for you," she said, pulling onto a side road and doing a U-turn. "We can pick up from here tomorrow. Jules needs to be back in the hotel by the time the sun comes up."

Gabriel leaned forward. She felt his eyes on her, though she refused to look in the rearview mirror to see what he was doing. "If the daylight becomes a problem, we can always put him in the trunk," Gabriel said.

"Sounds like fun. But no."

"I'll be fine, Hannah," Jules said.

She shot him a death glare.

He shrugged sheepishly. "He'll just use glamour to get his way, so it's not worth fighting."

"Dammit!" God, how she hated vampires!

As usual, Gabriel was amused by her outburst. She flipped him the bird as she made another U-turn. Beside her, Jules winced, but Gabriel ignored her gesture.

Hoping she wasn't about to run into any speed traps, she put the pedal to the metal in the vain hope that they could find Ian, kill him and his fledglings, and escape Gabriel all by the time the sun rose high enough to put Jules into his coma-like daytime sleep.

⁊⊃

ALTHOUGH DRAKE WAS FAMILIAR with how the Guardians hunted their quarry, he'd never done the tedious task of searching through the newspapers for clues. He didn't work on cases until well after the Guardians had confirmed the existence of a Killer and narrowed down his hunting grounds. Given Camille's state of mind, however, he didn't feel inclined to inform her of his lack of experience.

Even if he'd been a veteran at the job, he doubted he would have had an easy time of it with Camille hovering over his shoulder. The fledglings gathered downstairs weren't much help, either. With their maker under attack, the fledglings were

on edge, fighting amongst themselves, their raised voices breaking his concentration.

It was perilously close to dawn when he felt he had suffi-
ciently narrowed down the possibilities to report his findings
to Camille. A strange glow lit her eyes when she snatched the
map from his hands.

"You're sure he's around here somewhere?" She studied it
as if she could discern her son's whereabouts just by looking.

Of course he wasn't sure. It wasn't like vampire hunting
was an exact science.

"It seems highly likely," he said.

Her eyes fixed on him and narrowed. "But would you stake
your life on it? Because that's what you're doing."

He'd have been alarmed, except his instincts had already
told him this. "What about your agreement with Eli? I'm helping you in good faith, but I'm hardly infallible."

"Eli and his high-handed tactics have cost me my son!"

"Gabriel hasn't made all those fledglings in the last week.
Whatever's brewing in his heart was brewing long before Jules
and I came to Baltimore."

"That's right, Drake. It's been brewing ever since Eli broke
our family apart and drove me and Gabriel from Philadelphia."

He stifled any number of curses. Whatever arrangement
Eli'd had with Camille, it was shattered now. And that told
Drake more than he wanted to know. He wasn't staking his
life on this hunt. Camille was going to kill him anyway, to
hurt Eli. And she'd kill Jules and Hannah, too, if she could
get her hands on them.

"Come now," Camille purred. "You must be getting tired.

I'll see you to your room. And then I believe I'll have Roger take me on a relaxing drive to the country."

Drake was powerless to stop her from locking him in his room once more, so he preserved what dignity he could by not resisting. He hadn't wanted to die one hundred and ten years ago, when he'd become a vampire. And he certainly didn't want to die now. But unless Eli personally came to Baltimore to rescue him, he didn't see how he could avoid it.

❧

HANNAH GLANCED OVER AT Jules and was alarmed by what she saw. He had ducked his head and hunched his shoulders in an attempt to keep himself in the shadow of the brim of his hat, but she could have sworn the sun was rising faster than usual. His eyes were heavy-lidded with impending sleep, and his skin seemed to have a rosy cast that was all wrong.

"Please, Gabriel," she said, hating to beg. "We've got to get Jules out of the light."

Gabriel sighed. "Very well. We're almost there anyway." He leaned forward, putting his head between the two front seats and pointing. "Pull in to that driveway."

He was pointing at a picturesque white clapboard house, complete with a white picket fence and a red barn in the back. The place belonged on a postcard, though she'd seen more picturesque farmhouses in the last few hours than she could count. This just wasn't the kind of area you'd picture when you thought about vampire hunting grounds. All the more reason why Ian's kills stood out like the proverbial sore thumb.

Obediently, Hannah pulled into the driveway, but she

frowned at Gabriel in the rearview mirror. "What's the plan here, Gabe?" Surely they weren't going to go knocking on the door and ask if they could take shelter for the day here.

"There's no one home," he said. "Park the car around back and we'll spend the day in the barn. There shouldn't be much sunlight in there, and we can cover Jules with some hay just to make extra sure he doesn't fry."

If she weren't so worried about Jules, she might have objected to the plan. As it was, she pulled in and practically leapt from the car in her hurry to get him out of the light. He was alert enough to get his door open but faltered when he tried to get out. Hannah ran to his side, but Gabriel beat her there, dragging Jules's arm over his shoulders and hauling him out effortlessly.

"Get the door." he commanded, and Hannah hurried to pull the barn door open. This being sleepy farm country, it wasn't locked.

Gabriel dragged a semi-conscious Jules through the doorway, into the dark of the barn. The place stank of horses, though its occupants were apparently away from home today. Gabriel deposited Jules in one of the stalls, then started covering him with handfuls of hay.

"We're close," Jules murmured, at least half asleep.

"Yes," Gabriel confirmed. "I'd say they're about a quarter mile away."

"Can sense them," Jules agreed. Gabriel dumped a handful of hay on his face, and Jules pushed it away.

"We need to cover your face," Gabriel said, but Jules shook his head.

"There's a mortal . . ." Despite what looked like a massive effort, Jules's eyes slid closed and his body went limp. When Gabe tossed hay over his face again, he didn't protest.

Hannah leaned against the side of the stall and watched as Gabe made Jules disappear in the hay. "He won't suffocate, will he?" she asked.

Gabe stood up and brushed the dust from his hands. "No. He'll be fine. Why don't you lie down and get some sleep. I'll keep watch."

But Hannah shook her head. "What was Jules trying to say? There's a mortal . . . ?"

Gabriel gave her one of those assessing looks, then shrugged. "Ian's fledglings are very nearby. Nine of them, and one mortal."

Ian's fledglings, eh? He'd said that as if he knew none of the nine was Ian. "And what about Ian?" she asked, just to be sure.

Gabriel pursed his already thin lips and shook his head. "He's not there. They're all young fledglings."

"And how do you know that?"

She must have sounded too eager, for Gabriel gave her a suspicious look. "Why should I tell you? Surely for a mortal you know too much about vampires already."

Her curiosity was unabated, but she was too freakin' tired to play word games with Gabriel. Let him go all prickly and mysterious on her if he wanted. She yawned hugely and sat on the pile of hay, careful to avoid Jules. Sleep would be pure heaven right now, but she wasn't sure she could manage it with Gabriel looming over her like that.

"Don't *you* need some sleep?" she asked. "Or would answering that violate the Vampire's Code?"

The corner of his mouth lifted, and he came to sit on the hay a respectful distance away. "Yes, under normal circumstances, I need to sleep. Right now I'm too . . . wired, I guess you would say." He picked up a piece of hay and studied it with great concentration. "I'm sure you already know that as we get older, we get more powerful. When we're young, we sense each other's psychic footprints in a vague, amorphous way. The older we get, the more concrete that footprint is. I can practically 'see' the fledglings. And the footprint looks . . . darker, for want of a better word, as vampires age. These footprints are very light. I'm looking for one about the same as Jules's, and it's definitely not in that house."

Hannah was more than a little surprised that he was being so forthcoming, but she wasn't about to look a gift horse in the mouth. "What about mortals? Can you see our, er, footprints too?"

"How do you think I know there's a mortal in that house?"

"Yeah, yeah, I got that. I mean, do we look different?"

"You look . . . muddy." He grinned, then frowned. "Actually, the mortal in that house looks *very* muddy. I'd say he or she is badly injured."

Hannah's heart lurched. She'd somehow assumed the mortal was a henchman, like the idiots who worked for Camille. But if the poor soul was an intended victim . . .

"You said Ian's fledglings were all very young, right?" she asked.

He nodded cautiously.

"Then if Jules is asleep, they'll all be asleep too."

Gabriel smiled. "True. You're considering taking a little trip over there during the daytime?"

She hadn't been able to save whatever hapless mortal Gabriel had killed last night, but maybe she could save this one before Ian and his cronies made a meal of him or her. Assuming Gabriel wasn't going to stop her.

"There'd be no danger, right? Ian's no older than Jules, so it's not like he's going to show up and kill me."

"True. And what will you do with the fledglings?"

If she had the guts, she'd shoot them while they slept, but she'd already established that she couldn't shoot helpless victims.

Gabriel gave her another of his gentle smiles, the kind that made him look almost human. "It's all right. It's best that the fledglings stay alive anyway—the better to lure Ian into range." He gestured her toward the barn door. "Let's go."

She hesitated. "You're coming with me?"

"Why not? You make better company than Jules at the moment."

She narrowed her eyes at him. "I'm not going over there to get you a free meal."

One corner of his mouth rose in a lopsided grin. "Understood. I won't harm the mortal unless it turns out to be an accomplice."

She wasn't a hundred percent convinced, but it wasn't like there was any way she could keep Gabriel from coming with her. Besides, despite being a sadistic serial murderer, he seemed to be honest. If he wanted to kill the mortal, he'd probably tell her so and gloat that there was nothing she could do about it.

Hannah bit her lip and looked at the pile of straw that hid Jules. "Do you think he'll be all right in there? I mean, what if the owners come back?"

"He'll be fine. And we won't be gone long. Now let's go."

Nerves tingling with foreboding, she followed him out into the early morning light.

❧

HANNAH PULLED UP IN front of the building that Gabriel indicated and turned off the car.

"You've got to be kidding me," she said, shaking her head. The place was a quarter mile from where they'd stopped for the day but couldn't have been more different.

She supposed that once upon a time, this had been another lovely, picturesque farmhouse, surrounded by clucking chickens and tended by a farm wife in a frilly apron. Once upon a time being maybe fifty years ago.

She got out of the car and shaded her eyes against the glare of the sun, but the light just made the house look worse. She had no idea what color the wood had once been, but now it was a uniform shade of gray. Vines had pulled many of the boards apart. The front porch sagged in the middle, the railing that surrounded it warped in some places, broken in others. There wasn't a hint of glass in any of the windows, but the fact that they were all boarded up with new wood suggested it might be a vampire nest after all, despite its condition.

"What a charming home," Gabriel muttered. "I can't imagine why Ian chooses to spend the day elsewhere."

A breeze rustled through the vines that were still working at tearing the house to shreds. Hannah nearly gagged at the stink that wafted from the house on that breeze.

"Jesus!" she said, pinching her nose. "What the hell is that smell?"

Gabriel wrinkled his nose and stared up at the roof, which had cracked open in multiple places. "Bat guano."

"Bats?" She shivered. *Like big, furry cockroaches.* She suppressed a groan. "And I bet the place is just crawling with roaches, too."

"Wouldn't surprise me," Gabriel agreed, taking a step toward the front door. He pulled up so suddenly she almost bumped into him. His expression changed from mild disgust to . . . something else, though damned if she knew what it was.

"What's the matter?" she asked.

Gabriel turned to regard the road. His eyes hardened and his lips pulled away from his teeth to reveal his fangs.

"Gabe?" She wasn't at all sure she wanted to know what was wrong.

He shook his head. "Not here, not now," he said, but he was talking to himself, not to her. He turned to her and held out his hand. "Give me the keys."

"Huh?" So maybe it wasn't the most intelligent-sounding response she could have made, but she had no idea what was going through his head.

"The car keys. Give them to me. My mother is coming. I can assure you, you don't want to be caught in the middle if she and I face each other."

She bit her lip. Boy, would she ever feel like a sitting duck if Gabriel hit the road and Camille decided to stop by and chat.

Gabriel read her hesitation easily. "It's me she's after, not you. And now that she senses me near these fledglings, she'll be even more sure I've betrayed her. Now give me the keys."

"Do you know how to drive?"

He didn't answer, but suddenly she blinked, and he was gone, the car pulling out of the driveway at top speed. She squeezed her eyes shut and took a deep breath that was supposed to calm her. Would have worked better if it weren't for the bat stench. That had probably been the creepiest glamour she'd ever encountered. Usually, she at least had some sense that time had passed, some awareness that she'd been spaced out for a bit. This time, there'd been nothing.

"Dammit," she said, watching the car as Gabriel sped away. Perhaps he wasn't used to driving, but he seemed to have no hesitation about breaking the speed limit. The car practically turned the next corner on two wheels, tires screaming in protest. In the distance, she spied another car approaching. Could be anyone, of course, but it wasn't like this little country road saw a whole lot of traffic.

She had the choice of standing out here like an idiot and watching Camille approach, or going into the condemned, rotting house like an idiot and trying to rescue the poor mortal who was trapped inside. Giving the house another once-over, she decided that Camille was probably the only creature scary enough to make her think the house was the lesser of two evils.

The boards on the porch creaked and groaned ominously as she stepped on them, and she hoped she wasn't about to fall through. Camille's car was too close for comfort, so Hannah stiffened her spine and pushed the front door open.

Inside, the stench of bat guano was enough to make her eyes water. The boards over the windows blocked out almost all light, but after she'd stood blinking in the dark for a few minutes, her eyes adjusted. A little bit of light seeped in through cracks in the walls. Enough to allow her to see deeper pools of blackness in the shadows.

The house groaned and creaked around her, and she heard little scuttling sounds. Or maybe that was just her overactive imagination.

"My kingdom for a flashlight," she muttered. Or a crowbar, to pry the boards off the windows. She might not have been able to bring herself to shoot the sleeping fledglings in the head, but she figured she could handle letting the light in.

"Hello?" she called, but nerves made her voice come out in little more than a whisper. She clenched her fist and hit herself in the thigh. There was nothing to be afraid of. The vamps were fast asleep. And as far as she knew, bats slept in the daytime too. She cleared her throat.

"Hello?" she tried again, louder this time. No one answered. Was the mortal gagged? Unconscious?

Dead?

Shaking despite her reassurances to herself, she wedged the door open with a hunk of rotten wood that had once been a piece of baseboard.

The light revealed an inside as decrepit as the outside. Mildewed wallpaper hung in strips from water-stained walls. A patchy, moth-eaten rug covered a patchy, moth-eaten floor that was coated with a half inch or so of dirt. Little pellets of what she assumed were rat or mouse droppings added to the all-around lovely aroma. Her stomach gurgled unhappily, but she hadn't eaten any breakfast so she supposed she wasn't likely to up-chuck.

Doubting it would do her any good, she reached into her

pocket and pulled out her gun. At least it made her feel a little less helpless.

She ventured down the hallway and peered into the next room. Unfortunately, the light of the open door didn't reach this far. Once again, she paused, waiting for her eyes to adjust, wondering if they would adjust enough.

There looked to be an especially dark lump on the floor about a yard into the room, to her left. She stared at it hard, trying to force her eyes to penetrate the gloom, but she had no luck. Trembling in superstitious terror, her heart throbbing in her throat, she crept into the room, toward the patch of darkness. When she explored with the tip of her foot, she felt the yielding softness of flesh. She swallowed a cry of alarm, though she couldn't stop her reflexive jump.

Whoever it was she'd just poked with her toe made no move to attack her. In fact, it didn't move at all. Forcing a couple of deep breaths, she squatted beside the body and felt for its throat. It was a man, she discovered as her fingers encountered a flat, muscular chest. His chest rose and fell with even, steady breaths, and he showed no sign of waking up even when she slapped his face. A vampire, then. Not the mortal she was here to save.

Maybe she should wait, hope Gabe was able to lose his pursuit and come back to help. But what were the chances of that? Besides, the mortal might need immediate medical attention. Hannah didn't want to know how she'd explain anything on the 911 call, but she'd worry about that later.

She rose and squinted once more into the darkness. She thought she saw a tiny hint of light on the far wall. Perhaps that was a window. Maybe the wood around the frame was rotten enough that she'd be able to pull the boards off without the help of a crowbar. That would make for one less vamp in the world, at least.

She took a slow, deep breath—through her mouth—then started cautiously picking her way across the darkened room toward the window.

Not cautiously enough.

Her foot came into contact with what felt like another body. This time, her reflexive jump landed her on what felt like someone's hand. She listed to the side and took several staggering steps to try to regain her balance.

Her right foot landed on empty air. The gun dropped from her hand as she frantically windmilled her arms, but she was hopelessly off balance.

With a choked scream, she fell.

19

Hannah awoke to pitch darkness, an aching head, and a throbbing wrist. With a little groan, she pushed herself up into a sitting position, sending a stabbing pain down her left arm. She cradled her injured arm close to her body and shivered. She must have landed on it when she'd fallen.

Moving slowly and carefully, she checked out the rest of her body, making sure all her parts were intact. It seemed that in spite of the aching head and banged-up arm, she hadn't suffered much damage. She peered upward into the darkness, but could see nothing.

Great. Just great. How was she supposed to get out of here if she couldn't see her hand in front of her face? She wondered how long she'd been out.

Telling herself she'd moan about the pain later, she rose to her feet and began exploring the space around her, arms stretched out in front of her as she groped through the darkness. When she found a wall, her sense of relief was completely out of proportion, considering her still-dire situation. But at

least she had a point of reference. Even if that point of reference was slimy with what felt like wet moss. And probably
crawling with six- and eight-legged beasties.

She sucked in a quick breath. "Don't even *think* about pan-
icking!" she told herself sternly. She continued to feel her way
around the wall, one agonizingly slow step after another, looking for a door or a stairway. But when she found the door, she
discovered it was locked. She treated it to a few karate kicks,
but it didn't budge. A shiver crawled up her spine. Except for
the fortified windows upstairs, most of this house looked like
it would collapse if you breathed on it too hard. Which suggested this door had been reinforced. Not a good sign at all.

Panic hammered at her self-control, but she held it at bay.
When she remembered her cell phone, she practically wept
with relief.

Her hand shaking, she pulled the phone out of her pocket
and flipped it open.

The good news was it hadn't been damaged in her fall.
The bad news was she wasn't getting a signal. She tried reaching up on tiptoe, moving the phone around to every conceiv-
able angle, but to no avail.

At least she had a little light, while the battery lasted. She
held the phone out in front of her like a flashlight and examined the door. As she'd suspected, it was brand new, complete
with a heavy deadbolt.

Swallowing hard, Hannah turned to face the room. In the
dim glow of her cell phone, she made out the shape of a body,
lying on the floor not five feet from where she stood. Reluctantly, she went to kneel beside the body.

It was a young girl, probably in her early twenties. Her short hair had been dyed jet black and arranged in spikes that resembled Gabriel's 'do. A pair of metal balls pierced one eyebrow, and another pierced her nose. Blood crusted her throat, and Hannah discerned several punctures there. She touched her fingers to the girl's throat and found a thready pulse.

"Can you hear me?" she asked, giving the girl's shoulder a little shake. There was no response.

Hannah panned the cell phone's light down the rest of the girl's body, looking for other injuries. And she found them.

The girl's T-shirt had been ripped open, and her poor breasts were covered with bite marks. A pair of ratty jeans and torn white panties were gathered down around one ankle. There were more bite marks around her inner thighs, but there was more than just blood crusted between her legs. Hannah shuddered in sympathy. Along with the other injuries, the girl's arms and legs were covered with bruises, which suggested she'd been conscious and fighting during her ordeal.

Hannah glared upward at the hole in the ceiling. If she got out of here before the sun set, she suspected she'd now be able to get over her moral qualms about shooting sleeping vampires in the head.

Wishing she could do more for the girl, Hannah did her best to get her dressed before she froze to death in the winter chill. The girl remained a dead weight, and Hannah wondered what her chances of survival were.

Pretty damn bad, if they didn't get out of here.

Once more using her cell phone for light, Hannah examined their basement prison. With a shock, she saw two more bodies lying on the floor. Both women, one considerably older than the other, and when Hannah got close enough, she saw that they, too, had been raped and bitten.

Both were still alive, their pulses as thready as the punky girl's.

Her stomach lurched. Gabriel said he sensed *one* mortal in this house. Which meant two out of these three women were fledgling vampires. But Hannah had no clue how to tell which two.

"Oh, this is just getting better and better," she muttered.

She explored every inch of the basement, but she didn't find any way out. She *did* find her gun, which luckily had dropped into the basement with her. Great. Now she was armed. But she was still in deep, deep shit. After all, she could only shoot one vamp at a time, and this house was teeming with them.

The clock on her cell phone told her it was after four already. Which meant she had at most two hours before her future playmates rose. She made one more futile attempt to get a signal, then reluctantly closed the phone to save the battery. When the sun went down, she'd need that feeble light to have even a chance of killing some of the vamps.

ॐ

SOMEONE WAS SCREAMING. A high, shrill keen that overlay a cacophony of other sounds. Banging and crashing. Pleas for mercy. Cries of pain and terror. Sobs.

Drake jerked awake, his body awash with sweat. The house was eerily silent in contrast to the clamor of his dream. He took a deep breath to calm the hammering of his heart.

And that's when he smelled it. Blood. Strong and fresh.

He leapt out of bed, shaking his head to clear the lingering cobwebs, and saw that his door was standing open. The reek came from somewhere below. He reached out with his senses and felt two vampires down there.

Two vampires, and no one else.

What had happened to all Camille's fledglings? And her mortal pets? The air stank of doom.

Bracing himself, Drake cautiously left his cell and peered over the banister. What he saw sapped the strength from his knees, and he had to hold on to the banister for balance.

Gabriel stood in the entryway below, using a dampened white towel to wipe the blood from his face and hands. Around him, bodies and pieces of bodies lay strewn all over the floor.

The butler and Camille's other mortals lay together in one corner, their corpses stacked like firewood, intact, but very much dead. The others, though . . .

Drake couldn't even have said how many dead fledglings there were down there, based on the profusion of body parts. Except Gabriel had lined up the heads in a semi-circle around his feet. Eight heads. All eight of Camille's fledglings.

Camille sat huddled in one corner, her arms wrapped around her knees, her shoulders heaving with sobs. Gabriel finished wiping off blood, though his clothes and hair were still soaked with it, and tossed the towel onto the floor in front of his mother. She didn't look up.

"So," he said, his voice calm and level, "now you see what it would have been like if I really *had* been behind the attack, Mother. Do you believe now that it wasn't me?"

Camille raised her head, and Drake flinched to see what had become of this proud, arrogant creature. Her eyes were red and swollen with crying, her jaw slack with despair. Worse than that was the utter terror on her face. She was pressed into that corner as if she hoped to disappear into the wall, and her whole body shook with tremors.

What the hell had Gabriel done? And how had he managed it, when Camille was obviously older than he?

Gabriel glanced up and caught sight of Drake. "Oh, good. You're up. If you'd like to be reunited with Hannah and Jules, come with me. They most likely could use our help right now." He started picking his way through the carnage toward the front door.

Drake hadn't the faintest idea what to think of what he was seeing. Gabriel sounded as calm as if he hadn't just massacred his mother's minions, oblivious to the blood and gore that surrounded him. Was he completely mad?

"Are you coming?" Gabriel asked, his hand on the front door.

Numb and nauseated, Drake started down the stairs, trying not to look at the slaughtered bodies. For whatever reason, Gabriel had spared him the fate of Camille's fledglings. Drake supposed he should find out what he wanted.

When he reached the bottom of the stairs, Drake gave Gabriel a visual once over. He was dressed all in black, which helped disguise the blood, but there was so much of it no one could possibly miss it.

"You're going to attract a lot of attention if you don't change clothes and wash your hair." He was impressed with his own calm, considering he was obviously in the presence of a madman. A very dangerous madman.

Gabriel looked down at himself and shook his head. "Can't

be helped. I've led your friends to Ian's hiding place, and I've taken their car. They're in danger, and it's a half-hour drive. There's no time to waste. This," he said, sweeping his hand to indicate the carnage, "is none of your concern. Your friends are. Follow me or not. Your choice."

Then he was out the door. This could all be some bizarre kind of trap, but Drake could see no reason why Gabriel wouldn't just go ahead and kill him if he wanted to. And if what he said was true . . .

Drake made it out the door just in time to see Gabriel, driving Hannah's rental, pull out into traffic. Cursing, Drake sprinted for his own car. Luckily, Gabriel had to stop at a red light, or Drake might have lost him before he even got started.

A half-hour drive. Drake glanced at the darkening sky. Ian's fledglings wouldn't be up yet, but Ian would be. He could only hope that Jules and Hannah were well hidden, and that Ian wouldn't be looking for them.

The light turned green. Both Gabriel and Drake ignored the speed limit in their race against time.

࿓

JULES YAWNED AND GOT a mouthful of straw. He spit it out and sat up abruptly, shaking straw from his face and picking it out of his hair. He rubbed his eyes and looked around him, seeing the horse stall where he and Hannah and Gabriel had taken shelter this morning. Only Hannah and Gabriel weren't there.

He closed his eyes and reached out with his senses, but he was alone. Alarm shot through his system and he sprang to his feet. The only presence, mortal or vampire, that he sensed came from the distance—from the house that Gabriel claimed Ian's fledglings were in.

The house was barely in range of his "vamp-dar," but he sensed a strong vampire presence, as well as a much more feeble mortal one. He'd have to get closer to examine the psychic footprints more carefully.

Hoping against hope that Hannah was nowhere near that damn house, he jogged out into the failing light of late afternoon. The car was gone. Maybe that was a good sign, though he couldn't imagine why Hannah would have left him alone here in the barn. Was Gabriel up to some kind of trickery?

He hesitated only a moment before continuing his run across the fields. After a couple hundred yards, Jules paused and reached out again.

His unease redoubled. There were *nine* vampires in that house. And two mortals. Instinct told him that one of those mortals had to be Hannah, though he couldn't imagine what the damn fool woman was doing in that house without him.

The sun was setting rapidly, and soon even fledgling vampires would be up and about. There was no time to waste.

His jog turned into an all-out sprint, fueled by something akin to terror. If something happened to Hannah because of him . . .

Fear leant him speed, and soon he was dashing up the steps of a crumbling, derelict house that stank to high heaven. A flood of bats poured from the eaves, squeaking shrilly as they took flight.

The front door was propped open, and Jules plunged inside, only to find himself surrounded by inky blackness. The windows had been boarded over, so the fading sunlight didn't make it inside.

"Hannah!" he cried, looking frantically right and left though he couldn't see a damn thing.

"Jules!"

He wasn't sure whether the feeling that flooded him was relief, or even more terror. What the fuck was she doing in this house?

"I fell through the floor," she shouted, "and the basement door's locked. Be careful. There are vamps everywhere."

He felt the minutes ticking away like a physical force, but he had enough common sense not to go plunging blindly toward her voice without thinking. He'd do her no good if he found her hole in the floor and fell through it with her.

Adrenaline surging through his system, he grabbed one of the boards covering the window and tore it loose, letting in a stream of red-gold light. He tore off two more boards, and the light revealed a doorway to his right. A sleeping vampire lay on the floor near that doorway, and when Jules approached, he saw the hole in the floor. He needed to get Hannah out of here, but he wasn't sure how long it would take. Best to take out one of the enemies while he could.

Jules reached down and snapped the sleeping vampire's neck with one hard jerk. Two more lay on the floor on the other side of the hole, and he dispatched them with equal speed. Then he lay down on his belly and peered into the hole.

Hannah stood in what looked to be a basement, looking up at him by the light of her cell phone. He reached his hand down.

"Can you jump up and reach me?" he asked, but he already

knew the answer. She'd need springs in her legs to reach him. She tried anyway, but she didn't come close.

"The door's over there," she said, pointing, "but it's locked."

He looked in the direction she was pointing, but it didn't look like the entrance to the basement was in this room. Damn it, he didn't have time to go exploring! But he couldn't be sure he'd be able to force the door if he jumped down there, so he had no choice.

A quick psychic check showed him four vampires upstairs. And two downstairs, with Hannah.

"I'll see if I can find the door," he said, standing up reluctantly. "There are two vampires down there with you."

"I know. Unfortunately, there are three unconscious people, and I don't know which two are vamps."

"The two over there," he said, pointing vaguely, but he was already heading back to the entryway to see if he could find the basement stairs.

The sun was almost completely down, the missing boards no longer lighting his way. He took a page from Hannah's book and opened his cell phone. Its bluish light picked out three doorways that opened off the entryway. The first one proved to be a closet, or at least what had once been a closet. Now it looked like a nesting place for rats and spiders. The second opened into what might have been a bedroom.

The third opened on a set of crumbling stone steps, leading downward. He hurried to the bottom, almost tumbling down headfirst when his foot slipped on some loose rubble.

The door was brand new, and secured with a deadbolt and a bar. He twisted the deadbolt and raised the bar, then slammed the door open.

Hannah stood over the bodies of two women, her cell phone in one hand, her gun in the other. A psychic check confirmed the women were vampires, but as usual, Hannah seemed reluctant to shoot. He moved in quickly, meaning to snap their necks, but when he drew up beside Hannah, he saw exactly why she didn't shoot.

The wounds on the women's throats were fresh, not more than a day old.

"*Marde!*" he cursed. They were so new there was no way they'd had their first kill yet. Hell, they probably hadn't even awakened since they'd been made.

"They can't be Killers yet, can they?" Hannah asked. She didn't wait for his answer. "So they can be saved. Join the Guardians?"

He nodded reluctantly, knowing he was about to have a battle on his hands.

"There's also a mortal over there," Hannah said. "I don't know if there's a chance she's going to live or not. She hasn't woken up all day, and her pulse is very weak."

He shook his head, hating what he had to do. "We have to get out of here, Hannah. And we don't have time to drag three unconscious women out with us."

"We can't just leave them here!" she protested.

He stood up and glowered at her in the darkness. "There are four Killers still alive in this house, and they'll be waking up any second now. And one of them is Ian, who—"

"No, Ian isn't here. At least, Gabriel said he wasn't."

"And where the fuck is Gabriel?"

"Long story," Hannah said. She tucked the number pad of her cell phone into the waistband of her jeans, leaving it flipped open for a little light, then stuffed her gun in a pocket. She bent to grab the arm of one of the young fledglings and slung it over her arm. "Help me out here," she said, struggling to her feet, the fledgling a dead weight.

Jules didn't have time to argue with her. He was all for gallantly rescuing the three women, but Hannah had to come first, and if he didn't get her out of here *now*, she'd never get out alive. He met her eyes and wrapped her in glamour. The fledgling's arm slipped from her grip. He put his hand on Hannah's arm and gave her a little push toward the door. But it was already too late.

From upstairs, a voice howled in fury as one of the resident vampires discovered his dead friends. Hannah wouldn't move fast enough under the influence of glamour, and he doubted his concentration would hold anyway. He released her, stepping in front of her to take the lead and grabbing her hand.

"Run!" he said, jerking her toward the door.

ॐ

HANNAH CAME TO HERSELF and almost fell flat on her face because Jules was practically pulling her arm out of its socket as he shouted at her to run.

She wanted to tell him exactly what she thought about him and his glamour, but she heard the outraged cries from upstairs and realized there wasn't time for it. She managed to get her feet under her and stumbled after Jules as he dragged her up the stairs. She was too off-balance to get her gun out of her pocket.

"Let go, Jules!" she yelled, though she didn't slow down.

The jackass ignored her, naturally. She banged her shoulder against the doorway as the two of them burst into the hall. Her cell phone came loose and clattered to the floor. Its light shut off, leaving them in total blackness. Suddenly, she was glad for Jules's grip on her hand. She sure hoped he knew where he was going.

The house seemed to come alive with voices, all angry. No, furious. A body barreled into her, and she lost her grip on Jules's hand.

"Hannah!" he yelled, but she couldn't answer him because the impact with the floor knocked all the wind out of her lungs.

The guy on top of her felt like he weighed about two-fifty. He seemed to think that because he outweighed her, she'd cower in fear, for he made only the most half-assed effort to restrain her. Even before she could get any breath into her lungs, she jerked her head up, making solid contact with his nose. She felt and heard the cartilage crack. He howled in pain, and blood spurted her face. She hit him again as he put his hand to his broken nose, conveniently giving her some fingers to break. Another howl, and he rolled off of her.

Hannah lurched to her feet, trying to run toward the sound of Jules's voice, but someone grabbed her from behind, forearm pressing against her windpipe. Her back slammed into a wall of muscle. Immediately, she turned and bent her head, trapping his hand between her chin and her left shoulder. Then, she started turning to the right, bending his wrist at an unhappy angle. As he realized he was coming out on the losing side of this, she punctuated her point by stomping his instep. He yanked his hand free of her grip but was too stupid to know he was outmatched by the "little lady."

When he shifted his grip lower, she hooked one of her feet around his ankle, pulling forward as she sat down.

His feet flew out from under him, and her butt made solid contact with his groin when they landed. At last, he let go, and once more Hannah scrambled to her feet.

A hand clamped around her wrist, but though her immediate impulse was to counterattack, instinct or intuition told her it was Jules, and she didn't try to break the grip.

Together, they charged toward what she sincerely hoped was the doorway. But they didn't get far before a blinding white light seared their eyeballs.

Ian Squires laughed in delight.

20

Jules blinked in the blinding light of a Coleman lantern. He put himself between Hannah and Ian, but it was a futile gesture. Ian laughed and put the lantern down on the floor, its eerie white glow filling the room with alternating glare and shadows.

One of Ian's fledglings lay on the floor, clutching his groin. Another was using both hands to try to stanch the flow of blood from his nose. Two of the fingers on his left hand were bent at odd angles. Despite their dire situation, Jules couldn't help giving Hannah an amazed look. She managed a sickly grin and a shrug.

"Your woman seems to have a great deal of spirit," Ian said. "I'm sure you're going to enjoy watching me crush that spirit out of her."

The two uninjured fledglings eyed Hannah with lust and hunger. Surprisingly, she clutched Jules's arm and kind of tucked herself behind his back, as if hiding. But Hannah didn't back down from anything, and there was no way she'd be sheltering behind him. She was up to something.

Hoping to buy Hannah time for whatever she was up to, Jules swept a contemptuous glance over Ian's fledglings.

"Where did you get these guys from, Ian? It looks like you raided the local reform school." The four of them resembled nothing so much as a quartet of teenage gorillas, with bulging muscles and vapid expressions.

Ian smiled. "In point of fact, a couple of them have spent time in such an establishment. Have you any idea the kinds of things young hoodlums learn to do in reform school when girls aren't available?" He leered at Jules and licked his lips.

Once upon a time, that threat would have made him shudder. Now, he managed to face his maker with no change of expression. "Same things you learned from Gabriel?"

His taunt hit home. Ian snarled, showing fang. Dire though the situation was, Jules managed a hint of a smile, glad to know he'd scored a hit, glad to know he hadn't given his maker the satisfaction of flinching.

Ian regained his composure, glancing at Hannah for a moment before meeting Jules's eyes with an expression of gleeful malice. "Did you tell your woman all about our lovely night together, Jules? Did you tell her how you begged me to fuck you?"

The hateful memory still lurked in the background of his psyche, but he refused to let Ian win a battle of wills. He met Ian's eyes with what he hoped was cool aplomb. "Did you tell your fledglings that you couldn't get anyone, man or woman, to fuck you without force or glamour?"

Ian's control broke, and he took two furious strides forward before he pulled up. "No!" he said. "No quick death for you. The boys and I are going to take turns riding your woman while you watch. Then, when we've fucked her to death, we'll start on you. My dear mentor taught me far more than I've ever showed you, but that will soon change."

"Sounds like fun," Hannah said from behind Jules's back, "but I think I'll pass."

Ian laughed at her. Big mistake.

Out of the corner of his eye, Jules saw Hannah's hand rise up beside his arm. And in that hand was her gun.

The gun went off with a deafening boom, but her aim was off. The bullet slammed into Ian's shoulder instead of into his head. He roared in pain.

"Get down!" Hannah shouted, and Jules obeyed without thought as Ian's fledglings charged them.

The one with the bleeding nose was slightly ahead of the rest. The gun boomed again, and the fledgling's head jerked backward. He fell and didn't get up. Hannah squeezed off one more shot before she froze. Another fledgling fell, never to rise again.

Ian, his hand clamped to his bleeding shoulder, his face contorted in pain and rage, hit Jules with the full force of his glamour. Jules remained crouched on the floor, unable to move a muscle, while Hannah stood over him in her shooter's stance, unable to pull the trigger.

The two remaining fledglings looked half insane with hunger, their eyes bulging as drool dripped from their fangs. Ian must have been starving them, and the scent of blood in the air was overpowering.

Ian plucked the gun from Hannah's nerveless fingers and

tossed it over his shoulder into the darkness beyond. He shoved Jules aside with his foot.

"Play with him," he said to his fledglings, "but don't kill him. That pleasure will be mine. I'm going to punish the little lady for killing your brothers in arms."

Ian moved around behind Hannah, pulling her hair away from her throat. He raised his eyebrows when he saw the punctures that Gabriel had left there.

"I see someone has tasted her already." He looked down at Jules, who lay on his back on the floor, helpless to break the hold of his glamour. Ian clucked his tongue. "Naughty, naughty. But I'll show her how a *real* man does it." He punctuated that statement by grinding his hips against Hannah's backside. His hands looped around to the button on her jeans, and he pulled his lips away from his fangs.

"No!" Jules shouted as Ian sank his fangs into Hannah's neck.

The two fledglings came at him, but it was as if they moved in slow motion. The red haze was back, the haze he'd felt in the hotel room when he'd seen what Gabriel had done.

The red haze that shielded his mind from Ian's glamour.

Jules slammed into Ian and Hannah, the force of the impact knocking Ian loose. With a snarl of unadulterated hatred, Jules flung himself at his maker. Ian was so startled by his inability to control his fledgling that he didn't even get his hands up. Jules used his knees to pin Ian's wrists to the floor, then started swinging his fists.

He was barely aware of what he was doing as he landed one punch after another on Ian's face. Bone crunched with each blow. Blood coated his knuckles. Ian screamed, high and shrill, his body writhing as he tried to get out from under Jules, to no avail.

Jules was still battering his maker's face when the insane rage began to wear off. Ian was crying and begging for mercy, his face a pulpy mess, as Jules recoiled in horror at what he had done.

Ian's well-honed survival instincts must have alerted him that Jules's mind was back, because suddenly, Jules couldn't move. Dammit, even in his state of pathetic misery, Ian was too powerful a foe!

Ian's face was so ruined he couldn't open his eyes, but his hands rose and groped for Jules's neck. Jules struggled to call the blind rage back and break the glamour, but it stubbornly refused to come on command. Ian's hands found his neck and started to squeeze. Weakly, at first, but the grip grew stronger as Ian mumbled curses and threats through his broken teeth. Jules couldn't breathe and realized his maker wanted to knock him out so he could finish healing. Then, no doubt, he would pay Jules back in spades for every punch he had landed.

The sound of a gunshot shattered the air. Ian's head jerked and a gout of blood spurted from a bullet wound in the side of his skull.

The glamour let up, and Ian's hands fell away from Jules's neck. Gasping for breath, Jules looked toward the source of the gunshot.

In the doorway stood Drake, holding Hannah's gun. Beside him stood Gabriel, two dead fledglings at his feet.

Jules shook his head to clear the remaining fog, his eyes searching the room for Hannah.

His heart nearly stopped when he saw her.

She was lying on the floor on her back. Blood pooled by her head. Lots of blood. Way too much blood, and more of it continued to pour from the ragged tear in her throat.

With an incoherent cry of despair, Jules launched himself across the room to her, clamping his hand over the wound, trying desperately to stanch the flow as he cradled her head in his lap. Her pulse was weak and slow, her body limp.

"Goddammit, no!" he shouted, holding her more tightly against him as the life continued to seep out of her body.

"She's not going to make it," Gabriel said, coming to kneel beside her.

"Shut the fuck up!" Jules snarled. "She's going to make it! She has to!"

But he could feel it as clearly as Gabriel could. She was dying, and there wasn't a damn thing he could do about it.

"You have to change her," Gabriel said.

Jules blinked, wishing Gabriel would go away and leave him alone. If these were to be his last few moments with her . . .

"Bite her!" Gabriel said, more urgently. "Change her. But hurry up, she isn't going to last much longer."

Jules felt as if all his breath were sucked from his lungs at once. Change her? Change Hannah? He looked up and met Gabriel's eyes. The older vampire was dead serious.

"I can't do that," Jules said, despair heavy in his voice.

It was one of Eli's cardinal rules—there were more than enough vampires in the world already. There was no excuse for making more. He clutched Hannah more tightly, his heart bleeding as heavily as her neck.

Gabriel's voice was eerily calm, though his eyes pierced Jules with deadly malice. "So you're going to let the woman you love die because Saint Eli decreed 'thou shalt not make vampires?'" He turned his head to the side and spat as if the words tasted bad. "You're a weak-minded fool. And if you let her die, I will take both you and Drake apart limb from limb."

There was no doubt that Gabriel meant what he said. Obviously, he was more than just "fond" of Hannah. Jules doubted Gabriel could inflict any greater pain than that of losing Hannah, but he glanced up at Drake, hating that he, too, would pay the price if Jules refused.

Drake looked unruffled by the threat. "I'll stand by whatever decision you make. No matter what."

Jules let out a shuddering breath. If he changed her, Hannah would hate him forever. She was already uncomfortable with his superior strength and his glamour. How could she tolerate being his fledgling?

I own you, Ian's voice whispered in his memory.

But if he didn't change her, she would die. She might die anyway—not everyone accepted the psychic lifeline—but how could he not offer her the choice? If she hated him, if he hated himself, if Eli and the Guardians condemned him, that was just the price he'd have to pay.

Jules raised Hannah to a sitting position and covered her still-bleeding wound with his mouth.

It was the first time he'd tasted human blood since he'd become a vampire, and the rush of it was indescribable. No milk to make his stomach revolt, no medicinal-tasting chemicals to preserve the blood, no chill of refrigeration. He moaned in almost sexual pleasure as he drank, and he could see with total clarity how easy it would be to become addicted.

Even more compelling than the physical experience was the psychic one. As soon as he'd swallowed that first sip, he felt as though the psychic walls around his mind crumbled, and he could reach out as he never could before. He felt Hannah's life force like a physical presence in his mind, becoming weaker and weaker with every sluggish beat of her heart. She was pulling away, fading. He was losing her.

Acting on pure instinct, he reached out to her, straining against the limits of his own body, willing to follow her into the abyss of death rather than give up. He felt a connection, tenuous and shaky.

When Ian had changed him, Jules had grabbed onto that psychic lifeline in a reflexive gesture, no thought involved. Impending death had reduced him to mindless instinct, and Ian had gleefully reeled him in before Jules had any idea what he was giving up to save his own life.

But Hannah knew. Jules felt her hesitation and strained toward her, reaching desperately.

Hold on to me, Hannah, he urged as she started to slip away again. *Don't let go. Please don't let go.* Still, she was fading, and pain knifed through him, body and soul.

Don't let go, he begged again. *I need you. I love you.*

The words sent a shock through his system, but there was no denying the truth of them. He loved her, and he was *not* going to lose her!

Dammit, Hannah! You're too damn tough to die, so hold on tight and come back to me.

The pull slackened, but she still didn't come to him. He could feel her uncertainty, her fear. He imagined surrounding her in comforting warmth, drawing her away from the chilling abyss into the heat of his arms. She resisted, and immediately he stopped. He couldn't draw her away—she had to come to him of her own free will.

Steadying his nerve, feeling like his heart was in his throat even though he couldn't feel his body, he loosened his grip—not letting go, but letting her feel his surrender, letting her know he wouldn't keep her against her will. He visualized a strong, thin lifeline anchored immovably in his heart as he let go with his hands, spreading his arms to his sides and laying his head back.

She could follow that line back to him. Or she could slide into the abyss, ripping his heart from his chest and taking it with her.

I love you, he repeated. *I'm yours if you want me.*

For what seemed like an eternity, they balanced on the brink of the abyss. Jules had surrendered his heart to her, but it would mean nothing if she couldn't return the gesture, couldn't give him a little piece of her soul and thereby bind herself to him forever.

Then, suddenly, he was pulling away from the abyss, and Hannah was following. He practically wept with relief. The psychic connection broke, and he was back in his body, in the real world, with Hannah cradled in his arms. He withdrew his fangs and pressed a kiss on the wound, then gathered her in even closer, tucking her head under his chin. A tentative probe confirmed that she'd made the transition, though she was still unconscious.

"She'll be out for days," Gabriel said. "The transition—"

"I know," Jules interrupted. He and his fellow Guardians had rescued enough newly made fledglings to know what to expect. The next few weeks were going to be very difficult for Hannah. He rocked her in his arms, hoping that somewhere deep inside she felt the comfort he was trying so desperately to give her.

"So, what happens now?" Drake asked.

Jules didn't want to think about that. "There are two more new fledglings in the basement. And another mortal woman, too. She's badly in need of medical attention."

Drake and Gabriel exchanged a look. Gabriel sighed heavily.

"Take the fledglings to Eli," he said. "I very much doubt they were volunteers, not with Ian as their maker. Much as I loathe my father, I know he's very good with new fledglings."

"What about the mortal?" Drake asked.

"I'll take her to the hospital, but I doubt she's going to make it."

When Jules closed his eyes and concentrated, he could see what Gabriel meant. The mortal woman's psychic footprint was very faint, though not as faint as Hannah's had been. There was at least some chance she would survive.

He glared up at Gabriel. "You're not going to kill her." Who he was kidding by issuing orders, he didn't know, but Gabriel took his tone in stride.

"No, I won't kill her. I fed last night, remember? Unlike Ian, I'm not a glutton. When I kill, it's for a reason." He turned to Drake. "Help me get them out of the basement."

The two of them left the room, and Jules heard them descending the stairs into the basement. He sat numbly on the cold floor, holding Hannah and trying to absorb the enormity of what he'd just done.

He'd created a fledgling. Never in his wildest dreams would he have imagined he'd do such a thing. He swallowed hard, remembering the taste of her blood in his mouth. The memory was heady, and embarrassingly pleasant, but he didn't feel any unbearable compulsion to start killing people. Would he have become fatally addicted if she'd refused him and died? But then, he doubted he'd have survived. He'd thought his surrender was figurative, but it hadn't *felt* that way.

Drake and Gabriel returned, and Drake came to squat beside Jules. Jules met his solemn eyes. He was probably the only Guardian who wouldn't condemn him for what he'd done.

"Thank you," he said, more moved than he wanted to admit by the Killer's show of solidarity.

Drake nodded in acknowledgment. "I'll take her to Eli with the others," Drake said quietly. "He'll take good care of her, you know that."

Jules nodded tightly. He didn't want to, but he loosened his grip on Hannah and let Drake take her from him. They stood up together, and Jules planted one more soft kiss on Hannah's temple before Drake carried her from the room, leaving him alone with Gabriel.

He'd almost allowed himself to forget the deal he'd made with Gabriel, and what the consequences of breaking that deal would be. He should probably be very, very alarmed right this moment. But somehow he couldn't seem to feel much of anything except the heaviness of his heart. Perhaps he was in shock.

At the sound of Drake's car starting, Gabriel frowned and gave Jules a puzzled look.

"He's leaving without you?"

Jules shrugged. "It's not like I can go back to Philly after what I just did."

Gabriel cocked his head. "Why not?"

"Because Eli would kill me."

Gabriel looked disgusted. "So, you're going to make Hannah a vampire, and then you're just going to dump her in Eli's lap and wash your hands?"

Jules snarled at him. "You're not in any position to give lectures. And where the hell were you, anyway? Why was Hannah in this house? And why was she alone?"

To his surprise, Gabriel lowered his head and looked vaguely ashamed. "My apologies. Hannah and I were on our way here to try to rescue the mortal, but my mother caught up with us and I had to run for it." He shook his head. "I should have known Hannah wouldn't wait for me to come back."

For the first time, Jules took a really good look at Gabriel. The light of the Coleman lantern bleached a lot of the color out of his skin and hair, but Jules now saw the smudges of what he'd thought was dirt were actually blood. Dried blood, not the blood of Ian's fledglings.

"Is she dead?" Jules asked, wondering how Gabriel could have taken out a monster like Camille. He was strong, but she *should* be stronger.

An eerie light shone in Gabriel's eyes. "No, she's not dead. But right now I'm not sure she appreciates the distinction." He smiled, but it wasn't a pleasant expression. "I suppose I'm the new Master of Baltimore, though despite my mother's suspicions, I have no fledglings." He looked at Jules and curled his lips up to reveal his fangs. "I would have been here sooner, but I had to wait till her fledglings woke up enough to feel what I did to them. I wanted her to hear them scream. And I wanted her to know that sickening, helpless feeling that she could do nothing to stop me."

Jules took an involuntary step backward from the mad, dangerous creature who stood before him. The creature who'd promised him slow torture if he refused to give up everything he knew about the Guardians.

But Gabriel sheathed his fangs, that insane light fading from his eyes. The sneer turned into something almost like a smile. "Don't worry. I know you never intended to give me any information. You're a terrible liar."

"Then why did you give me Ian?"

A shrug. "Because it pleased me to do so. Of course, I'd intended to make you talk afterward."

"But you've changed your mind?" It sounded too good to be true, but Jules was sure of one thing—he didn't understand Gabriel worth a damn. Who knew what the freak was thinking, or what he would do?

Gabriel stepped closer and clapped a hand on Jules's shoulder. Jules managed to suppress the urge to pull away as Gabriel leaned in close.

"I've thought of a better way to strike at my father. Besides, Hannah needs you."

Those words were just a little more proof that Jules didn't get this guy. "Hannah's made it very clear she doesn't need anybody."

"That's what she thinks, but she's wrong. She was wrong even before you made her, and she's doubly wrong now. If I questioned you as I planned, you'd be broken when I was finished. You're no good to her broken."

Jules snorted. "I'm no good to her dead, either, which is what I'd be if I tried to go to her."

Gabriel released his shoulder. "Eli won't kill you."

"Somehow I don't think your assessment of his character is terribly reliable," Jules said.

"Why not? I've known him for almost five hundred years. He wasn't able to kill me, and I've done worse than you. Far, far worse."

About the last thing Jules had expected was for Gabriel to defend his father, but it was hard to miss the hint of wistfulness in his expression. It must have hurt like hell when Eli turned on him. Still, that didn't make his argument convincing.

"I used to think I knew him," Jules said, bitterness tingeing his voice. "Or at least, that I understood him. But that was before I knew he was a Killer who's been lying to me for almost eighty years."

Gabriel made a sound between a snort and a laugh. "Eli doesn't lie. He's a master of skirting the truth, but he's completely anal about not lying."

"For eighty years, he's been pretending that he's not a Killer, that he wants nothing more than to destroy Killers for the good of all humanity. As far as I'm concerned, that's an outright lie!"

Gabriel's eyes widened. "You don't know the truth about him, do you?" He chuckled. "That would explain a good many things."

"What truth? What are you talking about?"

Gabriel met his gaze squarely. "He *was* a Killer. But he cured himself." He smiled wryly. "Not on purpose. He was trying to kill himself in a fit of remorse but fucked it up." The smile turned into one of Gabriel's patented sneers. "That's when he decided all the rest of us needed to die. That's when he founded the Guardians." He sighed. "So no, Jules, he won't kill you for turning the woman you love into a vampire to save her from certain death. But if you're too chickenshit to go to her when she needs you, then I'd be happy to carry out my original plan."

Jules blinked, and suddenly his back was against the cold, crumbling wall, his feet off the ground as Gabriel crowded into his space.

"Don't misunderstand me, Guardian," Gabriel said. His breath reeked of blood and death. "I'm not the forgive and forget type. I *will* come to Philadelphia. And I *will* kill any Guardian who gets between me and my father when I come for him. If you truly love Hannah, then go to her. Let Eli help her through her transition. And then the both of you had better stay the hell out of my way. Now, should I take you to the train station, or should I start questioning you?"

It was hard to get a sound out with Gabriel's forearm pressed hard against his windpipe, but Jules managed to gasp the words "train station." The freak released him and gave him a shove out the door. Jules breathed deep of the fresh clean air, but Gabriel was walking briskly toward the car and he had to hurry to keep up.

The badly injured mortal woman lay across the backseat. Her skin was deathly pale, her breathing shallow. The life force Jules had sensed in her was growing even more faint.

"What are you going to do with her?" he asked as he got into the car.

Gabriel floored the gas pedal, and the car took off with a shriek of burning rubber and a fountain of gravel. Jules hastily fastened his seatbelt.

"I'll drop you at the train station," Gabriel said as the car continued to pick up speed. The maniac had to be doing about eighty on this quiet country road. "Then I'll take her to the emergency room."

Jules gripped the door handle and tried not to watch the road, figuring what he didn't know wouldn't hurt him. "Shouldn't we drop her at the emergency room first?"

"First or second, it doesn't matter. She's going to die anyway," Gabriel said with callous indifference.

"You don't know that! She might—"

"I've seen more human death than you can possibly imagine, Guardian. I know it when I see it. But I'll take her to the emergency room anyway. She'll probably last a day or two, maybe long enough for her family to come be with her at the end."

Jules would have argued further, but there was clearly no point in it.

They made it into the city in what had to be record time despite a stop at a convenience store bathroom to wash off the worst of the blood. Jules wondered how much glamour Gabriel used to avoid being stopped for any of the hundreds of moving violations he committed along the way.

True to his word, Gabriel dropped him at the train station. Jules had to pick up his luggage from the hotel before going anywhere, but he'd be extremely thankful to be out of Gabriel's presence and take a cab.

"I'll take care of returning the car for Hannah," Gabriel

said as Jules shut the door behind himself. "Take good care of her."

"I will," Jules said, once more bemused by Gabriel's apparent multiple personality disorder.

Then the car pulled out into traffic once more, and Jules was faced with a decision. He wasn't foolish enough to remain in Baltimore, but just because Gabriel had dropped him at the train station didn't mean he had to go to Philadelphia. For a moment, he entertained fantasies of leaving his past and all his troubles behind him, going somewhere new and starting over. Then, he returned to reality.

Maybe Gabriel was totally delusional, maybe Hannah didn't need him. And even if she did, maybe she wouldn't *want* him, not after what he'd done. But he owed it to her to let her make that choice herself.

Hoping that Gabriel was right about at least one thing— that Eli wasn't going to kill him on sight—Jules entered the train station and bought a one-way ticket to Philadelphia.

21

JULES STOOD OUTSIDE THE gates of Eli's mansion and shivered. Freezing rain pelted him, soaking through his clothes and chilling him to the bone, and yet still he hesitated. It had taken him three seemingly endless nights to work up the courage to come here, but now his courage was failing him.

Was Hannah awake yet? If so, would she hate him? He wasn't sure he could bear it if she did.

The intercom set into the gate suddenly squawked, nearly startling him out of his skin.

"How long are you planning to stand out there in the rain, Jules?" Eli's voice asked.

Jules groaned quietly. He'd told no one that he'd returned to Philadelphia. He'd shut off his cell phone and unplugged his home phone, needing the extra time to try to straighten out his thoughts. The time hadn't done him much good.

"How did you know it was me?" he asked, leaning closer to the speaker.

"Who else would stand at the gate in the rain for twenty minutes without ringing?"

"May I . . . come in?"

Eli didn't answer, but the lock on the gate buzzed. Gathering the remnants of his courage, Jules stepped through the gate and hurried up the path toward the house. At least it would feel good to come out of the cold, even if Eli was about to kill him. Or, worse, tell him that Hannah hated his guts and never wanted to see him again.

Eli met him at the door, silently handing him a towel. Jules took it gratefully and dried off as best he could, considering his clothes were soaked through. Eli led him to the library, where a merry fire crackled in the hearth. Jules stood so close to the fire he practically singed his eyebrows, drinking in the warmth of the flames. Behind him, he heard Eli sit down in one of the leather reading chairs. Bracing himself, Jules turned around to face the Founder.

He might have thought that after all he'd learned about Eli, he'd see the Founder with different eyes. But Eli still looked like Eli, a kind old man with a too-knowing stare.

Jules stuffed his hands into his pockets and resisted the urge to scuff his feet like a guilty ten-year-old. "So, are you going to kill me?" he asked.

One corner of Eli's mouth raised slightly. "Tempting, but no. I understand from Drake that there were . . . extenuating circumstances."

Yeah, that was one way to put it. He swallowed hard, shoving away his mental picture of Hannah lying bleeding on that floor.

"Was it worth it, Jules?" Eli asked softly. "Is everything all better now that you've had your revenge?"

Jules flinched. Eli always knew how to eviscerate a person with his words. Jules almost swallowed the rebuke without protest. But on second thought . . .

He sucked in a deep breath and met Eli's steady gaze. "If I hadn't gone to Baltimore to confront him, then I never would have been able to let go of the rage."

Eli raised an eyebrow. "Have you let it go then?"

It was tempting to give Eli the glib, easy answer, but Jules knew the Founder wouldn't settle for that. So he thought about it a long moment before he spoke. "I don't know if I'll ever let go completely. But what was once a bleeding wound is now no more than an ugly scar." His throat tightened. "If Hannah hadn't gotten hurt in the process, I'd have said it was worth it."

Eli's gaze frosted over. "You selfish, arrogant ass! Would it have been worth it if because of your pig-headed insistence on revenge Camille had destroyed the Guardians?"

Jules stood firm in the face of Eli's anger. "No, of course not. But she didn't."

"No thanks to you."

"It's not my fault you've lied to everyone for all these years."

Eli's eyes said he made no apologies. "I keep secrets for good reason, Jules. I know I can never atone for the things that I've done, but I'm going to keep trying anyway. The fewer people who know about my past, the better."

Jules shook his head. "So what you're saying is you're still going to keep your damn secrets."

"Yes. Drake has agreed not to share what he's learned about me. And if you start talking, he'll contradict you."

Jules knew he was playing with fire, practically daring Eli to change his mind about killing him, but he couldn't help himself. "Have you ever told Drake that the addiction is curable?"

For the first time Jules could remember, Eli looked genuinely stunned.

"Gabriel told me."

Eli shook his head and groaned. "How I wish I'd killed him when I had the chance!"

"I gather this means Drake has no idea."

Eli sighed. "No. And it's going to stay that way."

"Eli—"

"It's not curable. Not for someone his age, or someone who wants to live."

"What happened?" Jules asked, unable to repress his curiosity. "How did you do it?"

But Eli shook his head. "I'm not in the mood to share confidences. I tried to reproduce my results with others. Every one of them died, slowly and in terrible pain."

"But surely Drake has a right to know—"

"Don't push me on this, Jules." Eli's eyes flashed with anger. "If I thought telling him was the right thing to do, believe me, I would have done it by now."

"What gives you the right to decide that for him?" Jules's temper was stirring ominously, but he didn't feel any hint that he might lose control of it.

Eli steepled his fingers in front of his face and stared at the fire. "Drake is the most well-adjusted vampire I've ever known. And I've known a lot of vampires in my life. He's completely at peace with what he is because he's convinced he has no choice, and he's not the type to whine about his fate. But if he should start to think that maybe he has a choice after all . . . Do you really think it's fair to shatter his peace of mind when in all likelihood he'd die if he tried to beat the addiction?"

Jules wasn't sure that fairness was really the issue, but he couldn't deny that he saw Eli's point. Still . . . "All these secrets of yours may very well come back to bite you in the ass."

Eli shrugged. "Perhaps."

"No, I'm not talking hypothetically. Gabriel's gunning for you. He told me he plans to come to Philadelphia and confront you, and I believe him."

Eli's eyes hardened. "Let him come. This time, I won't lose my nerve."

Jules doubted a straightforward fight with Eli was what Gabriel had in mind. He tried to think of a delicate way to say that, but Eli slammed that conversational door in his face before he had a chance.

"Are you going to get around to asking about Hannah, or are you going to keep avoiding the subject indefinitely?"

Jules found himself holding his breath and forced himself to release it. "How is she?"

"She's come close to consciousness a couple of times, but she hasn't fully awakened yet."

Jules nodded and finally sat down. He'd forgotten his clothes were soaking wet and would probably ruin the leather of the antique chair he'd chosen. He started to stand up again, but Eli waved off his concern.

"How are *you*, Jules?"

Jules suspected his smile was as enigmatic as one of Eli's. "When I figure that out, you'll be the first to know."

"You should be there with her when she wakes."

"And if she hates me for what I've done?"

Eli's expression turned stern. "Then you'll just have to take it like a man."

Jules closed his eyes and absorbed that. He'd take it like a man, all right—a man who was hopelessly in love with a woman who might very well hate him. "Will you take me to her?"

"Of course."

⁂

WARMTH. THAT WAS THE first thing Hannah noticed. She had a vague memory of being cold. Shivering. Teeth chattering. Buried under piles of blankets, flickering firelight that failed to warm her. A voice, unfamiliar, speaking to her from far away.

She groaned softly and cuddled into the warmth, drinking it in through her skin. Not just warmth—safety. She'd been in danger, and now she wasn't anymore. She sighed in contentment and drifted away.

When next she woke, the warmth was still there, as was the sense of safety. She breathed deep, inhaling a bewildering bouquet of scents. Wood smoke. Furniture polish. The crisp smell of clean sheets. Something else—spicy, familiar.

Jules.

She opened her eyes.

She was in an unfamiliar room that looked like it could be a bed-and-breakfast inn. Cozy, with an English cottage look. Wood crackled in a fireplace fronted by an ornate iron screen. She wanted to move closer to the fire, closer to that tempting warmth, but for reasons she couldn't name, she didn't like the look of that iron screen.

Blinking bleary eyes, she tried to remember where she was. Her last clear, coherent memory was of being in the dark, cold and scared, fighting for her life. Then she remembered the flare of a Coleman lantern, Ian's evil laugh. Trying to shoot him. Failing. And then . . .

Groaning, not sure she wanted to know, she reached up to her throat where she remembered the sharp, stabbing pain of Ian's fangs. The skin felt smooth under her fingertips, and she frowned in puzzlement. Maybe she'd dreamed Ian biting her, but she *hadn't* dreamed Gabriel, she was sure of it. She felt all around her throat, but couldn't feel any sign of a scab or even a scar. What the hell . . . ?

More fragments of memory floated around in her brain. Falling. Falling down an endless black pit, terror dragging on her heels, sucking her down toward nothingness.

Then something else had a hold of her, slowing her fall. The memory crystallized. Jules. It was Jules who had a hold of her. Jules who offered her a lifeline.

Her stomach turned as her conscious mind finally made sense of the images. She'd been dying. And Jules had made her a vampire.

The fog continued to clear, and she realized she really did smell Jules's distinctive scent. Slowly, almost reluctantly, she turned over, her body so weak she could barely manage it.

He was lying beside her on the bed. It was his warmth she'd cuddled up to when she'd first awakened. He was fast asleep, but even so she could see the haggardness of his face, the shadows under his eyes. She swallowed hard, her newly acute senses reeling from too much input as she realized she could feel him there beside her without having to touch him.

"Gee, I have vamp-dar," she muttered to herself, but she didn't much feel like laughing at her own joke.

Beside her, Jules stirred, then woke with a start. He sat up abruptly and gazed into her face, his eyes widening.

"You're awake," he said. She wasn't quite sure what to make of the expression on his face, though she read relief and dread in it.

"Yeah." She should say something more, but words stuck in her throat. She closed her eyes, the room spinning around her as panic threatened. She was a vampire. A newly created creature of the night. She had psychic powers. She would have to drink blood.

And Jules was her maker.

Her hands fisted in the covers and she fought against the sting of tears. Surely this had to be a dream! If only she could wake up from it.

Jules's fingers brushed softly over her cheek, the touch so tender and tentative it made her heart ache. A tear spilled out from under her closed eyelid. He bent and kissed it away.

"I'm so sorry, Hannah." His voice was a hoarse croak, full of anguish. "I was too slow. I should have—"

It took every ounce of her energy, but she reached up and touched her fingers to his lips to silence him. Her memory of what had happened was spotty and vague, but she remembered four fledgling killers and Ian. How either of them could be alive right now was a mystery.

Her hand fell weakly away from his lips, and Jules wrapped his fingers around hers, squeezing tightly. He no longer looked like the cocky alpha male she'd known. His eyes were shadowed by uncertainty, his shoulders slightly hunched.

"Where are we?" she asked, glancing around the strange room.

Jules took a slow and shaky breath. "We're at Eli's." Haltingly, he told her what had happened after Ian bit her. She did her best to absorb it, and a long silence descended on the room, broken only by the crackle of the fire.

Finally, Jules shifted uncomfortably and squeezed her hand even tighter. "I can't stand it anymore—do you hate me?"

She looked up into his anguished face, and something stirred inside her. Something that most definitely was not hate. "Of course I don't hate you." She shivered in a sudden chill, and her whole body felt heavy. Her vision blurred. "What's happening?" she mumbled, sure she should feel alarmed, though her emotions seemed suddenly miles away.

"You're still recovering." Jules's voice was faint and distant. She had the vague impression he said something more, but her mind sank into the darkness and she didn't hear.

※

SHE WOKE AGAIN SOME unknown amount of time later. Her body felt a little stronger, and she managed a tentative stretch. Every muscle and joint ached and protested, but she struggled her way into a sitting position.

Jules was standing by the fire, looking at her with obvious concern.

Sitting on the edge of her bed was a man she'd never seen before, but whom she instantly recognized. She licked her dry, chapped lips.

"Gabriel has your eyes," she told Eli, who smiled faintly.

"I know. How are you feeling?"

"Like I've been run over by a truck. And I think it backed over me afterward to finish the job."

Still standing by the fire, Jules laughed. "That's my Hannah," he said with obvious affection.

My Hannah. She truly was *his* Hannah now, wasn't she? He was her maker. Her master. Bile rose in her throat, and she forced it back down.

"It will take you a few weeks to become accustomed to the changes that have occurred in your body," Eli said. "I'm afraid you'll suffer quite a bit of discomfort for a while, but it will pass."

She nodded, then looked over at Jules. Why didn't he come any closer? Why was he hanging back by the fire? And why was he sweating and chewing his lip?

She frowned at Eli. "So, what's going on here, exactly?"

"Jules broke a cardinal rule by making you," Eli said. He lost his kindly-old-man look and became coldly stern. "If it weren't for the extenuating circumstances, his life would be forfeit."

Something fierce stirred in Hannah's center, and she made a snarling sound she'd never heard from her own mouth before. "You're in no position to be throwing stones, buddy! Remember, I've met your fledgling up-close and way-too-personal." Her gums tingled strangely and her heart-rate accelerated as she struggled to sit up straighter, maybe even get out of bed and put herself between Jules and his hypocritical, holier-than-thou mentor. Though what she thought she could do against him was anyone's guess.

Eli smiled at her bravado and patted her shoulder. "As I

said, I understand there were extenuating circumstances. Jules is in no danger. Calm yourself and withdraw your fangs."

Fangs? She tentatively touched her tongue to her canines and discovered that they'd grown and sharpened. Ah, that's what the tingling feeling in her gums was. She frowned. How exactly did one withdraw them?

"They'll withdraw on their own when you calm down," Eli answered, as though she'd asked the question out loud. "You'll gain voluntary control of them eventually."

She forced a slow, deep breath, calling on her martial arts training to find a core of calm. Not that she'd ever been much good at that part. Still, her heart-rate was slowing, and her gums tingled again.

"As I was saying," Eli continued, "it's highly . . . irregular . . . for a Guardian to create a fledgling. Jules had a choice between making you or letting you die. My question to you is, are you comfortable with the choice he made?"

"Huh?" Boy, she was just full of intelligent questions to-day. A regular Einstein.

"If you had to choose between life as a vampire and death, which would you choose for yourself?"

Jules made a little choking noise, and she glanced over at him. He stood motionless by the fire, his eyes pleading with her, and she realized he was in the grip of Eli's glamour.

"Let him go!" she snapped at Eli.

"Answer my question first, then I'll release him. This is *your* life we're talking about, not his."

She opened her mouth for a retort, but when she met those implacable, ancient eyes, she swallowed her words. She had the distinct impression that if she said she'd choose death, she'd be dead before the words finished leaving her mouth.

A lot of things made sense now. She remembered Jules's question—*Do you hate me?*—and even now she saw the guilt in his face. Ignoring Eli, she met Jules's eyes and spoke only to him. She remembered that horrible falling feeling, and she remembered Jules extending his psychic hand to catch her.

She chose her words carefully. "Unlike most people, I knew what you were offering. I'm the one who decided to accept. You didn't force anything on me, I'm not mad at you, and I certainly don't hate you."

His shoulders sagged in relief and he came to the bed in two long strides. Eli stood so Jules could take his place. With a nod and an enigmatic smile, the Founder slipped out of the room.

Jules grabbed her hand and squeezed it, then seemed to decide that wasn't enough. He pulled back the covers and slipped into the bed beside her; pulling her into his arms. She went readily, laying her head against his chest and wrapping her arms around him.

"You know," she said, "there's nothing like a near-death experience to show you what's really important in life."

His arms tightened around her, and he pressed a kiss on the top of her head. "You know I would never take advantage of my power as your maker."

She thought about it a moment, feeling his muscles stiffen when she didn't immediately reply. She smiled and rubbed his chest. "Yes, you would."

"I would not!" he cried, and he couldn't have sounded more indignant.

She raised her head and looked up into his eyes. "If I were about to do something insanely dangerous, like walk all alone into a house filled with nine Killers, you'd freeze me in my tracks without a second thought. Hell, I'd do the same to you if I had that kind of power."

He frowned at her, no doubt trying to puzzle out whether he should be offended. She snuggled against him once more.

"Besides," she said, smiling against his chest, "you used glamour against me, and you even tied me up, and I managed not to hate you for it." *And to get the better of you anyway,* she thought but didn't say. Before, she'd thought letting a man have any amount of power over her was a sign of weakness. Now she understood that she'd given him power the moment she'd fallen in love with him. What's more, he'd given her the same power over him.

"Did you mean what you said?" she asked, thinking back to the moment when she'd been on the brink of death.

"What I said when?"

"When I was dying and you were trying to bring me back."

"You remember words?" He sounded startled.

"Yeah. I heard you talking to me, in my head." And she remembered the magic words that had made the decision for her. "Do you remember what you said?"

His hand stroked her back, and underneath her ear she heard the steady thump of his heart. "I think I said something about you being too tough to die."

There was a rumble of humor in his voice, and she smiled, realizing he knew perfectly well what she meant. "Before that."

"Hmm. I think I said something really incisive, like 'come back.'"

She slapped his chest, though she was too weak to put much force behind the blow. "*After* that, you jerk."

He laughed. "Oh! That!"

She raised her head to glower at him, but the warmth and sparkle of his eyes changed the glower into a smile again in no time.

He brushed a lock of hair away from her face. "I believe I said I love you." He swallowed hard. "And yes, I meant it."

She tried to raise up high enough to kiss him, but her strength was failing rapidly. He considerately lowered his head and brushed his lips over hers. She wanted more, but that would have to come later. Her body was insisting she needed to sleep again. And Jules's chest made quite the nice pillow, even if it was a little hard.

She let her eyes slide closed and sighed in contentment.

"Hannah?" His voice sounded strangely tentative.

Sleep was calling to her, an inexorable force she was too weak to fight.

"Yeah, I love you too," she managed to murmur before her last ounce of energy drained.

She could hardly wait until she got her strength back so she could show him how much.

Epilogue

GABRIEL SMILED DOWN AT the girl who lay sleeping in his bed. Blonde roots were sprouting under her jet black hair, and he'd removed all traces of eyebrow pencil and mascara as soon as he'd brought her back to his home. He suspected she'd be quite lovely in her natural state. The piercings on her eyebrow and nose were the next to go. He'd hesitated over the ugly, amateurish pentagram tattoo on her right shoulder. In the end, he'd decided to slice it off while she was unconscious, removing her most identifying feature. Her vampire body healed the wound with no scar.

The girl moaned in her sleep, and Gabriel brushed his knuckles gently across her cheek. Her eyes fluttered open.

When he'd made her, he'd created a link with her mind stronger than most master-fledgling bonds, another of the advantages of having been born vampire. Another advantage of his special birth neither his mother nor his father knew he had. He'd been under the thrall of first one, then the other, for too long. It was time to stretch his wings and see what he could do.

Someone tapped tentatively on the door. Gabriel smiled at the scent of fear in the air. "Go away, Mother," he said. "I'm busy."

He listened as Camille obediently retreated, then turned his attention back to his first fledgling, meeting her clouded eyes.

He saw the nightmare images flashing across the poor girl's mind—hitchiking on a quiet country road, being picked up by a man who instantly made her skin crawl. She was too smart to get into the car with him, and she'd been armed with a dainty little gun to protect herself from the predators of this world. But no weapon could protect her against glamour.

Then the images got worse—running through a darkened house, terror nearly stopping her heart. Falling through a hole in the floor. Men jumping through the hole after her, baring vicious-looking fangs. The screams of her fellow prisoner as he was raped, tortured, then killed. Hours spent alone in the dark with the corpse. Then the door opened and the vampires came again.

Fangs sinking into her throat, her breasts, her thighs while the man who'd picked her up took her virginity by force. Then the others mounting her one by one as she lay helpless in a pool of her own blood.

Tears streamed down her cheeks, and Gabriel brushed them away.

"Shh," he whispered, "it's over now. You're safe."

But even the considerable power of his glamour couldn't ease her remembered pain. She sobbed, her mind begging for help, desperate, nearly shattered. And she didn't even know what he'd done to her yet, didn't know she was no longer human. She would be no good to him in her current state of mind. He took her hand in his, giving her an anchor in the here and now.

"I can make the pain go away," he told her, leaning over her and capturing her eyes again. "I can push that memory to a corner of your mind where it won't seem real at all, and it will be almost as if it never happened."

She clung to his hand, her whole body shaking, tears still leaking from the corners of her eyes despite the surge of hope his words inspired. "What's the catch?" she asked between hiccups.

He couldn't help smiling to find the hint of her once-keen edge even in the fragments of her shattered mind. "The catch is that you'll have to do something you may find morally distasteful in return."

She sniffled and clung harder. Her grip would have broken a mortal's hand. She didn't know her strength yet.

"Do it!" she begged. "Make me forget." She closed her eyes hard, as if trying to shut out the images that still flashed through her brain. "Please make me forget."

"As you wish, my dear," he said, and with a quick jerk of the psychic leash that held her, he sent her back into a deep sleep.